Joyce S. Denney
45 Trail Rd.
Marietta. GA 30064

W9-CKE-425

Sept. 2007

And Then You Die...

And Then You Die...

IRIS JOHANSEN

DOUBLEDAY DIRECT LARGE PRINT EDITION

 BANTAM BOOKS

New York   Toronto   London   Sydney   Auckland

This Large Print Edition, prepared especially for Doubleday Direct, Inc., contains the complete, unabridged text of the original Publisher's Edition.

AND THEN YOU DIE...
A Bantam Book / January 1998

ISBN 0-56865-727-7

Published simultaneously in the United States and Canada

Bantam Books are published by Bantam Books, a division of Bantam Doubleday Dell Publishing Group, Inc. Its trademark, consisting of the words "Bantam Books" and the portrayal of a rooster, is Registered in U.S. Patent and Trademark Office and in other countries. Marca Registrada. Bantam Books, 1540 Broadway, New York, New York 10036.

PRINTED IN THE UNITED STATES OF AMERICA

This Large Print Book carries the Seal of Approval of N.A.V.H.

And Then You Die...

PROLOGUE

September 19
Danzar, Croatia

 The dogs were howling.

Sweet Jesus, Bess wished they'd stop.

Focus.

Shoot.

Move on.

Dark here. Adjust the light.

The babies . . .

Oh, God, why?

Don't think about it. Just take the picture.

Focus.

Shoot.

She needed more film.

Bess's hands were shaking as she opened the camera, took out the used roll, and inserted a new one.

"We have to leave, Ms. Grady." Sergeant Brock stood in the doorway behind her. His words were polite but his expression was full of revulsion as he stared at her. "They're right outside the village. You shouldn't be here."

Focus.

Shoot.

Blood. So much blood.

"We have to go."

Another room.

The camera was knocked out of her hand. Sergeant Brock now stood in front of her, his face white. "What are you? Some sort of ghoul? How can you do this?"

She couldn't do it. Not anymore. She was exploding inside.

She had to do it. She bent down and picked up the camera. "Wait in the jeep for me. I won't be long."

She scarcely heard his curse as he turned on his heel and left her alone.

No, not alone.

The babies . . .

Focus.

Shoot.

She could get through this.

No, she couldn't.

She leaned against the wall and closed her eyes.

Closed out the babies.

The dogs continued their howling.

She couldn't shut them out.

Monsters. The world was full of monsters.

So do your job. Let everyone see the monsters.

She opened her eyes and lurched toward the last room.

Don't think. Don't listen to the dogs.

Just focus.

Shoot.

Move on.

ONE

January 21,
4:50 P.M.
Mexico

She just might murder her.

"You see? I told you so," Emily said, beaming. "This is working out just fine."

Bess braced herself as the jeep drove into yet another pothole. "I hate people who say I told you so. And will you stop being so damn cheerful?"

"No, I'm happy. You will be too, when you admit that I was entirely right to persuade you to bring me with you." Emily turned to the driver in the seat next to her. "How far, Rico?"

"Six, maybe seven hours." The boy's cheerful smile lit his dark face. "But we should stop and set up camp for the night. I'll need to see the road. From here it gets a little rough." Another bone-jarring bump punctuated the sentence.

"This isn't rough?" Bess asked dryly.

Rico shook his head. "The government takes good care of this road. No one repairs the one into Tenajo. Not enough people to matter."

"How many is that?"

"Maybe a hundred. When I left a few years ago, there were more. But most of the young people are gone now, like me. Who wants to live in a village that doesn't even have a movie theater?" He glanced over his shoulder at Bess, who was sitting in the back. "I don't think you will find anything interesting about Tenajo to photograph. There's nothing there. No ruins. No important people. Why bother?"

"It's for a series of articles I'm doing for *Traveler* on undiscovered destinations in Mexico," Bess explained. "And there better be something in Tenajo, or the Condé Nast people won't be happy."

"We'll find something for you," Emily said.

"Practically every Mexican town has a plaza and a church. We'll go from there."

"Oh, will we? Are you directing my shoots now?"

Emily smiled. "Just this one. I approve of this assignment. I like the idea of you shooting nice, pretty scenery instead of having crazy idiots shoot at you."

"I enjoy my work."

"For God's sake, you ended up in a hospital after Danzar. What you're doing isn't good for you. You should have finished medical school and gone into pediatric surgery with me."

"I'm not tough enough. I knew it the night that kid died in the emergency room. I don't know how you do it."

"I suppose Somalia was easy and Sarajevo was a piece of cake. And what about Danzar? When are you going to tell me what happened at Danzar?"

Bess stiffened. "Stay out of my job, Emily. I mean it. I don't need supervision. I'm almost thirty."

"You're also exhausted and drained, and still you have an obsession with that damn camera. You haven't taken it off your neck since we started this trip."

Bess's hand instinctively went up to cup the camera. She *needed* her camera. It was part of her. After all these years, being without it would be like being blind. But it was no use trying to explain to Emily.

Emily had always seen things in black and white; she had absolute confidence that she knew right from wrong. And she had always tried to guide Bess into doing what she thought was right. Most of the time Bess could handle it. But Danzar had shattered her, and that had alerted all of Emily's protective instincts. Bess should have stayed away, but she hadn't seen Emily in a long time.

And besides, she loved the bossy bitch.

Now Emily's older-sister mode was in full bloom. Time to change the subject before she became any more dictatorial.

"Emily, why don't you try to get Tom on the cellular? Rico said we'll be out of range of any tower pretty soon."

Emily was immediately distracted as Bess knew she would be. Her husband, Tom, and their ten-year-old daughter, Julie, were the center of Emily's existence. "Good idea," she said, pulling out her portable and dialing the number. "It may be my last chance. They're taking off at dawn for Canada to do that wilderness thing. No telephone, no TV, no radio. Just Tom passing on his survival expertise to his heir." Holding the receiver to her ear, she listened intently, then scowled. "Too late. Nothing but static. Why couldn't you choose a civilized little village to bring me to?"

"I didn't choose, I was sent here on assignment. And *you* weren't invited."

Ignoring the jab, Emily turned to Rico, who had been politely ignoring the discussion between the sisters. "We can stop now. It's getting dark."

"As soon as I find a stretch of flat ground to set up camp," Rico said.

Emily nodded, then looked at Bess. "Don't think I've said all I want to say. Our conversation isn't over yet."

Bess closed her eyes. "Oh, my God."

"They've stopped for the night. They're setting up camp." Kaldak lowered the binoculars. "But there's no doubt they're on their way to Tenajo. What do you want to do?"

Colonel Rafael Esteban frowned. "This is most unfortunate. It could cause complications. When do you expect the report from Mexico City?"

"An hour or two more. I sent the order as soon as we caught sight of them this morning. We already know the license plates are registered to Laropez Travel. Finding out who the hell they are and what they're doing here is what's taking time."

"Unfortunate," Esteban murmured. "I detest complications. And everything was going so well."

"Then remove the complication. Isn't that why you brought me here?"

"Yes." Esteban smiled. "You came highly recommended in that area. What is your suggestion?"

"Put them down. Disposal should be no problem out here. It'll take me no more than an hour and your problem is solved."

"But what if they're not innocent tourists? What if they have awkward ties?"

Kaldak shrugged.

"That's the problem with people of your ilk," Esteban said. "Too bloodthirsty. It's no wonder Habin was willing to let you go."

"I'm not bloodthirsty. You wanted a solution. I gave it to you. And Habin has no ob-

jection to blood. He sent me to you because
he felt uncomfortable around me."

"Why?"

"His fortune-teller told him I'd be the
death of him."

Esteban burst out laughing. "Stupid ox."
His laughter faded as he stared at Kaldak.
That face . . . If the Dark Beast could be
personified, it would have a face like
Kaldak's. He could see why a superstitious
fool like Habin would be uneasy. "I don't use
fortune-tellers, Kaldak, and I've put down
better men than you."

"If you say so." He lifted the binoculars to
his eyes again. "They're spreading out their
sleeping bags. Now would be the time."

"I said we'll wait." He hadn't said any
such thing, but he wouldn't have Kaldak
pushing him. "Go back to camp and bring
me the report when it comes in."

Kaldak started toward the jeep parked a
few yards away. His instant obedience
should have reassured Esteban but it didn't.
Indifference, not fear, spurred that obedience, and Esteban was not accustomed to
indifference. He instinctively moved to as-
sert his superiority. "If you must kill someone, Galvez has offended me. It wouldn't

displease me to see him dead when I return to camp."

"He's your lieutenant. He may still have his uses." Kaldak started the jeep. "You're sure?"

"I'm sure."

"Then I'll take care of it."

"Aren't you curious what he did to offend me?"

"No."

"I'll tell you anyway." He said softly, "He's a very stupid man. He asked me what was going to happen at Tenajo. He's been entirely too curious. Don't make the same mistake."

"Why should I?" Kaldak met his gaze. "When I don't give a damn."

Esteban felt a ripple of frustration as he watched the jeep bounce down the hill. Son of a bitch. Having Kaldak obey his command to kill should have brought the familiar flush of triumph. But it didn't.

Kaldak would have to go the way of Galvez when it was convenient. At the moment, he needed the entire team to complete this phase of the job.

But after Tenajo . . .

. . .

"Are you awake?" Emily whispered.

Bess was tempted not to answer, but she knew that wouldn't do any good. She turned over in her sleeping bag to face her sister. "I'm awake."

Emily was silent a moment, and then she said, "Have I ever done anything that wasn't for your good?"

Bess sighed. "No. But it's still my life. I want to make my own mistakes. You've never understood that."

"And I never will."

"Because we're not the same. It took me a long time to find out what I wanted to do. You've always known you wanted to be a doctor, and you've never wavered."

"No job is worth going through what you did. Why the hell do you do it?"

Bess was silent.

"Can't you see I'm worried about you?" Emily continued. "I've never seen you like this. Why won't you talk to me?"

Emily wasn't going to leave it alone and Bess was too exhausted to fight her. She said haltingly, "It's . . . the monsters."

"What?"

"There are so many monsters in the world. When I was a kid, I thought monsters existed only in the movies, but they're all around us. Sometimes they're hiding, but give them an opportunity and they'll crawl out from under their rocks and rip you apa—"

Blood. So much blood.

The babies . . .

"Bess?"

She was starting to shake again. Don't think about it. "We stop the monsters when we can," she said unsteadily. "But most of us get bored and lazy and too busy. So when the monsters do crawl out, it has to be someone's job to show everyone that they're here."

"My God," Emily whispered. "Who the hell appointed you Joan of Arc?"

Bess could feel the flush burn her cheeks. "That's not fair. I know I sound like an ass. And some Joan of Arc I make. I'm scared all the time." She tried to make her sister understand. "It's not as if I go around looking for monsters, but in my job it happens. And when it does, I can do something about it. You save lives every day. I could never do that, but I can do this."

"And I can try to save you from yourself. Let's talk this out and see what—"

"Don't do this to me, Emily. Please. Not now. I'm too tired."

Emily reached out and gently touched her cheek. "Because of your job. You're too impulsive, and you're always rushing in and getting hurt. That trip to Danzar was almost as disastrous as your marriage to that good-for-nothing Kramer."

"Good night, Emily."

Emily made a face. "Oh, well, I have two weeks to do the job." She turned her back and drew her sleeping bag around her. "I'm sure you'll be much more mellow after Tenajo."

Bess closed her eyes and tried to relax. She was tired and sore from that jarring ride and should have no trouble sleeping.

She was wide awake.

She was raw and hurting and she didn't need additional pressure from Emily. So she had made a few mistakes. A bad marriage, a few false career starts. Her personal life might still be a disaster, but now she was in a profession she loved, she made a good living, and was respected by her peers. If there were thorns that ripped at her from time to time, that was something she just had to accept. Danzar was the exception, not the rule.

She might never know another horror like the one she had faced there.

All she needed were two peaceful weeks taking boring photos of town squares and cantinas, and she'd be ready to go back into the fray.

The trucks and equipment had arrived when Kaldak returned to camp. Galvez was directing the distribution of the equipment among the men.

Kaldak silently watched until Galvez finished and turned toward him.

Galvez smiled maliciously. "You'd better grab some of this crap yourself unless you think you can do without it. Can you walk on water, Kaldak?"

"I'll get mine later."

"You know what it is?"

"I've seen it before."

"But you didn't know you'd need it here. Esteban tried to keep it such a big secret, but I knew it was coming."

Esteban was right, Kaldak thought. Galvez was stupid to run off at the mouth. "Esteban sent me to check on the report from Mexico City."

Galvez shook his head. "Nothing. I checked the fax machine fifteen minutes ago. Only two from Habin and one from Morrisey."

"Morrisey?"

"He's always getting phone calls and faxes from Morrisey." Galvez raised his eyebrows. "You don't know about Morrisey? Maybe they don't think so much of you after all."

"Maybe not. Esteban really wants the report. Will you check again?"

Galvez shrugged and went into the tent. Kaldak followed him to the fax machine.

"Nothing," Galvez said.

"Are you sure? Maybe it's out of paper. Check the memory."

Galvez bent over the machine. "I told you, there's nothing here. Now, leave me—"

Kaldak's arm went around Galvez's throat. It took only a quick twist to break his neck.

January 22,
12:30 A.M.

"You've got it?" Esteban strode toward the jeep. "It took you long enough."

Kaldak passed him the fax. "No connections with any government agency. Dr. Emily Corelli, thirty-six, thriving practice in pediatric surgery in Detroit. Her husband, Tom, is a building contractor. One child, Julie, age ten."

"And the other one?"

"Her sister, Elizabeth Grady, twenty-nine, divorced. Photo- journalist."

"Journalist?" Esteban frowned. "I don't like that."

"She's freelance."

"I still don't like it. Why Tenajo?"

"She's on assignment for a travel magazine."

"But why now?"

Kaldak shrugged.

Esteban focused the flashlight on the passport photos transmitted with the fax. The two women looked nothing alike. Corelli's dark brown hair was drawn back, her features were fine and regular. Elizabeth Grady's mouth was large, her hazel eyes deep set, her jaw square, and her short, curly hair sun-streaked to a much lighter shade than her sister's.

"How long are they due to be gone?"

"Two to three weeks." Kaldak paused. "No one will search for them for at least a week. They have a cellular phone, but they're already out of range of any tower. Phone service is usually spotty from Tenajo, so the phone company won't be aware right away that the lines to the village have been cut. It may be another week before a crew comes out to fix them."

"Your point."

"Remove the complication. Why let them go on to Tenajo? By the time anyone starts searching, I'll have disposed of them where no one will ever find them."

"You are persistent."

"Let me do it tonight. It's the smartest course to follow."

"I'll decide on what course is wise," Esteban said. Arrogant peon. "You have no idea what's involved."

"And I have no intention of probing. I don't want to end up like Galvez."

Esteban searched Kaldak's face. "You did it? Already?"

Kaldak looked surprised. "Of course."

Pleasure rushed through Esteban. He had asserted control. But even that supreme feeling of power was spoiled by Kaldak's casual attitude. Esteban wadded the fax into a ball. "You can't have them. We'll let them go on to Tenajo."

Kaldak was silent.

He wasn't happy, Esteban realized with satisfaction. Good. Perhaps he should have let Kaldak do his job, but the lack of subservience stung him. Besides, it didn't really matter.

It would all come down to the same thing anyway.

"Are you coming back to camp?" Kaldak asked.

"No, I'll stay here for a while."

He turned back to the hills as Kaldak drove off. He didn't want to be distracted by the men at camp. He had decided it wasn't safe for him to go into Tenajo, but the anticipation was almost as good. He had set the plan in motion, now he deserved this time to savor. Habin with his political causes didn't really know the true meaning of what he was doing.

Excitement surged through him as he realized that even at that moment it was going on.

The night was clear, no tempest clouds

were swirling over those distant hills. Yet he could almost see the Dark Beast hovering, toying with Tenajo.

Holy Virgin, help them. Their immortal souls are writhing in Satan's fire.

Father Juan knelt at the altar, his gaze fixed desperately on the golden crucifix above him.

He had been in Tenajo for forty-four years and his flock had always listened before. Why would they not listen to him now in this supreme test?

He could hear them in the square outside the church, shouting, singing, laughing. He had gone out and told them they should be in their homes at this time of night, but it had done no good. They had only offered to share the evil with him.

He would not take it. He would stay inside the church.

And he would pray that Tenajo would survive.

"You slept well," Emily told Bess. "You look more rested."

"I'll be even more rested by the time we leave here." She met Emily's gaze. "I'm fine. So back off."

Emily smiled. "Eat your breakfast. Rico is already packing up the jeep."

"I'll go help him."

"It's going to be all right, isn't it? We're going to have a good time here."

"If you can keep yourself from—" Oh, what the hell. She wouldn't let this time be spoiled. "You bet. We're going to have a great time."

"And you're glad I came," Emily prompted.

"I'm glad you came."

Emily winked. "Gotcha."

Bess was still smiling as she reached the jeep.

"Ah, you're happy. You slept well?" Rico asked.

She nodded as she stowed her canvas camera case in the jeep. Her gaze went to the hills. "How long has it been since you've been in Tenajo?"

"Almost two years."

"That's a long time. Is your family still there?"

"Just my mother."

"Don't you miss her?"

"I talk to her on the phone every week." He frowned. "My brother and I are doing very well. We could give her a fine apartment in the city, but she would not come. She says it would not be home to her."

She had clearly struck a sore spot. "Evidently someone thinks Tenajo is a wonderful place or Condé Nast wouldn't have sent me."

"Maybe for those who don't have to live there. What does my mother have? Nothing. Not even a washing machine. The people live as they did fifty years ago." He violently slung the last bag into the jeep. "It is the priest's fault. Father Juan has convinced her the city is full of wickedness and greed and she should stay in Tenajo. Stupid old man. There's nothing wrong with having a few comforts."

He was hurting, Bess realized, and she didn't know what to say.

"Maybe I can persuade my mother to come back with me," Rico added.

"I hope so." The words sounded lame even to her. Great, Bess. She searched for some other way to help. "Would you like me to take her photograph? Maybe the two of you together?"

His face lit up. "That would be good. I've only a snapshot my brother took four years ago." He paused. "Maybe you could tell her how well I'm doing in Mexico City. How all the clients ask just for me?" He hurried on: "It would not be a lie. I'm very much in demand."

Her lips twitched. "I'm sure you are." She got into the jeep. "Particularly among the ladies."

He smiled boyishly. "Yes, the ladies are very kind to me. But it would be wiser not to mention that to my mother. She would not understand."

"I'll try to remember," she said solemnly.

"Ready?" Emily had walked to the jeep, and was now handing Rico the box containing the cooking implements. "Let's go. With any luck we'll be in Tenajo by two and I'll be swinging in a hammock by four. I can't wait. I'm sure it's paradise on earth."

TWO

Tenajo was not paradise.

It was just a town baking in the afternoon sun. From the hilltop overlooking the town Bess could see a picturesque fountain in the center of the wide cobblestone plaza bordered on three sides by adobe buildings. At the far end of the plaza was a small church.

"Pretty, isn't it?" Emily stood up in the jeep. "Where's the local inn, Rico?"

He pointed at a street off the main thoroughfare. "It's very small but clean."

Emily sighed blissfully. "My hammock is almost in view, Bess."

"I doubt if you could nap with all that caterwauling," Bess said dryly. "You didn't men-

tion the coyotes, Rico. I don't think that—"
She stiffened. Oh, God, no. Not coyotes.

Dogs.

She had heard that sound before.

Those were dogs howling. Dozens of dogs. And their mournful wail was coming from the streets below her.

Bess started to shake.

"What is it?" Emily asked. "What's wrong?"

"Nothing." It couldn't be. It was her imagination. How many times had she awakened in the middle of the night to the howling of those phantom dogs?

"Don't tell me nothing. Are you sick?" Emily demanded.

It wasn't her imagination.

"Danzar." She moistened her lips. "It's crazy but— We have to hurry. *Hurry*, Rico."

Rico stomped on the accelerator, and the jeep careened down the road toward the village.

They didn't see the first body until they were inside the town. A woman lay curled in the shadow of the fountain.

Emily grabbed her medical bag, jumped out of the jeep, and bent over the woman. "Dead."

Bess had known she was dead.

"Why is she just lying here?" Emily asked. "Why didn't someone help her?"

Bess got out of the jeep. "Go find your mother, Rico. Right now. Bring her here."

"What's happening?" Rico whispered.

"I don't know." It was the truth. This wasn't Danzar. What had happened there couldn't happen here. "Just find your mother."

He roared off down the street.

Bess turned back to Emily. "How did she die?"

Emily shook her head. "I don't know. No marks of violence."

"Disease?"

Emily shrugged. "I can't tell, not without tests. What do you know about this?"

"I don't know anything." She tried to steady her voice. "But I think there will be others. The howling . . ." She hurried toward the cantina across from the fountain. "Bring your bag and come with me."

They found four bodies in the cantina. Two young men were slumped at a table, a pile of chips and money in front of them. An old man lay behind the bar. A woman in a purple dress was crumpled on the stairs.

Emily went from one to the other.

"All dead?" Bess asked.

Emily nodded. "Come here." She opened her bag, drew out a face mask and rubber gloves, and handed them to Bess. "Put them on."

Bess slipped on the mask and gloves. "You think it's contagious?"

"It won't hurt to be careful." She moved toward the door.

"How did you know?"

"The dogs. When I was in Danzar, we heard the dogs howling from miles away. Everyone in the village had been butchered by the guerrillas."

"Everyone," Emily echoed. She straightened her shoulders. "Well, none of these people died of wounds, and I won't believe everyone is dead just because some stupid dogs are yapping. Come on, let's find someone who can tell us what happened."

They found no one in the first house they entered. Two dead in the shop next door. A woman behind the counter and a little boy curled on the floor. Chocolate malt balls were scattered beside him. More candy was clutched in his hand.

His hands were smeared with chocolate,

Bess thought dully. Children loved sweets. When her niece, Julie, was younger, she'd had a passion for M&M's and Bess had always brought her—

"What the hell are you doing?" Emily asked.

Bess looked down at the camera with which she'd just shot a picture of Emily and the little boy.

Focus.

Shoot.

Danzar again.

But she didn't have to take pictures here. There would be no secrets or hidden mass graves. "I don't know." She stuffed the camera in her vest.

"Stop crying."

She hadn't known she was weeping. She wiped her eyes with the back of her hand. "Whatever happened here, it happened quickly. Most people go home when they become ill."

Emily rose to her feet. "Maybe some of them did. I'll have to find out. It's crazy. I've never heard of a fatal outbreak like this except maybe Ebola."

Bess froze. "Ebola? In Mexico?"

"I didn't say that's what it is. There are all

kinds of new viruses springing up, and, for all I know, it could be some contaminant in the drinking water. Maybe cholera. Outbreaks are still too frequent here in Mexico." She shook her head. "But I've never heard of it attacking with this kind of totality and swiftness, and I don't see signs of vomiting or diarrhea. I just don't know." She went behind the counter and picked up the receiver of the telephone on the wall. "Whatever it is, we need help. I'm not qualified to diagnose—" She hung up. "No dial tone. Great. We'll have to try the next house."

In the next house they found no dead, but the telephone there didn't work either. "I want you to leave Tenajo," Emily told Bess.

"Go to hell."

"I didn't think you'd go, but I had to try." Emily shrugged. "We've probably already been exposed anyway. Let's go see if we can find any survivors."

During the next three hours they found forty-three dead. A good many were in their own homes. In their beds, in their kitchens, in their bathrooms.

And they found Rico's mother.

She lay on a faded sofa and Rico knelt on the floor beside her, holding her hand.

"Oh, damn," Bess whispered.

"There wasn't any use bringing her to you," Rico said numbly. "She's dead. My mother's dead."

"You shouldn't be touching her," Emily said gently. "We don't know what killed her."

"Father Juan killed her. He made her stay here."

Emily opened her bag and pulled out a mask and gloves. "Put them on."

He ignored her.

"Rico, you need to—"

"He killed her. If she'd been in the city, I could have taken her to the hospital." He stood up and moved toward the door. "It was the priest."

Bess stepped in front of him. "Rico, it's not—"

He knocked her aside and ran out of the house.

"You keep looking," Bess tossed over her shoulder to Emily as she started after Rico. "I'll go after him."

Why was she even bothering? she wondered. The priest was probably dead too. Like everyone else in Tenajo.

God, she wished those dogs would stop howling.

Rico was standing over the priest when she burst into the church.

"Get away from him, Rico."

Rico didn't move.

She pushed him aside and knelt by the priest. He was gasping for breath but was still alive, she saw with relief.

"Did you hit him?"

Rico shook his head.

"Get me some water."

Rico didn't move.

"Get it," she said fiercely.

He turned reluctantly and moved toward the holy water by the door.

She didn't think the water would do any good, but it got Rico temporarily away from the priest. "Father Juan, can you speak? We need to know what happened here. Do you know if anyone else is still alive?"

The priest's eyes opened. "The root . . . the root . . ."

Was he saying they had been poisoned? Perhaps Emily's guess about the contaminant was right.

"What happened here? What killed those people?"

"The root . . ."

"Let him die." Rico was back beside her.

"Where's the water?"

His gaze was fixed on the priest's face. "It doesn't matter. He doesn't need it now."

Bess looked at the priest.

Rico was right. The priest was dead.

"What's the closest village to Tenajo?"

"Besamaro. Forty miles."

"I want you to drive to Besamaro and phone the public health officials. Tell them there's a problem here. Try to stay away from everyone as much as possible in case you're contaminated."

Rico was still glaring down at the priest, his face twisted with rage. "He killed my mother. Him and all his talk of the glory of poverty and humility." He kicked viciously at the poor box lying next to Father Juan and sent it skidding across the floor to lodge beneath a pew. "I'm glad he's dead."

"You may be dead too if you don't get help," she said. "You're young. Do you want to die, Rico?"

That broke through to him. "No, I'll go to Besamaro." He walked out of the church, and a moment later she heard the roar of the jeep.

She probably shouldn't have sent him away. He might spread the contagion. But what else was she supposed to do? They couldn't handle this nightmare by themselves.

The priest's eyes were open, staring up at her. Death. So much horror and death. Shuddering, she stood. She had to get back to Emily. Emily might need her.

To search for more dead. No, they were searching for the living. She had to remember that. There might still be life in this hideous place.

The sun was descending as she paused on the top step. Blood- red. Death red.

She sank down on the step and wrapped her arms about herself. She was ice cold and couldn't stop shaking. In one minute she would go back to Emily. She would take just this one minute for herself. She needed the time to prepare for the night ahead and to be as strong as Emily.

Wouldn't those dogs ever stop wailing? Danzar.

This wasn't Danzar. But what if it were?

The dead. A town cut off from communication. The first thing the guerrillas had done at Danzar was cut the telephone lines.

But Tenajo wasn't war-torn Croatia. It was a small Mexican town in the back of beyond. There was no reason for it to be destroyed.

But had there been any real reason for Danzar?

Stop it. It's all supposition. You don't have to do this.

But who else was here to do it? What if her instincts were right? Was she going to turn her back and walk away? Maybe a few pictures . . .

Just in case.

She slowly stood up and took her camera out of her vest. She immediately felt a rush of confidence, a sense of rightness. Just a few pictures and then she'd go back to Emily.

Just in case.

The woman lying by the fountain, staring at the sky with blind, dead eyes.

Focus.

Shoot.

Move on.

The bartender in the cantina.

Focus.

Shoot.

The old woman curled up beside a rose-bush in her garden.

Dead. So many dead.

Was she still taking pictures? Yes, the shutter was clicking as if by its own volition.

She wanted to stop. She couldn't stop.

Oh, God, two small boys lying together in a hammock. They looked like they were asleep.

She staggered to the side of the house and threw up. She leaned against a wall, her cold cheek pressed against the sunwarmed adobe. Shudder after shudder convulsed her body.

It only seemed as if the entire world was dead. But she was alive. Emily was alive. Hold on to that truth.

She would go find her sister and help her. She would pretend to be as strong and brave as Emily.

She mustn't let Emily see how terrified she was.

Emily wasn't at Rico's mother's house.

No, of course she wouldn't wait for Bess to return. She would go on and do her job. No weakness. No hesitation.

Bess went back out into the street. It was dark now. "Emily."

Silence.

She walked one block, two.

"Emily."

The dogs howled. Did one of them belong to the little boy in the store?

Don't think of him. It's easier when you don't remember them as individuals. She had found that out after Danzar. "Emily."

Where was she? Panic suddenly soared through Bess. What if Emily were ill? What if Emily were lying in one of those houses unconscious and unable to call out?

"Emily!"

"Here." Emily came out of the house two doors up the street. "I've found someone."

Relief poured through Bess as she hurried to her sister. "Are you okay?"

"Of course," Emily said impatiently. "I've found a baby. Everyone else in the house is dead, but the baby is alive. Come on."

Bess followed her inside. "Why would the baby live?"

Emily shook her head. "I'm just glad to find someone who did." She led Bess toward a crib covered by mosquito netting. "If the disease is airborne, the netting might have protected her."

The baby was a plump little girl, not over

twelve months, with curly black hair and tiny gold hoops in her ears. Her eyes were closed, but her breathing was deep and steady.

"Are you sure she's not ill?"

"I think so. She woke up a minute ago and smiled at me. Beautiful, isn't she?"

"Yes." Beautiful, cuddly, and wonderfully *alive*.

"I thought you needed to see her," Emily said quietly.

"I did." She swallowed hard.

They stood there for several moments looking down at the baby.

"I'm sorry, Emily," Bess said. "I should never have brought you here. I never dreamed this—"

"It's not your fault. I'm the one who nagged you into taking me."

Bess couldn't take her eyes off the little girl. "Now, how do we keep her alive?"

"Get her out of this town." Emily frowned. "I don't even want to touch her until I've been sterilized. There's no telling what we've picked up."

"Should we take a hot shower? Boil our clothes?"

"The water might be contaminated." She shrugged. "But I guess we've no choice."

"I sent Rico to the nearest town to call the public health officials."

"It will take them time to muster a crew and get here. I don't want to stay and wait for them."

Neither did Bess. She'd rather camp out in the center of a volcano than stay in Tenajo. "How long will it take you to sterilize what you have on?"

"Forty minutes."

"Find something here for me to wear and sterilize that too. I'll be back."

"Where are you going?"

"We didn't finish searching. There might be someone else."

"There're only three more blocks. The percentages are against it."

"Babies don't know about percentages. Maybe that's why this one lived."

Emily smiled. "Not logical. Be sure you're back in forty minutes. I want to get Josie out of here."

"Josie?"

"We have to call her something besides 'that one.' " She began to strip off her shirt.

Bess walked out the door and braced herself. She was probably going to find nothing but more horror.

Unless there was another Josie.

So don't think about it. Just do it.

She clenched her hands into fists and started down the street.

No more Josies.

Just death. And the howling of the dogs.

She stopped on the porch of the last house and took a deep breath.

That's when she saw the string of lights coming down the hill.

Cars? No, the vehicles were too large. Trucks, then, coming fast. They would be here any moment.

Thank God.

Rico must have reached someone. But had there been time for Rico to make contact and mobilize help? Not likely.

Three trucks roared by her, army trucks heading for the plaza. Fear iced through her. There had been army trucks in Danzar too.

She was being paranoid. It could be help. Or it could be—

Emily. She had to get to Emily.

She flew down the steps, out the gate, and down the block.

Emily looked up as she ran through the door. "What is it? I heard the—"

"Get out. You've got to get out." She hurried to the crib and threw up the mosquito netting. Josie beamed up at her. "Take her away."

"What the hell do you mean?"

"Army trucks have arrived. But it's too soon." She scooped Josie up and wrapped her in a blanket. "They shouldn't be here yet."

"You shouldn't be touching—"

"Then you take her. Just get out. Those trucks shouldn't be here yet."

"You don't know that. They could be—"

"It's not *right*. It doesn't feel right." She thrust Josie at Emily. "Leave now. Go out the back way and run up to the foothills. I'll go to the plaza and check the situation out. If everything's okay, I'll come and bring you back."

"Are you crazy? I'm not going to leave you here."

"You've got to go. You've got to take Josie away. She's only a baby. She's helpless. What if— They could hurt her, Emily."

Emily looked down at Josie in her arms. "No one would hurt her."

"They could. They might." Tears were

streaming down her face. "You don't know what— Oh, Christ, get out of here."

"Then you come with us."

"No, one of us has to see what's going on."

"Then let me do it." Emily started for the door.

"No!" She grabbed Emily's shoulders. "Listen to me. You're a doctor. You have a child of your own. What do I know about babies? It's only logical that you be the one who—" Emily was shaking her head. "Don't risk Josie because you want to protect me. I won't have it, Emily." She pushed past her toward the door. "Don't be an ass. Do what I tell you. I'll come for you when I know it's safe." She could feel Emily's stunned gaze on her.

"Bess!"

"Don't you dare follow me. Get *out*." She ran toward the plaza.

Don't come after me, she prayed. Run, Emily. Be safe, Emily.

Men were pouring from the army trucks. Men dressed in white decontamination suits and helmets, gleaming in the darkness like ghosts. One man was moving toward the fountain. The others were fanning out, entering the houses on three sides of the square. One man stood silent, watching, beside the back of a truck.

Bess took a deep breath. It could still be all right. "You've come too late," she called as she hurried forward. "They're almost all dead. Everyone is—" The man who had reached the fountain was pouring something into the water. "What are you doing? It's too late to—"

The man by the truck turned toward her.

She inhaled sharply as the headlights illuminated his face behind the transparent visor. She instinctively whirled away to run.

His gloved hand fell on her shoulder. "You're right, it's too late."

The last thing she saw was his fist arching toward her face.

THREE

White walls. The strong smell of antiseptic.

The same smell that had assaulted Bess when she woke up in the hospital after Danzar.

No.

Panic raced through her as her eyes flew open.

"Don't be afraid." A man was smiling down at her. Fortyish, dark skin, Indian features, a hooked nose, faintly gray at the temples. She had never seen him before.

She started to sit up and then collapsed back on the bed as dizziness overcame her.

"You mustn't move too quickly," the man

said soothingly. "You've been very ill. We're not sure the fever is gone yet."

"Fever?"

Was he a doctor? He was wearing a gray military uniform. Decorations beribboned his chest. "Who are you?"

He bowed slightly. "Colonel Rafael Esteban. I've been put in charge of this unfortunate situation at Tenajo."

Tenajo.

Sweet Jesus, Tenajo.

He considered what happened unfortunate? What an understatement. "Where am I?"

"San Andreas. A very small military medical facility."

"How long have I been here?"

"Two days. You were brought here directly when my man found you at Tenajo."

"Your man?" Memory flooded back to her. Cold blue eyes, high cheekbones, and a face that was hard, ugly, brutal. "He hit me."

"Kaldak has been disciplined. You were running toward him and he was afraid you'd contaminate him."

He hadn't been afraid. And she had been running away from him, not toward him. "I wasn't ill. He knocked me unconscious."

"Yes, it was after you woke up that he realized you were ill. You were screaming and out of control. He had to give you a shot and brought you here. You don't remember?"

"Of course I don't remember. It didn't happen. If he told you I was ill, he lied."

He shook his head.

"I tell you, he deliberately attacked me. And contaminate him against what? What happened at Tenajo?"

"Cholera. A particularly virulent strain."

"You're sure? Emily said the symptoms were—" Terror surged through her. "Emily. Where's my sister? Is she ill too?"

"Yes. She's not doing quite as well as you, but don't worry. She'll soon be on her way to recovery."

"I want to see her."

"That's not possible," he said gently. "You're too ill."

"I'm not ill. I feel fine." It was a lie. She felt sluggish and lightheaded. "And I want to see my sister."

"Tomorrow or the next day." He paused. "In the meantime, I have a great favor to ask of you. You can imagine the panic that would ensue if news of what happened at Tenajo got out before we could complete our investigation."

She couldn't believe what he was implying. "You're saying you want to cover it up?"

He looked shocked. "Certainly not. We merely need a little time. Water samples were taken and are on their way to the Centers for Disease Control. As soon as we have results we'll be able to take appropriate action."

She supposed that made sense. Damage control was common in government and military circles. Esteban's request wasn't really that unusual. And maybe she had been ill and was just being paranoid.

But Esteban had said they'd taken water samples. Yet she had seen something put *into* the fountain. What if the Mexican government had committed some sort of environmental foul-up and was trying to cover it up? "And what do you want from me?"

He smiled. "Nothing very much. Just your patience and your silence for the next few days. Is that too much to ask?"

"Maybe. I want to see my sister."

"In a few days."

"I want to see her now."

"Be reasonable. Neither of you is well enough."

She tried to think through her growing uneasiness. That he didn't want her to see Emily could mean one of two things. Either Emily and Josie had escaped, or Emily was a prisoner. "I want to speak to someone from the American embassy."

He clucked reprovingly. "You don't seem to realize your position. You're very ill and in no shape to have visitors."

"I'm not ill and I want to see someone from the American embassy."

"In time. You really must be patient." He went to the door and motioned someone to come in. "It's time for your shot now."

"Shot?"

"You need to rest. Sleep is so healing."

She went rigid when a white-coated orderly entered the room carrying a hypodermic tray. "I don't need to go to sleep. I just woke up."

"But sleep brings wisdom," Esteban said.

"I don't need—"

She jerked as the needle entered her right arm.

The next twenty-four hours were lost in a haze.

She woke, she slept. She woke again. Sometimes Esteban was there, looking at her. Sometimes she was alone.

Emily, where was Emily? She had to find—

The needle again.

And darkness.

Esteban was standing over her. He wasn't alone.

That hard face, those blue eyes gazing down at her with dispassion—they were familiar. *Kaldak.* The man in Tenajo. The one who had hit her. Esteban had said he had been disciplined, but that was a lie. This man wouldn't tolerate being disciplined.

"You can't put it off much longer," Kaldak said. "She's a witness."

"Don't be so eager. There's still a little time. Habin is uneasy about disposing of an American citizen. I can wait." Esteban smiled down at Bess. "Ah, awake again? How do you feel?"

Her tongue felt thick, but she managed to form a word. "Bastard."

His smile faded. "Actually, I am, but how unkind of you to comment on it. Maybe you're right, Kaldak. Perhaps I've been indulging Habin."

"Emily . . . Have to see Emily."

"Not possible. I told you that she was still ill. Though she's being much more polite and cooperative than you."

"Liar. She's—not—here. She—ran—"

He shrugged. "Think what you like. Come along, Kaldak."

They were gone. Darkness was closing in again.

She had to fight it. She had to think.

What Esteban and Kaldak had said meant something.

Disposing of an American citizen.

They were going to kill her.

Kaldak had wanted to do it immediately, but Habin had objected to—

Who was Habin? Didn't matter. Only Esteban and Kaldak were the threat.

What had she witnessed? A cover-up?

That didn't really matter either. Keeping herself alive mattered. And keeping Emily alive.

Esteban wouldn't let her see Emily, so

she must have escaped. Dear God, she hoped her sister had escaped.

But he might already be searching for her. She had to get to Emily and warn her, protect her . . .

She was so weak, she couldn't even lift a finger.

But she wasn't ill. Esteban had lied. She had a sore jaw where Kaldak had hit her and a Band-Aid on her arm covering the needle punctures. She'd be as strong as ever if she could shake off the sedatives.

Fight the sedatives.

Think. Plan.

There had to be a way out.

It was nearly sunset when Esteban came back into her room. She quickly closed her eyes.

"I'm afraid you'll have to wake up, Bess. You don't mind me calling you Bess, do you? I feel very close to you."

She kept her eyes shut.

He shook her.

She slowly opened her lids.

He smiled. "That's better. Those drugs are so annoying, aren't they? I know you must feel dreadful. Do you remember who I am?"

"Bastard," she whispered.

"I'll ignore that insult, since our time together is rapidly drawing to a close and I don't want to part on a sour note. I need some information. We've had to be extremely careful about tapping into our usual sources, and Kaldak has unearthed practically nothing of value about you. I tried to tell my associate, Habin, that such painstaking methods weren't necessary, but he believes it's unsafe to take any action blindly." He gently touched her cheek. "I hate to make Habin unhappy."

She wanted to bite his hand. One twist of her head would put her within range. No, that would be futile. That wasn't what she had planned.

"You won't mind me asking you a few questions, will you?" he asked. "Then I'll let you go back to sleep."

She didn't answer.

He frowned. "Bess?"

"When you let . . . me see my sister."

His frown cleared. "Oh, is that all? After you tell me what I need to know."

Bullshit. "You . . . promise?"

"Of course," he said. "Now, you came here to do a travel article."

She nodded.

"Who hired you?"

He was almost on top of her. That wouldn't give her a chance; he'd easily overpower her. Take a few steps back, she prayed. "John Pindry."

"You knew him before?"

"I did an article about San Francisco for him a few years ago." She kept her voice slurred. "Now may I see my—"

"Not yet. Tell me about your family."

"Emily."

"Your parents?"

"Dead."

"When?"

"Years ago." She faked a yawn. "Have to go to sleep . . ."

"Soon. You're being very good." He moved away from the bed and strolled toward the window.

Yes.

"No husband? No other close relatives?"

He was trying to find out if her next of kin were going to be a problem for him. "No."

"Poor child, you must be very lonely. A roommate?"

"No. I'm never in the U.S. long enough to share expenses." She'd have to be careful. That sounded a little too coherent.

"You travel extensively?"

His back was still turned to her. The arrogant son of a bitch thought she was too weak to pose any threat to him.

"It's my job."

"And what is the—"

The metal bedpan hit the back of his head. He slumped to his knees.

"Bastard." She jumped on his back and hit him again. He fell to the floor and she straddled him. She hit him again. His head was bleeding. She hoped she'd cracked his skull open. "Who's your next of kin, you sleazy—"

Arms encircled her rib cage from behind. She was jerked off Esteban's back.

Kaldak.

She struggled wildly.

"Don't fight me."

The hell she wouldn't fight him. She kicked backward at his shin.

"Stop it."

"Let me go."

Esteban was stirring. She hadn't killed him after all.

Panicked, she fought frantically against Kaldak's grip. He muttered a curse and one hand moved from around her body to her neck, beneath her left ear.

Darkness.

She woke a few minutes later and discovered she was strapped to the bed.

Her heart was beating so hard, she could scarcely breathe. She tugged upward. No use. She was pinned down.

Kaldak was helping Esteban to his feet. Blood was running down Esteban's temple, and he swayed on his feet. He looked down incredulously at the bedpan on the floor.

"Come on," Kaldak said. "I'll bandage you."

Esteban stared at Bess. "The whore hit me with that goddamn bedpan."

Fear knotted her stomach. She had never seen such hatred in anyone's face.

"You can punish her later," Kaldak said. "You're bleeding."

"I'm going to kill her."

"Not now. You've attracted too much attention already." He was guiding Esteban toward the door. "I strapped her down. She's not going anywhere. We'll take care of her later."

Later.

Esteban was going to kill her. Nothing could be more certain to Bess. She had humiliated him and she was going to die for it.

Esteban jerked away from Kaldak and lurched across the room toward her.

"*Puta*. Bitch." He raised his hand and slapped her. "Did you think you could kill me? You know nothing about—"

"I know you're a weakling and a coward who beats up helpless women." Her head was ringing from the blow, but the words tumbled out. Why not? She had nothing to lose. "I know you're a stupid man. Emily is too smart for you. She'll get away and show them all what an asshole you—"

He slapped her again, harder.

She glared up at him.

He leaned over the bed, so close she could feel his breath on her face and see the urine from the bedpan running down his cheeks. "You think so much of that sister of yours, don't you?"

"I know she's more clever than you'll ever—"

"Did you really think she got away from Tenajo?"

Terror seized her.

"We captured her shortly after Kaldak brought you in. She's been here at San Andreas all the time."

"You're lying. She got away."

"No." His gaze was narrowed on her face, drinking in her fear and uncertainty. "She's here."

It couldn't be true. "Prove it. Let me see her."

He shook his head.

"Then you *are* lying."

"It would only distress you to see her. It's such an unpleasant place."

"Where?"

"Four floors down in the basement." His lips curved in a malicious smile. "She's lying in a drawer in our morgue. Just as you will be soon. Your sister is dead."

He walked out of the room.

Pain crashed through her.

Emily dead.

She didn't know it was true. The sadist enjoyed hurting her and she was sure he had lied about other things. Why should she accept what he said about Emily?

But it could be the truth. Emily could be dead.

She's lying in a drawer in our morgue.

The hideous picture was like a knife twisting inside her.

It wasn't the truth. He had just wanted to hurt her.

Emily could be alive.

Her fingernails dug painfully into her palms as her fists clenched.

Four floors down in the basement. She's lying in a drawer in our morgue.

"Is it the truth?" Kaldak asked as he bathed the cuts on Esteban's head. "Is the Corelli woman here?"

Esteban ignored the question. "I want that Grady bitch dead. I'm through with her. To hell with Habin."

"As you like."

"Now."

Kaldak nodded. "But not here. It mustn't be connected directly with you. Some of the hospital personnel aren't in your pocket, and the orderly saw us leaving her room."

Esteban's head was pounding with pain and fury . . . and humiliation. He felt as helpless as when he was a boy, before he had discovered how easily he could change his life.

"I want her to die slowly and I want to watch it. I want to do it myself."

"Then we'd better wait. Unless you can arrange to leave San Andreas?"

"Not for at least another day. I expected to move much faster, but we're still running tests. Too many of the people died at different times. There may be something wrong."

Kaldak threw the cloth into the sink. "Then let's deal with the Grady woman now so that you can go on to more important matters. It probably doesn't matter if anyone's suspicious. I was being too careful."

It did matter, Esteban realized with frustration. He couldn't afford to have any investigation getting in his way.

His hesitation disappeared at Kaldak's next words. "If you want me to take care of it, just tell me how you want it done. I know a lot of ways. It doesn't have to be quick."

He wanted it too, Esteban thought. "Take her away from here. Make her disappear."

Kaldak nodded.

"But I want to hear every detail and I want her to hurt for a long time."

"Oh, she will." Kaldak smiled. "I promise you."

FOUR

No one came near Bess the rest of the evening. It was sheer torture lying there bound and helpless with Esteban's words playing and replaying in her mind.

But she wasn't helpless. She was alive and able to think. There had to be something she could do. If she could talk him into releasing her, she would find a weapon, even if it was another bedpan.

Impossible. He would never release her. Why should he, when she was staked out ready for slaughter? He was just taking his time making her suffer. . . .

The door was opening. A man stood in the doorway, a huge, dark silhouette outlined against the bright lights in the corridor. He was carrying a canvas bag. Not Esteban. Not the orderly. She couldn't see his face, but she knew who it was.

Kaldak.

He closed the door and came toward her. He stopped near enough for her to make out his face, and it was no more reassuring than when she had first seen it at Tenajo. Why was it so frightening? It was just flesh and blood like any other. Maybe because it looked as hard as granite. Maybe because of the way the features had been put together. Whatever it was, she couldn't take her eyes off him, and the more she looked, the more terrified she became.

"Do you know why I'm here?"

"I can guess." She tried to steady her voice. "Esteban sent you to do his dirty work."

"Esteban sent me to kill you."

She opened her mouth to scream, and he covered it with a hand.

"I didn't say I was going to do it."

Her teeth sank into his palm.

"Christ." He jerked his hand away.

She felt the copper taste of blood in her mouth as she again opened her mouth to scream. This time he hit her in the face. The room swam around her.

"I could have just as well knocked you out," he said roughly. "The only reason I didn't is that I don't want to have to carry you. You've caused me enough trouble."

He was unbuckling the straps, she realized vaguely. Why . . .

He unzipped the canvas bag, drew out jeans, shirt, tennis shoes, and tossed them on the bed. "No disturbance. Everything has to go smoothly. Get dressed."

She slowly sat up. "What are you doing?"

"I'm getting you out of here."

"Why?"

"Do you want to go or do you want me to strap you back up?"

"I want you to tell me why I should go anywhere with a man who just punched me."

"Because your choices are nil. It doesn't matter if you trust me or not. And, if you cause me too much trouble, I'll drop you by the wayside."

Reassuring, she thought bitterly. But he was right, she had no choice. She was far better off now than she had been a few minutes earlier. She picked up the jeans. "Turn your back."

"And have you bean me with a bedpan?"

It was as if he had read her mind. Too bad. She started pulling the jeans on. She was so weak, she could barely stand up. "What makes you think you can get me out?"

"Esteban doesn't want an awkward death here. I told him I'd take care of you somewhere away from here."

"What about my sister? He said he killed her." She looked up, holding her breath. "Did he?"

"I don't know."

"You have to know. You work for Esteban. You were at Tenajo."

He shrugged. "Esteban doesn't want his left hand knowing what his right hand is doing. He gives out only bits and pieces to prevent anyone from putting together the whole picture. I knew about you because I was the one who brought you in. I didn't see your sister, but that doesn't mean she wasn't taken later."

She fought the despair and panic. Kaldak could be lying too. She pulled off the bedgown and picked up the shirt. "How about Josie?"

"Who?"

"There was a baby, a little girl. She was alive."

"She's here. She was brought in several hours after I delivered you."

Her gaze flew to him. "Where? Is she still alive?"

He nodded. "Three doors down. Esteban has visited her several times."

Her initial joy immediately changed to fear. Emily would never have left Josie if she could possibly help it. "Then Emily must have been with her."

He shook his head.

"She wouldn't have left Josie."

"She wasn't brought in with the kid. Hurry up."

"Who are you?"

"Kaldak."

"I know that. Who . . . why would you want to help me?"

"You're in my way. I'm just shifting you to one side." The words were said with such cool indifference that they sent a chill through her.

"They'll just let us walk out of here? He trusts you that much?"

"He doesn't trust me at all. But he knows I'm efficient in what I do."

It didn't take an Einstein to deduce in what skill Kaldak excelled. She buttoned her shirt and slipped on the tennis shoes. "Then it's reasonable that he'd talk to you about Emily."

"No, it's not."

"He said she's dead."

"Then she might be."

"You must know—"

"We're out of here." He headed for the door. "Keep your mouth shut and stay close to me."

She didn't move.

"Would you rather stay here and wait for Esteban?"

As he had said, she had no choice. She'd go along with him until she found a way to escape.

She blinked as she stepped into the brightly lit corridor.

It was after midnight and the corridors were empty. Three nurses were gathered at a nurses' station by a bank of elevators. "Won't they stop us?" she whispered.

"I've already told them Esteban wants you released. They won't argue."

It seemed impossible that in a matter of minutes she could be out of there.

She glanced down the hall. Only three doors away from Josie. A matter of yards, and yet the idea of crossing that distance frightened her to death. "Wait a minute."

"Wait, hell," he said through his teeth as he grabbed her elbow. "Come *on*."

"Do you think I don't want to go?" she said fiercely. "But I'm not going to leave Josie. If you can get me out, you can get her out."

"I can't risk—"

"I'm not going without her."

She moved quickly down the hall, and to her surprise he followed.

She opened the door to Josie's room. It was dark, but she could see the shadowy outline of a crib.

Kaldak closed the door and turned on the light.

She gasped.

Josie, sound asleep, was hooked up to an IV bottle and looked too pale.

"I thought you said she was all right," Bess whispered.

"She's healthy enough." He disconnected the IV. "Esteban didn't trust the hospital personnel to take care of her, so he warned them she was contagious. He didn't want anyone becoming attached to her."

Clearly there was no danger of that happening with Kaldak. "So he stuck needles and tubes in her. Just look at her. The son of a bitch drugged her."

"Good. Maybe we'll be able to get her out of here without getting our heads blown off. Stay here. I'll be right back."

He left the room and was back in seconds with the canvas bag in which he'd brought her clothes.

"Give her to me."

"I'll do it." She carefully laid Josie in the bag and stuffed some diapers and a blanket in with her. It was a tight fit. "Do we have to zip it?"

"Yes." He was already zipping the bag. "Let's go."

"What if there's not enough air for her—"

"Go." He pushed her through the door and down the hall, carrying the canvas bag as if it weighed nothing, swinging it slightly. "Go straight to the elevators. Don't even look at the nurses. Things have been going on that worry them, and I make them uneasy. They'll probably try to ignore me."

He was right. The nurses suddenly became very busy as she and Kaldak approached the desk. When they were inside the elevator and the doors had closed, she unzipped the bag a few inches. "She might not be able to breathe."

Kaldak shook his head but didn't stop her. He punched the lobby button. "I have a jeep parked in front. We may be challenged at the gate, but I have credentials and I've already made sure the men on duty know who I am. It should go smoothly."

Smoothly. He had used that word before. He wanted everything neat and tidy.

The doors opened, and Kaldak took her elbow, nudging her forward into the deserted lobby. They passed the emergency fire stairs. They walked out the door and climbed into the jeep.

Four floors down.

She's dead.

Kaldak turned on the ignition.

No!

Bess jumped out of the jeep. "I can't leave yet. I have to go to the morgue. He said my sister was there."

"Oh, no, not again." His hand closed on her arm. "You don't go anywhere but out that gate."

"First I have to find out if he lied to me."

"The hell you do. The morgue is a sensitive area and it's guarded."

"Don't you understand? I have to *know*." She jerked away from him, darted back into the lobby, and ran toward the fire stairs.

She heard him cursing behind her as she ran down the concrete steps and threw open the basement door. Around the curve at the end of the corridor a soldier stood in front of the double doors to the morgue. He raised his rifle.

Kaldak knocked her aside and dove for the soldier's knees.

He went down and Kaldak straddled him. He struck downward with the edge of his hand, and the soldier went limp.

Kaldak glared at her. "Damn you to hell."

He was angry. Things weren't going smoothly for him any longer. "I have to know." She stood up and moved toward the doors.

"Wait." He got to his feet and pushed her aside. He went in ahead of her.

A gangly, white-coated attendant jumped up from behind the reception desk. "Who are you? No one is allowed in—"

"Shut up," Kaldak ordered. "Get down on the floor."

"It's not—"

Kaldak's hand chopped down on the side of his neck, and the attendant slumped forward.

"Come on," Kaldak said as he headed for the door next to the desk. "Let's finish this and get out of here."

She followed him into a room of stainless steel and glass-fronted cabinets full of instruments. An autopsy room. A chill went through her.

"No bodies," Kaldak said. "Can we go now?"

She swallowed to ease the tightness in her throat. "He said . . . she was in a drawer." She walked slowly toward the white metal door at the far end of the room.

Kaldak got there before her. He pushed open the door.

She saw two refrigerated drawers set in the far wall. Drawing a deep breath, she forced herself to walk toward them.

"Only two. Good. At least, that will save time." Kaldak stood beside the drawer on the left. "I think you should know Esteban received an autopsy report this morning."

Her gaze flew to his face. "You said you didn't know whether—"

"I don't know who the report was on. I

don't ask Esteban questions." His face was without expression. "Have you ever seen a corpse after an autopsy?"

She shook her head.

"It's not pleasant. I don't want you fainting and forcing me to carry you out of here."

Oh, no, that would cause a ripple in his plans.

He reached for the drawer pull. "I'll look for you."

She stopped him. "I don't trust you."

He shrugged and stepped back. "Suit yourself."

She drew another deep breath and reached for the pull. The door slid open easily.

Empty.

Relief poured through her. She shut the drawer, then moved to the next one.

Please, God, let this be empty too, she prayed desperately. She could feel Kaldak's gaze on her as she reached for the pull.

Let it be a lie.

Please . . .

The drawer slid out as easily as the first one.

But it was not empty.

Her stomach heaved as she whirled

away from the drawer. She barely made it to a sink in the next room before she threw up.

"I told you it wasn't pretty." Kaldak stood beside her, his hand on her waist supporting her. "If you'd listened to me, you wouldn't have had—"

"Shut up."

"Was it your sister?"

She shook her head. "Rico."

"The guide."

"I sent him to the nearest town to call the public health department. I thought when the trucks came that he'd reached— I never dreamed anything had happened to him. He wasn't ill when he left Tenajo." She whirled on him. "What happened to him? Did you—"

"I didn't touch him. I didn't even know he'd been intercepted."

"He wasn't sick, I tell you," she said fiercely. "Not any more than I was."

"It's been two days. If he took ill after he left Tenajo, he could have died within six hours after he manifested symptoms."

"That soon?" she whispered.

"Quicker if he wasn't strong and healthy."

He had been strong. Young and strong and full of life. She shuddered as she remembered the Rico she had seen in that drawer. "I don't know if I believe you."

"I don't care if you do or not," he said flatly. "But he probably died of the disease. Otherwise there wouldn't have been any reason to perform an autopsy." He turned away. "Wash your face. I want you looking normal when we drive through the gates."

She automatically turned on the water and started splashing water in her face.

"Open the door." Kaldak was dragging the guard from outside through the autopsy room.

"What are you doing?"

"I don't want him found right away." He shouldered the door open himself and pulled the guard toward the refrigerated drawers.

"Is he dead?"

Kaldak nodded.

"Did you have to kill him?"

"No, but it was surer." He pulled out the empty drawer, fitted the guard inside and slammed it shut. "Dead men don't get in the way."

Cold, calm, without expression or feeling. "What about the morgue attendant?"

"He's alive. I tied him up and put him in the broom closet down the hall."

"Why didn't you kill him too?"

He shrugged. "He's only a scared rabbit. No threat." He took a towel from beside the sink. "Stand still."

"What are—" He was rubbing her left cheek with the towel. She knocked his hand aside and stepped back. "Stop that."

He tossed her the towel. "Do the other cheek. You need color. You're too pale."

And everything must look normal, everything must go smoothly. Never mind that dead body stuffed in the drawer. Never mind Rico, whose life had been snuffed out.

"Do it. We have to get out of here. I left your Josie in the jeep and there's a chance she might wake up and start howling."

Josie. Yes, she had to think of Josie.

She scrubbed her right cheek with the towel, then threw it on the counter.

He picked it up and hung it neatly on the rack. "Let's go."

Within a few minutes they had climbed into the jeep and reached the guard post at the high gate surrounding the facility.

"Keep your mouth shut." Kaldak leaned

forward so that the light fell full on his face as the guard came out of the booth. "Open the gates."

The guard hesitated.

"What are you waiting for? You know me," Kaldak said. "Open the gates."

The guard peered uneasily past him at Bess and then at the canvas bag at her feet. "I've no instructions about a woman leaving the facility."

"I'm giving them to you now. Open the gates." He smiled. "Or better still, let's call Esteban. Of course, waking him up will make him very angry. Almost as angry as this delay is making me."

The guard hurriedly stepped back and pushed the lever to open the gates.

Kaldak pressed the accelerator, and the jeep leapt forward. The gates closed behind them.

"Will he call Esteban?" she asked as she reached down for the bag. She unzipped it and lifted Josie into her arms. She was still sleeping deeply.

"Maybe." He pressed the accelerator harder. "Although Esteban wouldn't be surprised that I took you away from here. He wanted it clean. But everything will be blown the minute they discover the kid missing and the guard in the morgue."

A chill went through her. Very little about her escape had been clean and smooth and neat. And fool that she was, she was driving away from the hospital with a killer. "Where are we going?"

He glanced at her and bared his teeth in a smile. "Scared? Good. You just sit there and think about it. At the moment I can't think of anyone whose neck I'd like to break as much as yours. I might have gotten around killing that guard but you had to take the damn kid, didn't you?"

"Yes, I did." For some reason his anger caused some of her fear to ebb. After watching the cool precision with which he had killed the guard, she doubted if threats were part of his modus operandi. If he really intended to kill her, he would just do it. She hoped. She repeated, "Where are we going?"

"Away from San Andreas. Now, go to sleep. I'll wake you when we get there."

"You think I'd trust you enough to go to sleep? You just said you want to break my neck."

"It was only a passing thought. And you decided that I didn't mean it, didn't you?"

He read her too well. His perceptiveness made her more uneasy than his brutality. "I believe you're capable of anything."

"Oh, I am. So shut up and don't provoke me."

"Why did you help me leave that place?"

His hands clenched the steering wheel. "I'll make a bargain with you. If you'll just keep your damn mouth shut and let me think, I'll answer your questions once we get there."

"Get where?"

"Tenajo."

She stared at him in shock. "We're going to Tenajo? Why?"

"After we get there."

"Now."

"My God, you're stubborn." He turned and stared directly into her eyes. "I'd think you'd want to go back. The last time you saw your sister was in Tenajo."

"She can't still be there."

"Then maybe she left a message for you. Do you have anywhere else to start looking?"

"I could start with you. What do you know about Emily?"

"If you don't shut up, I'll gag you until we get to Tenajo."

This was no threat. He meant what he said. "How far are we from Tenajo?"

"Three hours."

She slowly settled back in the seat and cradled Josie's small, warm body closer. Three hours and she'd be back in Tenajo. The knowledge swept over her like a dark cloud. Hold on. It would be all right. Don't start shaking.

Had the dogs stopped howling?

They reached the hill overlooking Tenajo. The same place Rico had stopped that first day.

No lights.

No movement.

No sound.

"What happened to the dogs?"

"The public health team swept through here yesterday. They rounded up all the pets and are keeping them under observation to make sure they aren't carriers. When the relatives of the dead are notified, they'll be given a chance to adopt the pets." He smiled cynically. "It's one of those humane gestures that make politicians look good."

"The relatives haven't been notified yet?"

Kaldak shrugged. "An entire town wiped out isn't small potatoes. The government wants facts before it exposes itself to the media."

"They want to cover it up."

"Probably."

"What are they covering up? A nuclear waste foul-up?"

"No."

"It wasn't cholera."

"No, but that's what the CDC report will say."

"How could—" She remembered the man pouring something into the fountain. "You contaminated the water supply yourself."

He nodded.

"If it wasn't a waste foul-up, what happened at Tenajo?"

"Don't you want to go look for your sister?"

He had again hit on the one objective sure to distract her. Smart. Very smart. Every moment she was with him she was becoming more and more aware of the intelligence behind that frightening face. "Why have you come back?"

"Where do you want me to drop you?"

"Third house on the right." Where Emily had found Josie. The little girl who had beaten the odds. Bess's arms tightened around the baby. "Were there any other survivors?"

Kaldak shook his head. "Just you."

"I mean any townspeople other than Josie."

"Not that I know about." He stopped the jeep. "When you finish searching, come to the plaza. I'll pick you up there."

She got out. "Aren't you afraid I'll run away?"

"It doesn't matter. I'd find you."

The absolute certainty in his voice unnerved her. She felt a rush of fear that she tried to smother. "Why are you here? What are you looking for?"

"Money."

She stared at him in bewilderment. "Money?"

"If you find any, don't touch it. It's mine."

FIVE

Emily was not in the house.

But there were signs that she had been there. The huge pot of water for sterilization was on the stove and her leather medical bag was on the table.

Emily always took her medical bag everywhere. Why hadn't she taken it with her? Maybe she had not wanted to burden herself with the bag. Maybe she had just stuffed some emergency supplies in her pockets.

Bess carefully set Josie down on the couch, crossed to the table, and unfastened the bag. Everything was neat and nothing seemed missing.

But Emily was always neat, and Bess

didn't actually know what Emily carried in the bag.

She crossed the room to the crib. It, too, appeared undisturbed. The mosquito netting was still thrown up the way Bess had left it when she had snatched Josie and given her to Emily.

Bess moved through to the next room, which bore poignant evidence of the people who had lived there. A wooden crucifix over the bed. Photographs of a smiling older man and woman on the nightstand. Josie's grandparents? Were they also dead?

Stop it. She had come for a purpose. She started to search. No note. No other sign that Emily had been there. Disappointment swamped her. She had told herself not to expect anything, but she had felt a fugitive hope that Emily was still in Tenajo. No, she must have taken Josie and run as Bess had begged her to do.

But Josie had been taken by Esteban. And the only way that could have happened was if Emily had been captured and killed by Esteban.

Or Kaldak. In the short time she had known him he had shown himself capable of anything.

No, she wouldn't permit herself to consider the possibility that Emily was dead. Just the thought of it caused her to panic. Emily had escaped.

A sound came from the other room. A whimper. Josie was stirring at last.

She knelt down beside the couch. Josie's big, dark eyes were open and she was smiling.

"Hi," Bess whispered. "Here we are again. Now what am I going to do with you?"

Josie gurgled at her.

She stroked the baby's cheek. There was nothing softer or more satiny on earth than a baby's skin. "Where did you lose Emily? You'd be much happier with her. She knows a lot more than I do about babies. I'm a rank amateur."

Josie reached up, caught a strand of Bess's hair, and tugged.

Bess laughed softly. "What the hell, we'll get along. We just have to decide what to do."

And whom to trust.

She changed Josie's diaper and then went looking for food. She found a few jars of sealed baby food in one of the cupboards. She opened one and got half the minced beef down Josie before she started playing with her food.

"No games," Bess told her firmly. "We've got serious stuff here." She picked Josie up and carried her out onto the porch. She looked up at the hills. Was Emily somewhere in those hills, trying to reach the coast?

Lord, she hoped so.

She was tempted to run toward those hills herself. Well, why not? She had a good sense of direction and a certain amount of experience in rough country. Three years before she'd found herself stranded in Afghanistan and made it all the way to the Pakistani border. There was a good chance she could make it to the coast.

I'd find you.

Just try, Kaldak.

Josie whimpered and Bess loosened her grasp, which she had unconsciously tightened. No, this wasn't the time to run. Hiking through the hills by herself was one thing, but toting a baby around a wilderness was another. She had to be responsible and not act impulsively.

She would wait and see. Kaldak may not

know where Emily was, but he understood more than she did about what had happened at Tenajo.

She went down the porch steps and started toward the plaza.

Kaldak was coming out of the cantina carrying a shiny metal briefcase when she reached the fountain. "That didn't take you long," he said.

"She's not there. You knew she wouldn't be."

"I knew it wasn't likely. So did you." He glanced at Josie. "She woke up. Is she okay?"

"Fine. I fed her and changed her and she couldn't be happier."

"You've been busy." He paused. "Did you find any money?"

"No," she said, repulsed. "I didn't look."

"I haven't found any either." He crossed the street to the general store. "Wait here."

Robbing the dead. He was even worse than she had thought.

He was frowning as he came out of the general store a few minutes later. He clearly hadn't found anything. Good.

"Any money you find belongs to those poor people's relatives."

He shook his head. "It belongs to me." He was climbing the steps of the church.

She followed him. "My God, what are you doing? This is a church."

"The priest is dead, isn't he?"

"Yes. And that makes stealing from the church all right?"

"You found him?"

She nodded.

"Where?"

She pointed to the spot. "Next to the poor box."

"What poor box?"

She shrugged. "It was beside him. Rico kicked it."

His gaze raked the area and then focused on the second pew. She stood watching in disbelief as he walked over, pulled the poor box from beneath the pew, and lifted the lid.

"Jackpot," he said softly.

She moved closer and looked down into the box at stacks of violet-blue and lilac twenty-peso bills.

"You've found what you're looking for," she said coldly. "May we leave now?"

He unfastened the metal briefcase. "Stand back a few feet." She did and watched him empty the poor box into the briefcase. His expression was no longer impassive but filled with savage satisfaction. The amount of money in the poor box must have been substantial to stir a man like Kaldak.

"Let's go." He picked up the briefcase and went out the door.

She followed him. "Why do you want that money?"

"So I won't have to go back to San Andreas and risk getting my head blown off."

"It's not that much money. It wouldn't set you up for life."

He didn't answer. "Get in the jeep. I'll make one more sweep and be right with you. We've got to get out of here. We've stayed longer than I like."

She didn't move. "Where are we going?"

"Into the hills. Esteban has scouts all around here. We're bound to have been seen. We have to get out of town."

"I'm not going anywhere until you tell me what's going on."

"I don't know how much to tell you."

"You haven't told me *anything*."

"I've probably told you more than I should."

"For my good?"

"No, for mine."

"Of course, why would I assume anything else?"

"You shouldn't. I've already done more for you than I should have. I'm an ass. I should have handled it better." He started toward the general store. "Now there's only damage control."

"And the money is damage control?"

"Get in the jeep."

A chill went through her. Damage control could mean mending fences with Esteban by killing her and Josie. Why should she trust him? He was a murderer and a grave robber.

But who else could she trust?

Herself. Nobody but herself. Any other choice could be fatal.

She spun on her heel and started across the plaza. "I have to go back to Josie's house and get food and diapers for her. You can pick us up there."

She could feel his gaze on her, but she resisted the temptation to look back.

The gesture would have looked suspiciously fugitive.

. . .

She was gone.

Shit.

Kaldak walked out of Josie's house and jumped into the jeep. She couldn't have been gone longer than ten minutes; she was on foot and had the baby. She shouldn't be that difficult to run down. Dammit, the situation was difficult enough without having to drag her with him kicking and screaming.

But if that was the way it had to be, then so be it. There was no way he could let her get away from him.

Kaldak and the woman were in the hills above Tenajo, but they had separated.

Esteban hung up the phone, leaned back in bed, and contemplated the report. Kaldak's recent actions added up to a disturbing total. Was he CIA? Very possibly. And, if he was CIA, how much did he know? How much had he found out here and how much in Libya?

He reached for the phone again and called Habin.

"There's a slight problem," Esteban said. "The man you sent me has disappeared."

"Kaldak?"

"He killed one of my guards and took the Grady woman out of the facility."

Habin swore vehemently. "How could you let that happen?"

"You're the one who sent me Kaldak. I assumed he could be trusted. What do you know about him?"

"He came excellently recommended by Mabry in Iraq and he behaved impeccably while he was with me."

"But you still shoved him off on me when you got the opportunity."

"Not because he wasn't trustworthy. That would be cutting off my nose to spite my face."

"Oh, yes, your fortune-teller."

"Are you mocking me?" Habin asked.

Esteban retreated. Now wasn't the time to alienate Habin. "Merely a remark. How much does Kaldak know about your end?"

"Nothing. He had a job to do and did it."

The idiot probably wouldn't have realized it if Kaldak had found out everything. "We need to know about Kaldak."

"What if he's not CIA?"

"Then we'll hear from him."

"You should have killed the Grady

woman at once. It was dangerous to keep her alive."

Habin was forgetting that he, too, had hesitated about ending her life. But Esteban chose not to argue. "That mistake can be rectified. They've not made it out of the country yet. They were sighted in Tenajo an hour ago."

"Then what are you doing talking to me? Go after them."

"That's my intention. Don't worry, I'll take care of it."

"You had better be right. I can continue without you if you don't repair this bungling ineptitude."

"I'll repair it. Just see what you can find out about Kaldak. He's our prime concern."

Esteban waited politely for Habin to hang up first. It was difficult to display courtesy to assholes, but he had learned a discipline and control they would never know. He would be glad when he no longer needed them. His own plans were almost in place. He needed only a linchpin to launch the first phase, and Morrisey should be calling any day with the location of a suitable tool. He needed to be patient just a little longer.

"Perez," he called.

Sergeant Perez appeared in the doorway.

"Order my car. I'm going to Tenajo."

Perez nodded and vanished.

He wasn't as bright as Galvez, but he was silent and obedient and he lacked the curiosity and greed that had made Galvez dangerous. At least, Kaldak had gotten rid of that problem. Too bad he now presented a far greater one.

Still, it shouldn't take more than a day or two to find him and the woman. And then Kaldak would be vanquished. The thought sent a surge of excitement and eagerness through Esteban.

Where are you, Kaldak?

Suddenly Esteban had a vision of Bess Grady before him. Of course, the bitch had to die. It was absolutely imperative, but she was only a woman.

And women were so easy to kill.

They'd found her tracks again.

Bess wiped the sweat out of her eyes and moved to the side of the trail. The shale was slippery, but it left no mark of passing.

She could hear the soldiers calling to

one another on the other side of the hill. Soon they would reach the crest and she would be in view. She had to find a hiding place before that happened.

She was so scared. She had thought she was home free when she'd lost Kaldak the second day, but then the soldiers had come. Had that been his doing?

Josie whimpered in the blanket sling Bess had fashioned. "Hush," Bess whispered.

She couldn't blame Josie for complaining. Josie was as hot as Bess and hungry. She'd run out of food the third day and refused almost all the edible plants and berries Bess had found on the hillside.

But Josie mustn't cry now. Not now. To keep her silent, Bess had been forced to give her sedatives she had taken from Emily's bag. But the pursuit today had been so intense, Bess had had no time to administer a new dose, and the drug had almost worn off.

She skidded, fell, rose to her feet, and fell again.

A grove of trees lay ahead, balanced precariously on the sloping hillside.

The soldiers were closer to the crest.

She was almost there.

Oh, God, let there be somewhere she could hide.

She was in the grove.

Nothing.

The pine trees were leggy, the leaves sparse. Even if she climbed one of them she would be seen.

A fallen tree. Its branches spread over the ground.

She dove for it, under it, digging furiously in the hard earth to form a cover. The dead branches created a canopy, but she could still be seen by anyone who stooped and peered through the foliage. Or heard, if she couldn't control the harshness of her breathing.

Or if Josie didn't quiet down.

"Please, Josie. Please, baby."

Josie's whimpers increased.

The soldiers were close. They must have entered the grove. They were talking.

Let them keep on talking. Maybe they wouldn't hear Josie.

They had stopped talking.

She held her breath.

Josie fell mercifully quiet.

The tree shifted above her.

She braced herself.

No, they were stepping on the tree, jumping over it. She could see their legs as they landed on the other side.

Josie stirred in her sling.

No.

The soldiers were talking again. They didn't like the heat or spending the day climbing hills. They didn't like Esteban. He was a son of a bitch.

Amen.

Josie whimpered again.

Bess's heart stopped.

A bird?

Perez turned to look back at the grove.

They should probably check it out. They'd been instructed to follow every lead. Esteban would be furious if they lost the woman. He'd sent everyone climbing these fucking hills, even him. Perez had thought he'd inherited a soft job when he'd been elevated to Galvez's position, but here he was again sweating and swearing with the rest of the ordinary soldiers.

"You see something?" Jimenez asked.

The grove was in deep shadow. Perez saw nothing.

But had he heard something?

He'd almost fallen on that damn slippery shale when they'd gone down the slope. His ankle still throbbed.

Screw Esteban.

It was a bird.

"I was just catching my breath." He turned around and started down the hill. "I don't see anything."

Thank you, God.

Bess could feel every muscle go limp as she realized the soldiers hadn't heard Josie.

They were leaving the grove, searching the hillside beyond the trees for more signs of her passing through.

If she was very still, if she could keep Josie still . . .

There was a chance.

The soldiers were almost out of sight. In a moment it would be safe to move out and try to find another hiding place for the night.

Or maybe she should keep moving. How far was she from the coast? she wondered wearily. She must have come at least thirty miles from Tenajo, and that left another twenty to go.

Twenty miles. The distance seemed so small when you were driving it in a car. It was an eternity on foot. It seemed impossible to—

It wasn't impossible. That was only a stupid excuse because she was so tired. She would not give up. Josie needed her. Emily needed her.

Josie whimpered again.

"Don't nag, kid. We're on our way." She carefully edged out from beneath the tree. "But I need a little help. Okay?"

She needed more than a little help.

But she'd take what she could get.

Darkness was falling. They could no longer see to track the Grady woman. She would be safe for the night.

Esteban clenched his hands into fists as he gazed up at the hills.

Four days. Those fools had been searching for four days and they still hadn't found her. Kaldak had vanished without a trace, but there was no reason his men should not have been able to capture the woman. He could almost imagine the bitch laughing at them.

No, they had pushed her too hard for her to be amused by the hunt. They had found blood on the rocks that afternoon.

Why would she not give up?

A hand clamped over Bess's mouth, jarring her awake.

Someone was astride her. Sweat. Musk. A man . . .

Esteban's soldiers. They had found the cave. . . .

She rolled to the side and struck upward with her fist. She connected with flesh.

"Be *still*. I won't hurt you."

Kaldak!

She struck out again.

"Dammit, I'm here to help you."

Josie let out a shrill wail from the pallet Bess had made for her against the cave wall.

Kaldak stiffened. "What the hell?"

He had relaxed his hold. Bess heaved up and to the side, dislodging him, and jumped to her feet.

Do it right, she told herself. Do it right.

She whirled, her fist punching at his stomach as he got to his feet. She grabbed his arm, swiveled, and flipped him over her shoulder to the ground.

She heard him swearing as she snatched up Josie and took off for the cave entrance.

He brought her down with a tackle. She fell on her left side, instinctively protecting Josie, and rolled the baby away from her. Her knee sliced up into Kaldak's groin.

He grunted with pain but flipped her over and straddled her. His hands closed on her throat.

He was going to kill her. Oh, God, she didn't want to die. Her fingernails dug viciously into the backs of his hands.

"Stop it," he said through his teeth. "I'm not used to pulling back. I could break your neck without—" He drew a deep breath and slowly loosened his grasp. "Listen to me, I'm not going to hurt you. I'm not going to hurt Josie. I'm trying to help you."

"Bullshit."

"Then run away. Be stupid. In one day, maybe two, Esteban will catch up with you. He's camped not four miles from here right now."

She glared up at him. "How do you know that if you aren't with him?"

"He tracked you. I tracked him. He was easier than you."

She shook her head. "When I lost you, you called out the soldiers."

"I didn't have to call them. They were pouring through these hills eight hours after you took off from Tenajo. If I'd joined Esteban, wouldn't they be here right now?"

Josie let out another wail.

"She needs you," Kaldak said. "And we need her to be quiet. I'll let you up if you promise to hear me out."

"Would you trust me?"

"No, but I think you're an intelligent woman who will weigh the consequences. I can get you out of these hills."

"I can get myself out."

"Maybe. But you can't radio a helicopter in for a pickup. Do you want to dodge Esteban for the next week and risk getting Josie captured again?"

She went still. A helicopter.

"Get off me."

"Will you listen?"

"I'll listen."

His heavy bulk was lifted off her and she sat up and reached for Josie.

The baby wailed again.

"She has to be quiet," Kaldak said. "There are guards around the perimeter of Esteban's camp."

The warning caused her suspicions to ease a little. "What do you expect? You scared her." She cuddled the baby closer. "And she's hungry and probably wet again." She felt Josie's diaper. Damp. "I'm out of diapers. I was able to snatch only a few when I left Tenajo, and I had no time or way to keep them clean. Do you have anything I can use?"

"Maybe. I'll look in my backpack." He shrugged the pack off his back. "I wasn't prepared for this."

"Neither was I," she said dryly.

Kaldak switched on the flashlight he had taken out of his backpack.

"Turn it off. They'll see it," she said frantically.

He shook his head. "It's okay. We're far enough into the cave." He shoved aside the metal briefcase at the bottom of the pack, pulled out a white T-shirt, and tossed it to her. "How's this?"

"It will have to do." She glanced at him as she tore the shirt in two. "Do you have any food?"

"Field rations."

"Get it out and open it. I'll try to feed her." She knelt and changed Josie's diaper. "How did you find me here?"

"I tracked you."

"So did the soldiers. They didn't find me."

"They almost did this afternoon. In the grove."

She went still. "How did you know that?"

"I was tracking them at that point. I was pretty sure they were on the right scent."

"I didn't see you in the grove."

"I saw you."

"And you tracked me to this cave without my seeing you? How? When I saw Esteban's soldiers?"

"Maybe I'm better than they are," he said simply.

"Why are you better? Have you done this for a living?"

"Sometimes. My profession often calls for hunting skills." He watched as she sat Josie on her lap and began feeding her. "You do that very well."

"Anyone can feed a baby. Talk to me. I'm listening."

"You shouldn't have run away from me. I'm trying to help you."

"As I recall, when you weren't ordering me around, you were threatening me. I was in your way."

"That didn't mean I wouldn't get you safely away from Esteban. I never had any other intention."

She studied him. It was difficult to read the expression on that face, but instinct told her he was telling the truth. "I couldn't know that. You wouldn't talk to me."

He shrugged. "I made a mistake. I was hoping it wouldn't be necessary. I'll talk to you now."

"What happened at Tenajo?"

"Are you sure you want to know?"

"Don't be stupid. You're damn right I do." Her voice vibrated with feeling. "You *listen* to me. I don't give a damn about your damage control. All I care about is what's happened to Emily and me in the last week. I have a right to know. Now, you tell me."

He was silent a moment. "Okay. Ask me questions. I'll answer what I can."

"How did those people die?"

"I'm not entirely sure. I think it may have been an artificially produced disease."

She stared at him in shock. "Some kind of germ-canister foul-up?"

He smiled sardonically. "You keep thinking it's an accident."

"Are you saying that the Mexican government purposely loosed that sickness on Tenajo?"

"The Mexican government has nothing to do with it."

"Isn't Esteban a colonel in the Mexican army?"

"A convenience that allows him a certain amount of power and freedom. It also allowed him to neatly cover up the results of the experiment."

"Experiment?"

"They had to see if the biological agent worked. Tenajo was a testing ground."

A little boy lying on the floor of the store with chocolate smeared on his palms.

Tears stung her eyes. "Damn you to hell."

"I didn't know," he said roughly.

"You had to know. You worked for him."

"I knew something was going on at Tenajo, but I didn't suspect what it was until the night it happened. For the past few

months there were some cases of minor ill-
ness in the Tenajo area. Nothing fatal. I think
Esteban must have been practicing. I
thought it was going to be the same thing—
Esteban didn't let anyone—" He stopped in
mid-sentence. "I didn't know."

"Why did—" She tried to steady her
voice. "Why would they do this?"

"When a test takes place on a limited
plane it's usually meant to be applied on a
larger scale somewhere else."

"Where?"

"I don't know."

She felt dazed. It was difficult to think.
"You said the public health department did a
sweep. Why didn't they pick up on something?"

"Esteban didn't call them in until after the
cleanup and the cholera was planted. He
has his own doctors in the Mexico City
morgue who will give autopsy reports to the
effect that it was cholera that killed Tenajo."

"All this trouble . . . It must have been in
the planning stage for a long time."

"Two years that I know about."

"If you work with Esteban, why did you
help me?"

"I don't work with Esteban." He added

dryly, "Can't you tell? I'm one of the good guys."

"No, I can't tell. I watched you kill a man."

"Then don't trust me. Don't trust anyone. But let me help you. I *can* help you, Bess."

"How? Are you some sort of government agent?"

"Some sort."

"Be specific, dammit."

"I've been with the CIA for a number of years."

She felt a rush of relief. "You could have told me."

"I wouldn't have told you now if I could have found a way around it. Besides, would you have believed me?"

Did she believe him now? He could be lying.

But to what end? He had gotten her out of San Andreas and there was no reason for him to show up here without Esteban's soldiers if he meant to turn her over to them. "You should have told me."

"You know now." He held her gaze. "Listen to me, Bess. I'll take care of you. I intend to get you out of here and safely to the U.S. There's nothing I won't do to make sure of that. I *will* do it. If you don't believe anything else, believe that."

She did believe it. No one could doubt his sincerity.

He reached for the baby. "Now, let me finish feeding her while you eat something yourself."

Her arms tightened around the baby. "I can eat later."

"Actually, you can't. I had to leave the jeep in the lower foothills. We have a long trek out of these hills. I want to get started right away." He took Josie and the food from her. "Dig another can out of my pack and eat."

She hesitated and then did as he told her. She needed strength to get through this. She wrinkled her nose at the first bite. No wonder Josie had been tentative.

But the baby was now contentedly devouring the rations Kaldak was feeding her with surprising gentleness and skill. "She seems to have stood the trip well," he said. "She looks healthy."

"She's a survivor. Most babies are if you give them a chance."

He smiled down at the baby and wiped her mouth. "I like survivors." He looked up at

Bess. "You don't look so bad yourself. I expected to have to lug you over the hills in a sling after four days on the run."

"You still might. Or I might be the one dragging you." She put the spoon back into the pack and tossed the empty ration can aside. "Let's go." She picked up Josie's blanket. "Give her to me. I'll carry her on my back."

He wrinkled his nose. "That's very unpleasant-smelling. Urine?"

"What do you expect? I had a chance to wash the blanket only once. If it bothers you, stay away from us."

"It bothers me. I have a very delicate nose. But I can get used to anything." He picked up the backpack. "I think I can manage to stand you for a day or two."

"Is that how long it will take? What about the helicopter?"

"You made good time, but Esteban is too close. We'll have to backtrack and go around to the north. The hills are too rough here to land a helicopter." He placed Josie in the sling and helped Bess put it on. "So I've arranged a set-down about thirty miles from here. As soon as we get clear of these hills, I'll call for a pickup."

He seemed so sure, almost casual. For the first time, hope surged through her. She had never given up, but now she could see a light at the end of the tunnel.

And she wasn't alone any longer.

"Then what are we waiting for?" She strode past him and out of the cave.

Kaldak raised a brow as he followed her. "Me, evidently."

SIX

 The rats.
Esteban jerked upright on his cot. *"No."*

No rats. Only a nightmare. He was sweating, shuddering. The odor of garbage and decay filled his nostrils.

Why wouldn't the rats go away?

He stood up and moved naked to the washstand and splashed water in his face. The rats had not come to plague him in a long time. There must be a reason.

The Grady woman. The nightmare had first come the night after she had escaped with Kaldak. When he found and killed Bess Grady, the rats would flee back into their holes.

He moved to the tent entrance and stared out into the darkness. Bess Grady was out there somewhere. Close. His instincts seldom failed him when he was this near a prey.

To hell with the darkness. He couldn't wait for morning.

"Wake up, Perez!" he shouted as he pulled on his clothes. "Rouse the men. We leave in ten minutes."

"We can stop here and rest for a few minutes." Kaldak shrugged off his backpack. "You'd better change the baby and give her some water."

"Of course I'll do that," Bess said, bristling. "You don't have to tell me. We managed quite well without you."

"Sorry. I guess I'm used to running things."

"You don't have to tell me that either." In the last eight hours he had demonstrated that characteristic time and time again. The decisions had all been his, and he had made them easily and surely, pushing and prodding her every step of the way.

"You're cross with me." His brows lifted. "I'm surprised you didn't let me know earlier."

"I don't like being left out of decisions." She finished diapering Josie and held her hand out for the canteen. "But this is your area of expertise. It was clear you knew what you were doing. I would have been stupid to argue with you."

Kaldak's gaze focused on Josie. "She's a very good baby."

"Yes, she is," Bess said, softening. She fed Josie a little more water and wiped her forehead and neck and then did the same for herself. Though the poor kid was hot and sweaty, and a heat rash was starting on her neck, she had let out only a few whimpers during the journey. Josie was a true miracle.

She tenderly brushed the baby's dark wispy hair away from her face. Josie smiled up at her and Bess couldn't resist giving her a quick hug. "Do you have children?"

He shook his head. "Do you?"

"No, but I've always been crazy about kids." She smiled. "Emily has a daughter, Julie, and she's a charmer. When she was Josie's age, she was cute as a button. Red hair and a yell that nearly brought the house down. Not placid like Josie."

"Josie has a pretty good pair of lungs herself."

"But she uses them to make her needs known. Julie usually just wanted to make a statement. I remember once we took her to the lake and she saw—" Good God, she must be tired. What was she rambling about? And to Kaldak, of all people. "I'm sorry, you can't be interested in this."

"I'm interested." He stood up. "Are you rested enough to go on?"

"What would you do if I said I wasn't?"

"Tell you we have to keep pushing anyway."

"I thought as much," she said dryly as she put Josie into the sling. "I'm ready." Her gaze went to the hills behind them. "Do you suppose they're close?"

"Closer than I'd like. I caught sight of them two hours after we started."

"Why didn't you tell me?" she asked, startled.

"Why worry you? It was still dark and they were having trouble tracking. I did some weaving and lost them again." He frowned. "But I didn't expect them to start before dawn. Esteban is driving them hard." He started down the trail. "He wants you."

Her lips tightened grimly. "Well, he won't get me. How much longer do we have to go?"

"Another few hours before we're clear to radio for the helicopter. After that, maybe two hours to the rendezvous point."

Relief rushed through her. Not much longer. "Thank God."

"Oh, yes, and me, of course."

Good heavens, Kaldak was actually smiling at her.

She smiled back. "Of course."

Esteban looked down at the tracks. "Two of them?"

Perez nodded. "Joaquin says a man is with her. A large man. He must have joined her last night. It was only a single set of tracks before." He looked back over his shoulder. "Benito is motioning to me. Do I have your permission to—"

"Go."

She had help. The Grady bitch had help.

Kaldak? He was a big man.

Yes, probably Kaldak; he had already demonstrated his skill in making his way through these hills. Now he was with the woman and if he was CIA, he might be able to pull in more help.

If Esteban didn't reach them before they got out of the hills.

Perez was back. "We've intercepted a radio signal."

"Where?" Esteban asked.

"Southwest. Six miles."

They had cleared the hills and were radioing for assistance. Probably a helicopter.

Goddammit.

"*Get* them."

Bess staggered and then caught herself before she could fall.

"All right?" Kaldak asked, not looking back.

No, it wasn't all right. Kaldak had increased the pace in the last hour and she was bone weary, hot, and had a stitch in her side. "Can we go just a little slower?"

"No."

"Why not? We're close, aren't we?"

"Close isn't home."

"Josie needs changing."

"She'll have to wait. Hurry."

The last word was so fraught with tension, her stride automatically accelerated. She glanced back over her shoulder. "What's wrong? Are they close?"

"They've always been close and they're bound to have picked up the signal."

Josie whimpered.

Poor baby. "How far do we have to go?"

"Another hour. And Esteban probably is no more than twenty minutes behind us."

"What if the helicopter isn't there?"

Kaldak didn't answer.

He didn't have to answer.

In the valley below, the army-green helicopter shimmered in the twilight. It looked beautiful.

Bess's pace hastened in response to the hope leaping through her. "It's there. We're going—"

A bullet whistled past her ear.

"Shit." Kaldak grabbed her arm and pulled her down. She stumbled on a tuft of grass, caught her balance.

A second shot. Kicking up dirt ahead of her.

She glanced over her shoulder.

Soldiers. Streaming over the hill.

The helicopter door was open.

Another shot.

She jerked as pain streaked along her side.

They reached the helicopter. Kaldak tossed her onto the floor and followed her.

"Up, Cass," he shouted.

The door was still open as the helicopter rose jerkily.

One of the soldiers leapt upward and caught hold. Kaldak ground his heel on the man's hand and he fell back to the ground.

Bullets sprayed the helicopter.

What if they hit the fuel tank?

Clear. They were high above the ground. Surely out of range.

She looked at Kaldak. He nodded and she went limp with relief.

"You're bleeding." He was looking at her shirt. "You were hit?"

"My side. It's all right. Just a graze I think. I'll tend to— Oh, my God."

Josie was too still.

Bess frantically shrugged off the sling. The blanket was stained with blood.

Josie.

"Son of a bitch. Son of a bitch. Son of a bitch." Tears were running down her cheeks.

"They shot her. They shot Josie." The bullet that had grazed her side must have gone through the baby. "Goddamn baby killers."

"Is she dead?"

"I'm trying to find out." Hip wound. Blood. Too much blood. "She's alive. Barely."

"Can we save her?"

"I don't know. I know first aid, but I'm not a doctor. Maybe. If I can stop the bleeding." She was working quickly. "You get her to a hospital."

"I can't risk you. We can't land until—"

"Don't tell me that. I don't care where you take us." She shot him a fierce glance. "You get me to a medical facility where I can get help for her."

Kaldak nodded. "I'll find a place." He headed for the cockpit.

"Son of a bitch." She couldn't stop crying. She had sworn never to open herself to this kind of agony again. Yet here it was, deeper than ever before. "Hold on, Josie," she whispered. "We've gone through too much together. Don't leave me now, baby."

"We're going to set down." Kaldak was back. "How is she?"

"Unconscious. I've managed to stop the bleeding. Unless there's internal bleeding. Where are we?"

"Gulf of Mexico. I've located an aircraft carrier, the USS *Montana.* They'll have a doctor and full medical care. We should be down in ten minutes." He headed back to the cockpit. "One way or the other."

"What do you mean?"

"Aircraft carriers don't like uninvited guests. They're proving a little difficult and threatening to shoot us down." He glanced back over his shoulder. "Don't worry, I'll take care of it."

She cuddled Josie closer. She couldn't worry about anything but the baby. Let Kaldak take care of everything else.

Esteban's fists clenched as he watched the lights of the helicopter fade in the distance.

She was gone. She had escaped him.

No.

He drew a deep, ragged breath.

Kaldak had taken her away. He was probably already thinking that she was out of Esteban's reach.

He was wrong. There was always a way to bring down any prey. He would find her.

"Tell the radioman to get up here, Perez."

The woman had to die. And no one was ever out of reach.

Bess leaned her head on her hands. She felt utterly helpless.

"The baby?"

She looked up to see Kaldak standing beside her by Josie's bed.

"Dr. Caudill did what he could," she said wearily. "He thinks there's a severed vertebra but he's not a specialist."

"Do you want me to get one for you?"

She smiled crookedly. "Are you going to kidnap a specialist and fly him to the aircraft carrier? Not a good idea. Captain Hodgell wasn't at all pleased to have us land here. You're right, we were lucky we weren't shot down on the approach."

"For all they knew, the helicopter could have been loaded with dynamite." He shrugged. "It was the best I could do."

"It was a very good best. Thank you."

"You order. I obey." He squatted down before her chair. "You didn't answer me. Do you want me to go for a specialist?"

She shook her head. "That can wait. He wouldn't operate anyway until she's in better shape. She may not make it, Kaldak."

"When will you know?"

"An hour, two. If she stabilizes . . ."

He looked at the baby in the makeshift crib they'd fashioned out of the hospital bed. "Did she wake up?"

"No." She tried to steady her voice. "She may never wake up again."

"I've got a hunch she will. She came this far. She survived Tenajo. I don't think she's meant to die."

"And was she meant to be shot?" she asked fiercely. "She's a little baby. God shouldn't let things like this—"

"Shh." His hand closed over hers. "Don't blame God. Blame Esteban."

"I do blame Esteban. I want to burn him at the stake."

"Entirely understandable." He released her hand, stood up, and headed for the door. "I'll be back in a minute. You need food, but I know I can't get you to eat. I'll bring coffee instead. It may be a long wait for us."

"You don't have to wait with me. There's nothing you can do."

He paused at the door. "I'm not doing it for you. I think Josie will know I'm here. I'll be right back."

It was four hours later that Josie's vital signs stabilized. An hour later she opened her eyes.

"She's smiling," Bess whispered in wonder.

"I told you she wanted to live." Kaldak gently touched the baby's cheek. "Some things are meant to be."

"I'm in no mood for philosophy. I still don't know if she's ever going to be able to take her first step." But relief and joy were soaring within her. At least, the baby was going to live.

"Dr. Caudill said the best man for spinal injuries is Dr. Harry Kenwood at Johns Hopkins," Kaldak said. "I've arranged an air ambulance to take us there early tomorrow morning."

"You have?"

"And now, I believe it's time for you to eat." He wrinkled his nose. "And shower.

Josie may have a relapse when she rouses enough to get a whiff of you."

"I'm surprised you bore with me all these hours," she said tartly.

"I considered it an exercise in discipline." He turned away from her. "Go shower. I'll send in the nurse to watch Josie and get you some food and fresh clothes."

"Wait."

He looked back at her.

"Emily."

He shook his head. "I contacted our people in Mexico City. No word. But, if she's on foot, it's possible she hasn't reached the coast yet."

"Then I have to go back for her."

"No." The swift, harsh negative startled her. He hadn't used that tone with her since Tenajo.

"I won't abandon her."

"No one's suggesting you abandon her." He glanced at the baby. "Do you want to leave Josie before you know her condition?"

Bess's gaze followed his to Josie. She was as torn as Kaldak had known she'd be. "You know I don't. But I have to go. You can take Josie to—"

"You're handing her over to me? You scarcely let me touch her all the way here."

"I can't leave Emily there."

"For God's sake, Esteban will snatch you up as soon as you set foot back in Mexico."

"I'll go to the embassy and—"

"No, we'll talk about it later. Let me think about it. I may have a solution."

She watched him walk away. If he had a solution for this, he'd rival Solomon, she thought wearily. Then again, he'd managed to get her out of Mexico and saved Josie by finding a medical facility. Maybe he could work this miracle too.

Two hours later he knocked on the door of the tiny cabin she'd been allotted. "Come on. We're going to the radio room. I've arranged to radio someone."

Frowning, she fell into step with him. "Who?"

"Yael Nablett. He's one of my contacts in Mexico City."

"CIA?"

"No Israeli intelligence. They sometimes work together with us on certain agendas."

"This agenda?"

"Most particularly this agenda." He glanced at her. "I can't let you go back, Bess. You'd make too many ripples."

"Good. What's wrong with telling the Mexican government they've been had?"

"No one can know about Tenajo yet. It might trigger a nasty backlash from Esteban."

"Not if the police catch him first."

"Not likely. He has informants in every phase of government. Besides, he's not alone. We can't be sure they won't act as soon as Esteban is brought down."

"Who would act?"

"Habin, a Palestinian terrorist, located in Libya. And chances are you'd never reach the police. You'll be on Esteban's contract list. There's a lot of slime who want to curry favor with the good colonel."

"All the more reason why I should get Emily out of there."

He looked away from her. "She may be able to get herself out. Did you ever think of that? If she's managed to get away from Esteban, she's done pretty well so far."

"She doesn't know about Esteban."

"Is she smart?"

"Of course she's smart. Very smart. What does that have to do with anything?"

"After Tenajo, do you think she'd trust anyone? You didn't. You woke up in that hospital bristling and ready to take on everyone in sight."

"She might go to the police and you said that was almost a death sentence."

"But first she has to get through the hills."

"Then I should go and help her. I've been through them. I know them now."

"But it would be a risk."

"I don't have any choice."

"Yes, you do." He paused. "You could let Yael find her. I could have him do a discreet search and, when he finds her, smuggle her out of the country."

He had said when, not if, and the distinction gave her the first hope she'd had since Esteban had told her Emily was dead. "Could he do that? Could he find her?"

"I'll radio him to start the search now. In a few days she could be across the border."

It seemed too good to be true, so it probably was. "How do you know he'll find her?"

"I don't, but if she's alive, we stand an eighty percent chance. I've seen Yael work.

He can't find a needle in a haystack, but he comes close."

Eighty percent. She wanted it to be a hundred percent. "That's not good enough."

"That's seventy-five percent better than your chances alone." He added bluntly, "Don't be stupid. If you go back, you'll get her killed. Yael will get her out."

She stared at him in helpless frustration. What he said made sense but she didn't want to believe it. She didn't want to be hundreds of miles away from Emily with her hands tied. "You could call this Yael and I could meet him, help him to—"

Kaldak was shaking his head.

"Why not?"

"Because if you go back, I won't tell Yael to help you. You'll be on your own." He paused. "And your sister will be dead."

She stared at him in disbelief. "You're bluffing."

He grimaced. "You're right. I couldn't let you go off alone. But I'm telling the truth about your sister's chances. The sooner I get Yael on it, the sooner you'll see your sister again. Think about it."

What he had suggested went against

every instinct. Emily had always been there for her. She had to go to her.

And if she did, she might cause her death.

"I'll give him a few days," she said finally. "If he hasn't located her by that time, I'm going down there myself."

"It may take longer than that . . . if she's alive."

"Stop *saying* that. She *is* alive. Emily is one of the strongest women I know. She's not dead, I tell you."

"Easy."

She drew a deep breath. "Call him right away."

A few minutes later he was sitting at the radio, putting on the headphones. After a short wait a deep voice with the faintest accent crackled over the line. "It's about time. I've been waiting for you to call, you ugly son of a bitch. Are you ready for a pickup?"

She felt a little ripple of surprise. The cheerful voice was completely free of the fear she sensed in everyone else whom Kaldak encountered, and the words were certainly irreverent.

"No, I radioed Cass," Kaldak said. "We're on our way out now."

"How did Tenajo go?"

"Not what we expected. Bad."

"You're not going to tell me more?"

"Not now."

"Don't close me out. I want them as much as you do."

"I can't talk now."

"You blew your cover with Esteban?"

Kaldak glanced at Bess. "In a manner of speaking."

"Then why didn't you call me?"

"I have another job for you. We think there's a woman in the hills near Tenajo. Esteban is probably looking for her. You have to find her first."

There was a silence. "I don't like killing women, Kaldak."

"No problem. Just find her and get her safely out of the country."

Nablett sighed. "Nasty job. It would be easier to kill her. How quick?"

"Very. Esteban has been delayed, but my disappearance may push him to move."

"And the woman is important?"

"Get her out, Yael."

"It will be done, your royal gargoyleship. Where do you want her delivered?"

"I'll be in touch. She's Dr. Emily Corelli. About five foot six—"

"Seven," Bess interrupted.

"Five foot seven, thirty-six, dark hair and eyes, attractive. American but she speaks Spanish."

"Great. Do you know how many Mexican women fit that general description? Now, if she has a face like yours, I might have a chance."

"But if she did have a face like mine, she wouldn't have a chance. Give the woman a break."

A slight smile was curving his lips, and Bess realized Kaldak was joking. The idea of humor connected with that face and intimidating demeanor was totally incongruous. But she had found on the journey that many things about Kaldak were not as they seemed.

"She may not be willing to cooperate. She'd be an idiot to trust me if she's on the run. Can you give me anything to reassure her?"

"I'll ask her sister." Kaldak looked at Bess.

Bess thought for a moment. "Her daughter, Julie, has an Internet buddy named Linda Hankins. She's her best friend."

Kaldak repeated the information.

"I'm on my way," Yael Nablett said.

He didn't sign off but the radio went dead.

Kaldak turned to Bess. "Satisfied?"

She wasn't satisfied, but Nablett had seemed confident if bizarre. "A few days."

"Thanks," Kaldak said to the radio operator as he removed the headphones. He took Bess's arm and urged her toward the door. "Those few days will at least allow you to get the baby up to Johns Hopkins and into Dr. Kenwood's hands. You'd better check on Josie and then get to bed. The air ambulance will be here pretty early."

She nodded wearily. "I was going to do it. Will you please stop giving me orders?"

"I said I'd take care of you," he said quietly. "I meant it."

She went ahead of him down the narrow corridor. "Just take care of my sister. Good night, Kaldak."

"Good night."

He watched her disappear around the corner. He had avoided the confrontation but only temporarily. He wouldn't make the mistake again of underestimating Bess. Right now she was absorbed with worry about the baby and Emily, but he would have to walk very carefully.

Take care of my sister.

He wished he could promise her that.

Lies and deceit and manipulation. Press the right buttons, shade the truth, and twist reality. God, he was tired of it all.

But it was the coin he dealt in and he would spend it whenever necessary.

He went back to the radio room to call Yael again.

Johns Hopkins

"She looks like she did in that room in San Andreas," Bess whispered as she looked down at Josie. "All those tubes . . ."

"Dr. Kenwood says they're necessary. She needs nutrients. She lost a lot of blood," Kaldak said. "And you said you liked and trusted him."

She nodded. "But I wanted him to operate right away. I want to know she's going to be all right."

"He said she's got a good chance."

"I want to *know*. I don't want to wait another week." She bent down and brushed her lips across Josie's forehead. "He's going to fix you, baby. Just be patient."

"She's sedated and out of it. You're the one who's impatient." Kaldak gently guided her from the room. "Come on, let's go to the waiting room. We have to talk."

Her gaze flew to his face. "Did Dr. Kenwood tell you something he didn't tell me?"

"No." He pushed her into a chair. "He's a smart man. He wouldn't have dared."

She relaxed. "You scared me."

"This situation scares me." He sat down beside her. "I know you asked Dr. Kenwood to find you a bed here." He paused. "You can't stay, Bess."

She stiffened. "The hell I can't."

He shook his head. "It's too dangerous."

"No one knows I'm here."

"They probably will soon. It's just a matter of time. Esteban has established a network here. You'll have to go underground. I'm going to take you to a safe house."

"I won't leave Josie."

"Oh, you'd rather see her dead?" he asked bluntly. "That's what will happen. You're a witness. Esteban wants your head.

As long as you're close by, Josie is in danger. Is that what you want?"

"You know that's not what I want."

"I've called headquarters and arranged a guard for Josie at the hospital just in case Esteban tries to use her to get to you. But you're the one he wants. If he doesn't hear you're hovering over her, he may think she's not important to you. Without you, Josie is much more safe." He added softly, "Give her a chance, Bess. She's got a long way to go."

Bess felt tears sting her eyes. "He might not find her."

"Do you want to take the chance?"

"She'll be all alone."

"She'll be well guarded and besides, Josie's a heartbreaker. The nurses will be hovering over her every second of the day."

"But I want to—" But she couldn't do what she wanted, not if she wanted Josie to be safe. She hadn't wanted Kaldak to be right, dammit. "I want reports every day. Do you hear me? And I want to talk to Dr. Kenwood every other day. And she'd better be safe or I'll cut your throat, Kaldak."

"She'll be safe. I give you my word. Trust me."

She did trust him, she realized. Where

had it come from? The trek through the hills, the night he had stayed with Josie after the operation? However it had happened, the trust was there. She stood up. "I want to say good-bye to her."

He nodded. "Ten minutes? I have to make a few arrangements."

It was stupid to say good-bye, she thought as she looked down at Josie. The baby didn't even know she was there. "I'll be back," she whispered. "They're going to take good care of you but I have to leave for a little while. I'll be thinking about you." She blinked hard to keep back the tears. "You think about me too. I know you're going to be pretty occupied with all these doctors and nurses, but remember I'm the one you came with."

She couldn't take any more. She was going to blubber like a baby herself. She strode blindly out of the room and into Kaldak.

He handed her a handkerchief. "Okay?"

"No." She wiped her eyes. "Get me out of here. Where are we going?"

"To the airport. I have a helicopter waiting."

"And then?"

"Atlanta."

"To your blasted safe house?"

He shook his head. "We're in transition. I need to see a friend who may help us. And the safe house isn't set up yet."

Transition. Her life seemed to be nothing else since the day she arrived in Tenajo. "I'm not going to stay in any safe house unless you bring Emily there."

"Okay, I promise." Kaldak opened the door for her. "The minute we find her."

SEVEN

"You've found no sign of her?" Habin asked.

"That's not quite true," Esteban said. "My men said one of the bullets hit her. We're checking the hospitals for anyone who fits her or the baby's description."

"What else?"

"Kaldak himself is a lead. He went back to Tenajo before leaving Mexico. Does that suggest anything to you?"

There was a silence. "Yes."

"Then we have an idea where he's headed, don't we?"

"But will he take her there?"

"Oh, yes, most definitely. He's not going to let her out of his sight until it's confirmed.

I've sent for Marco De Salmo to take care of the matter. He's leaving Rome right away. Don't worry, we'll find Bess Grady before she can interfere."

"She's already interfered. She's in our way and you're doing nothing about it."

"I'm doing a great deal about it. I'll call you when I know more." Esteban hung up the phone. Habin was nervous and this time Esteban couldn't blame him. Time was of the essence, and he had hoped to locate the woman much more quickly. With any luck, De Salmo would get to her and make the kill in time.

But Esteban seldom relied on luck. A backup plan was always wise.

If Mohammed wouldn't come to the mountain . . .

He smiled.

Habin would appreciate the proverb.

It was almost noon when the helicopter landed at a deserted airport several miles north of Atlanta. There was no tower; one runway and only a few hangars dotted the scraggly landscape. It was the middle of the day, but no one was in sight.

"What is this airport?" Bess asked as she jumped from the helicopter.

"It doesn't have a name." Kaldak grabbed his knapsack and followed her out. "It's used by a few legitimate private pilots and a lot more illegitimate ones."

"Drugs?"

"Maybe. It takes money to buy this kind of privacy. I don't ask." He turned to the pilot. "Stay with her. There's supposed to be a car parked behind the hangar for me."

She shivered as she watched him walk away. It was actually warmer there than in Maryland, but she felt chilled anyway.

Something heavy settled over her shoulders. The pilot, Cass, had given her his leather flight jacket. "Thank you."

He smiled. "You're welcome. I guess you've been a little too busy to worry about a jacket."

"I guess I was. You get around. You're the pilot who picked us up in Mexico."

He nodded. "I've been put at Kaldak's disposal for the next month or so."

"Is that usual?"

He shook his head. "Not with all the budget cuts lately."

"Kaldak didn't introduce us. I'm Bess Grady."

"Cass Schmidt."

"I suppose you're used to picking up people in unusual circumstances. You're CIA?"

He nodded.

Her gaze went back to Kaldak. "Have you worked with him before?"

He nodded, then made a face. "The last time I screwed up, and I thought he was going to break my neck. I was surprised when he radioed me to pick him up this time."

"Maybe he realizes you're a good pilot."

"Well, I could have done without the honor. He scares me shitless."

"Does he?" She had almost forgotten how intimidating she had found Kaldak at first. "Have you known him long?"

"Two years. Libya and then Mexico."

Kaldak had mentioned Libya in connection with Esteban's partner, Habin.

"The car's here," Kaldak said as he reappeared. "Take off, Cass. We don't need you any longer."

Cass nodded. "Good-bye, Ms. Grady."

"Your jacket." She slipped it off and handed it to him. "Thanks again."

He grinned. "My pleasure."

Kaldak took her elbow and urged her forward. "Did you find out anything interesting about me from Cass?"

She didn't bother to deny that she had tried. "No, except that he was in Libya with you."

"Too bad. He may have been your last chance. You won't find many people in my circle as loose-lipped. The CIA has lowered its standards drastically of late."

They had reached a beige sedan parked by the road. "I don't want to question people like Cass about what's going on. I want you to tell me."

"When I know myself." He opened the passenger door for her and got in the driver's seat. "There are clothes for both of us in the trunk. I radioed ahead and told them we'd need clothes and new identification. We'll be staying at a motel north of town while we're here. Your name is Nancy Parker."

False names. New identification. It was all so unsettling. "I never liked the name Nancy."

"Then we'll get you another later."

She shook her head. He didn't understand. It wasn't really the name. She was beginning to feel as if everything was drifting out from under her. Emily and Josie had slipped away from her. She didn't even have her camera.

And it was her fault.

She'd been so worried and exhausted, she'd let herself coast along, letting Kaldak make his arrangements with Yael Nablett and Josie's doctors, and now he was trying to arrange her own life. "We need to talk, Kaldak."

He didn't speak for a moment as he studied her. Then he glanced away and started the car. "Okay, no problem."

By the time they had driven to the Residence Inn, it was close to eight. The motel was an older kind, with separate units, and after checking in they had to drive a short distance to their quarters.

Kaldak locked the door behind them. "It's their penthouse unit. The penthouse is just a loft. Not as grand as it sounds but convenient. Bed and bath upstairs, the same setup down here together with a kitchenette, dining area."

"It's fine," she said. "I don't care. I just

need a shower. Do I go upstairs or stay here?"

"Upstairs."

She picked up her suitcase and headed for the curving stairs.

"I'll carry that for you."

"I'm not helpless." But she was feeling powerless and frustrated, and she needed this little bit of control.

"God forbid I infringe on your independence." He turned away. "I need a shower myself."

In the bedroom Bess opened the suitcase and found two pairs of black slacks, a black jacket, two white blouses, blue striped cotton pajamas, a black chemise, a pair of black high heels and ballet flats, and five sets of black bras and panties. Amazingly, except for the shoes, which were a half-size too large, everything fit perfectly. It shouldn't have surprised her. The clothes Kaldak had brought to the hospital had fit too. He had a good eye.

A black leather shoulder bag was in the bottom of the suitcase. Inside she found a cosmetics case and wallet with two hundred dollars in cash, three credit cards, and a driver's license with her picture and Nancy

Parker's name. How had they managed to put all this together so quickly?

She grabbed the pajamas and headed for the shower.

The warm water felt wonderful as it beat against her body. She closed her eyes and tried to relax. Some of the tension began to ease out of her. She had been coiled tight as a spring, and that didn't bode well for clear thinking. It was good to be cocooned there away from Kaldak.

She stayed in the shower a long, long time.

"Kaldak, I've had news from Interpol," Ramsey said when he answered his portable phone. "The word is Marco De Salmo is heading for New York."

Kaldak tensed. "De Salmo?"

"Esteban has used him before."

"So have a lot of others."

"I just thought you should know. He could connect to anywhere from New York."

Including Atlanta.

"You should get her to a safe house," Ramsey said.

"I can't, dammit. Not yet. Keep me informed."

He hung up the phone. De Salmo. Not good.

He didn't have to be heading for Atlanta. Esteban might not have made the connection.

Kaldak couldn't take the chance. He had to move fast.

Kaldak was standing by the microwave in the kitchenette when Bess came down the stairs. He was wearing jeans and a dark blue sweatshirt and his close-cropped hair was wet. He slammed the microwave door shut. "I hope you like chicken. I had them stock the freezer with frozen dinners. But it's all chicken."

"Most frozen dinners taste the same." She sat down on the stool at the breakfast bar. "I need answers, Kaldak."

"The chicken will be seven minutes." He glanced at her towel-wrapped head. "You have time to go dry your hair."

"There wasn't a blow-dryer in the suitcase."

"How remiss of them. Any other omissions?"

"Imagination. Everything but these pajamas and a couple of shirts is black."

"It's standard procedure. Navy blue or black and everything wash-and-wear. Anything else?"

"A camera. I want my camera."

"I can't help you. I didn't see it after I took you to San Andreas. I assume Esteban has it."

"But I *need* it." She knew she was being unreasonable, but it was the final frustration for her. Without her camera she felt depleted . . . lost.

"Do you want me to pick up another one for you?"

Pick up? You didn't just pick up a camera. You had to examine and probe and get the feel of it. "I've had that camera for eight years. It's my favorite."

"Sorry, I'm not going back for it. Do you want me to replace it?"

"No, I'll do it myself." She went back on the attack. "I want answers. What you've told me about Tenajo has to be just the tip of the iceberg."

"Not now. You already have me at your mercy, so there's no reason for you to push. You're exhausted."

She *was* exhausted and her mind felt so blurry, she didn't know if she'd comprehend anything he told her anyway. Maybe she'd cope better after dinner. Kaldak was being evasive, and she was relieved not to have to be on the attack for a while. "You're not off the hook." She took off the towel and began to dry her hair.

"I see you're making do without the blow-dryer. That adaptability must have come in handy in some of the places you've had to go. Croatia isn't long on beauty salons these days."

She stopped in mid-motion. "How do you know I was in Croatia?"

"Esteban requested a report on you and your sister when you were sighted heading for Tenajo. He wanted to make sure you weren't with an agency that would bring dif-ficulties down on his head." He opened the refrigerator door. "So I tried to convince him he should let me come after you and termi-nate any threat."

She stiffened.

He took out a carton of milk and set it on the bar. "He wouldn't let me do it. I realize now he wanted to let the disease kill you."

"You would have killed us?"

He shook his head. "If I could have done it without blowing my cover, I'd have warned you and tried to get you out of the area without Esteban knowing."

"And if it would have blown your cover?"

He got down two glasses from the cabinet. "Then I would have had a decision to make."

"But you blew your cover at San Andreas."

"It was a calculated risk, and by that time I'd found out a lot more about the operation." He poured milk into the two glasses. "I'd been trying to work my way into Esteban's confidence for over two months. I *needed* that information."

The passion in that last sentence caused her eyes to widen. "Why are you telling me this?"

"So you'll know how important stopping Esteban is to me." He looked straight into her eyes. "If I'd needed to do it, I would have killed you, your sister, and your guide."

"Nothing should be that important."

"Tell that to the people who died at Tenajo."

"But you didn't save Tenajo."

"No." His lips tightened. "No, I didn't." He

turned his back on her and reached up into the cabinet.

He was feeling guilt, she realized suddenly. Terrible guilt. Underneath that harsh exterior, he was human after all. The knowledge came as a shock.

He brought down two plates from the shelf. "Take the milk into the dining room. I'll bring the chicken."

His face was once more without expression. She got off the stool and picked up the glasses. "Frozen dinners seem more suited to the kitchen."

"My mother taught me that dinner should always be served in the dining room. It's a habit I can't shake." He paused. "And yes, I did have a mother. I didn't crawl out from under a rock."

She found herself smiling. "I was thinking more along the lines of a metal egg from an alien planet."

He blinked. "My God, I believe you're joking with me."

She had been joking. Incredible. Not only had she found humor in the moment, but she had also felt enough at ease with Kaldak to indulge in it. "A temporary lapse."

He made a face. "Don't worry, I won't grow on you. Too many rough edges."

Rough edges, an alarming perceptiveness, and an almost fanatic intensity—he possessed all those things. He had shown a moment of weakness, but he had recovered with lightning swiftness. She had been crazy to think he was vulnerable in any way.

"Sit down. I'll get the silverware." Kaldak was behind her, setting the steaming plates on the table. "It's not very nourishing but it's food and you haven't had anything to eat since yesterday. I heard your stomach growl in the car on the way from the airport."

"It's rude of you to mention it."

"It would be ruder not to feed you."

She *was* hungry. Yet, there was something wrong with that reality. When you were worried or depressed, your body should just stop being beset by basic needs.

He was back with the silverware and napkins. He sat down opposite her. "Dig in."

She picked up her fork. "Is that what your mother would have said?"

He shook his head. "Part of my rough edges. Some things are ingrained. Some things we learn for ourselves."

But his table manners were impeccable, she noticed. "Is your mother still alive?"

He shook his head. "She died a long time ago. So did my father. How about your parents?"

"My mother died when Emily and I were small. My father was killed in an automobile accident when I was fifteen."

"That's an especially bad time to lose a parent."

"But I had Emily. She was in medical school and had an apartment in the city. We sold Tyngate, the house we grew up in, and she moved me in with her."

"No problems?"

She grimaced. "A few. I wasn't the most stable kid and I missed Tyngate. At first I gave her a pretty rough time, but we worked things out."

"Tyngate," he repeated. "It sounds like an estate."

She shook her head. "Just a big old house on the river. Nothing fancy."

His gaze was fixed intently on her face. "But you loved it?"

"Sure. I still miss it sometimes. But Emily's right, we had to move on. It's wrong to cling to the past."

"Tell me about this Tyngate."

"Why?"

"Just curious."

"I told you, it wasn't much. Comfortable. We had a pier and a boat. I don't know why it meant so much to me." She looked down at her plate. "You know, I read Katharine Hepburn's autobiography once, and Tyngate was something like the place where she grew up. It was sort of . . . golden. Emily and I had wonderful times when we were kids. We swam and sailed and built a tree house. I always felt safe there. No matter how complicated and weird the outside world became, Tyngate stayed sort of safe . . . and innocent."

"Innocence is at a premium these days. You should have kept the house."

She shook her head. "There wasn't much insurance and Emily had enough trouble supporting the two of us. No, she was right." She hadn't thought of Tyngate for a long time. She felt a sudden wave of nostalgia. "But every kid should be able to grow up at a place like Tyngate. It should be written into the Constitution."

"Write your congressman. They're always ready to embrace anything that touches kids. It's politically correct. Drink your milk. That's politically correct too."

She was glad of the change of subject. Memories of Tyngate would always be tied with Emily, and they sharpened the anxiety she was feeling. "I'm drinking it. I told you to stop giving me orders."

"I wouldn't want to ruin my image by being polite."

The words were said without a smile, and it took a minute for Bess to realize they were meant to be humorous. "I wouldn't worry about that."

"But I do. All the time." He picked up his milk. "It's necessary." He drank deeply before lowering the glass. "Perception is everything. It's what makes the— Why are you laughing?"

Without thinking, she took her napkin and wiped his upper lip. "You have a mustache. You remind me of Julie. She always ends up with—" The thought of Julie reminded her of the wrenching reality of Emily's situation. How could she have forgotten it for even a short time?

"Julie is your sister's child? The one who has the friend on the Internet?"

She nodded.

"Is she like Emily?"

"No, she's not like anyone. Emily says she's a little like me, but I think she's an original."

"You're close to her and Tom Corelli?"

"I love her, and Tom has always been kind to me. I like him very much." She became aware of the tension that hadn't been there a minute earlier. "Why do you ask?"

"What about anyone else? Who else are you close to?"

"You sound like Esteban. He was giving me the third degree too."

"Esteban's reasons and my reasons aren't the same."

"I hope not. He was interested in any next of kin who might bother him if he cut my throat."

"And I'm interested in keeping you from getting your throat cut. You're divorced, aren't you? Do you still maintain a relationship with your ex?"

"No." She wrinkled her nose. "We were married only nine months. One big mistake. Emily told me he was a loser, but I didn't believe her."

"Why not?"

"My hormones got in the way. Matt's a

musician. He's gorgeous, sexy, and he could even hold a conversation if it didn't get too deep. He didn't like deep." She sipped her milk. "And he had no use for fidelity. He was sleeping around two months after we were married."

"But the marriage lasted nine months."

She shrugged. "I'm stubborn. I didn't want to admit I'd made another mistake. So I tried to make it work. But there wasn't anything there to build on."

"Another mistake?" he repeated.

"I'm not perfect like Emily."

"Tell me about your friends. Is there someone special?"

"No, I travel a lot because of my job. It's hard to maintain friendships when you're always missing anniversaries and birthdays and— Why?"

"Where do you live?"

"I sublet an apartment in New Orleans."

"Any neighbors that you're fond of?"

"I like all my neighbors."

"No one in particular?"

She shook her head.

"Pets?"

"You shouldn't have pets if you're not there to take care of them."

"So you have no one but Emily and her family?"

She frowned. "I have friends, lots of friends. All over the world."

"I'm sure you have. Don't be so defensive."

"Well, you're making me sound like Little Orphan Annie."

"I'm just trying to determine where you're vulnerable."

"I'm not vulnerable." Sudden uneasiness overcame her. "Am I? Julie and Tom?"

"Maybe. Your New Orleans apartment is already under surveillance, but after dinner I want you to give me Corelli's address and phone number. I'll arrange protection for them."

"Done. But I don't think we have to worry right away. Tom and Julie are in Canada on a camping trip. They're away the three weeks Emily and I were supposed to be in Mexico."

"How accessible?"

"Not unless you're a grizzly bear. Tom's a wilderness expert, and when they go camping, it's serious stuff. They always park their car at a ranger station and live off the land."

"Radio?"

"No, but they take flares in case of emergency."

"You'd better give me the location of that ranger station so I can put a man there to meet them when they come out."

"Good idea." She leaned back in her chair. "Now tell me what we're doing in Atlanta, Kaldak."

"I told you, I need help from a friend."

"What kind of help?"

He didn't answer.

"What kind of help?"

He scowled. "You're not going to let it go, are you?"

"Why should I? It's my life. It's Emily's life. You've been very kind to me, but I don't want protection if it means not knowing what's going on. I can't function like that. Everything has to be clear and out in the open. You've not been telling me everything, have you?"

"No," he said. "I can't tell you everything. Not yet."

"When?"

"I'm not sure."

"That's not good enough, Kaldak. I've let you push me and prod me and run the show. From now on, if you want me to cooperate, you cooperate with me."

He studied her face and then slowly nodded. "Okay. But I don't know everything myself yet. It would be guesswork. Let me go see my friend and we'll talk afterward."

"I want to go with you."

"He's in a very sensitive position. I'm going to ask him to break some rules. He may not go along with me if someone else is there." He picked up the dishes and carried them to the sink. "Don't worry, I don't intend to skip out on you. I'll be back tomorrow evening."

She hadn't been worried about that. "And I'm supposed to sit here and twiddle my thumbs?"

"Sorry."

So was she, but it was obvious she wasn't going to get any more concessions from him. "And do you promise me that you'll be honest with me?"

"Would you believe me if I gave you my word?"

"Yes."

He inclined his head. "I'm honored. I promise you that I'll tell you all about my meeting when I get back tomorrow evening."

The words still held a note of evasion. "The truth."

"The truth." He grimaced. "You're very good at probing. It's no wonder you've won so many awards."

She looked at him in surprise. "You know a lot about me. Esteban said you weren't able to get much information."

"I didn't want him to know any more than he had to." He shrugged. "I've admired your work for some time. I liked the pictures you took of that bandit in Somalia."

"So did I." She stood up. "Which reminds me, I have to call John Pindry and tell him I can't complete my article for his magazine."

He shook his head.

"He has deadlines. It wouldn't be responsible to just leave him hanging."

"Let it go for a while. We don't want any mention of Tenajo to leak out yet."

"I wouldn't tell him about—" Oh, well, they wouldn't expect to hear from her yet anyway. "I'll write Emily's address on the phone pad and then I'm going to bed. I'm so tired, I'm about to fall into a coma."

"I'm surprised you lasted this long." He began washing the dishes. "You've been through a hell of a lot in the last week. You handled it well."

She felt a rush of surprise mixed with

pleasure. "I guess we do what we have to do."

"I guess we do." He added solemnly, "When we're not perfect like sister Emily."

Was he teasing her? she wondered in astonishment. It was hard to tell. "She is perfect. Well, almost."

"And you're chopped liver?"

He *was* teasing her. She smiled as she wrote Emily's address and phone number on the pad. "Hell, no. I'm a damn good photographer and a magnificent human being."

"I notice you put the profession first."

Her smile faded. "So?"

"Nothing. I just found it interesting."

He was digging, trying to get at what he deemed the truth. "Back off, Kaldak."

He nodded. "Okay, sorry. I have an analytical mind too. It's automatic for me to probe."

Had she been under the microscope all evening? He certainly had asked a lot of questions and not all of them concerning her close associates. For some reason, the idea stung. "Good night."

"Good night, Bess."

She started up the stairs. She had almost reached the loft when she looked back at him. Kaldak washing dishes was an incongruous sight. And yet every movement was precise and clean, just like the way he had killed the guard at San Andreas.

He looked up suddenly. "What?"

She searched for something to say. "You do that very well. Did your mother teach you?"

He nodded. "She always told me to clean up after myself. It's smart. A clean deck makes life much smoother."

Everything has to be smooth.

He had said those words at the hospital.

But she had spoiled his careful plans and a man had died. He had been angry with her, angry that he had been forced to kill. "Go to bed," he ordered. "I'll be gone when you wake up. There are eggs and bacon for breakfast. Don't leave the room. Don't open the door for anyone. Do you understand? Not for anyone."

"Okay, I heard you the first time. When will you be back?"

"As soon as I have what I need."

She turned and started up the stairs.

"Bess."

She looked back at him.

"There's no way you're chopped liver."

. . .

"I can't do this, Kaldak," Ed Katz said. "I work with a team. Someone would know."

"Give them the day off."

"Why can't you go through regular channels?"

"There would be reports and reports on the reports. I don't want any leaks."

"You could do this yourself."

"I don't have the facilities."

Katz bit his lower lip. "I don't like this. It's too scary."

"You like it. You're practically salivating to get started."

"So I'm curious."

"You owe me."

"Shit." Katz ran a hand through his long, dark hair. "Why don't you take my firstborn child instead?"

"You don't have any kids."

"Well, it's not that Marta and I haven't tried. We're trying a new hormone therapy that may work. When do you need this?"

"By tonight."

"Impossible."

"Do as much as you can. I need something, anything."

Katz scowled. "Then get out of here so I can get started."

"I'll wait."

"Nothing like a little pressure."

Kaldak smiled. "Exactly."

EIGHT

What the hell was he going to tell Bess?

Kaldak's hands tightened on the steering wheel.

He'd thought it would be bad but not this bad. He'd had no idea Esteban was so close. He should lie to her. The Company would say she had no real need to know, and he was good at lies. They came easily these days.

He didn't want to lie to her. He was sick to his soul of lies.

And he liked Bess Grady. She was such a complicated combination of fragility and strength, uncertainty and boldness. He liked her guts and her honesty and even the stubbornness that was causing him so much trouble.

And he had made her a promise.

To hell with "need to know." He would tell her what he could. It probably didn't matter anyway.

Not now.

"Well?" Bess said as soon as Kaldak walked into the room. "You took long enough."

"I did some driving around. I wanted to make sure I wasn't followed." He headed for the kitchen. "Do you want coffee?"

She crossed her arms over her chest. "No, I want you to talk to me."

"Well, I need it." He measured coffee and water into the machine and turned it on. "Why do they always have these two-cup jobs in hotel rooms?"

"Where did you go today, Kaldak?"

"I called Ed Katz with the CDC and had him meet me at the center."

"And?"

"I brought him the money I took from the poor box at the church to analyze."

After everything that had happened, she had forgotten about the money.

"When Esteban sent his men into Tenajo for the cleanup, we had orders to go through the town and collect any twenty-peso bills we found. They were put in specially insulated bags and later burned. We evidently missed the poor box then. Esteban will be most upset."

"Pesos?"

"Counterfeit pesos printed with a very special ink. According to Ed, a genetically mutated anthrax bacteria was added to the lilac ink."

"Anthrax," she whispered. "My God."

"What do you know about it?"

"Just what I learned while I studied medicine for a couple of years. Most people get it from handling infected material like leather or animal furs."

"It usually occurs as cutaneous, intestinal, or pulmonary infection. The kind released in Tenajo was pulmonary. It affects the lungs and pleura and the mutation causes it to kill within six hours of contact. But it didn't act on everyone in the same way. From the condition of the corpses, it was clear some died within minutes, while others took hours."

The little boy in the store looked struck down, as if by lightning. "But everyone died."

"Yes, but the time difference bothered Esteban. I think that's why he's delayed going forward. But he's close, too close."

"There's serum for anthrax. It usually works very well."

"Not for this mutated version."

"No cure?"

"Working twenty-four hours a day for the next eight months might produce one. We're not going to be given that luxury."

"And Esteban used money to kill all those people," she whispered.

"Can you think of a better way? Who's going to refuse money? Tenajo was a poor little village. When Esteban's men drove into town and distributed the pesos to everyone, they probably thought they'd died and gone to heaven."

"And then they did die." It was hard for her to comprehend such calculated malice. It was like those twisted people who laced Halloween candy with poison and gave it to children. "How could Esteban's men pass out the money without harming themselves?"

"They put the money in specially sealed see-through plastic envelopes. It took almost as long to develop those envelopes as it did to mutate the anthrax."

Like the envelopes he'd taken out of the poor box. "Was your metal briefcase specially sealed too?"

He nodded. "But I wasn't too worried. Esteban wasn't afraid to let the public health team into Tenajo. He'd tried to pick up every peso, but there's no way he would have chanced one of those officials dying of anthrax. The bacteria had to have a built-in dissipation factor. I think its life must have been at least twelve hours, because Esteban was sure you and your sister had been infected."

"Rico died."

"The circumstances may have been different. He may have come in direct contact with the pesos at some point."

"The root . . ." she said numbly. "The priest kept saying 'the root' before he died. I thought he was referring to poison. He was talking about the money."

"The root of all evil? Possibly."

"What does Esteban want that would make him do this?"

"I'm not sure what the crazy bastard wants." The coffee was done and he poured a cup.

"You have to know. You worked for him."

"He wants to use it as a blackmail tool,

so money is an obvious answer. And power. But I think there's more." He sipped his coffee. "He's a wild card."

"He's like some cartoon monster."

"Don't even think it," he said soberly. "He's very intelligent, or he wouldn't have been able to establish his network. Esteban's lab developed the anthrax and Habin was handling the counterfeit branch of the operation. Habin thinks he's in control, but I wouldn't bet on it."

"What about this Habin?"

"He's an international terrorist stationed in Libya. He's doing it for politics. He's been trying to pressure the United States for the past year to influence Israel to release Palestinian prisoners."

Shock jolted through her. "The United States."

"I told you that Tenajo was just a test."

"You didn't tell me that the United States would be the target."

"I think you suspected it."

Maybe she had, but she hadn't wanted to admit it to herself. "You're sure?"

"Eighteen months ago a set of twenty-dollar plates disappeared from the Denver Treasury."

"But I've heard our currency is impossible to reproduce."

"They could come close enough and the setup would be just like Tenajo. Who's going to check if money falls from heaven?"

"What city?"

He shook his head. "I don't even know if it's been decided."

"We have to warn someone."

"Who do you want to call? The president? If he contacts Mexico, he's going to be assured Tenajo was decimated by cholera. The CDC will confirm it."

"But you have the contaminated money."

"That's another drawback. Even if the president accepts the fact that there's danger, he can't make a public announcement. To make the public suspicious of our currency would send the economy crashing. Can you imagine what would happen to the stock market?" His hands tightened on the cup. "That would please Habin. It would accomplish his purpose without the bother of unleashing the anthrax."

"So you're going to chance letting more people die?" she asked in disbelief.

"I didn't say that. We just have to know more before we send out any warnings."

"And how are we going to find out any more? You can't go back to Esteban."

"I could if I brought him your head."

She stepped back.

"I was joking," he said roughly.

She glared at him. "How am I supposed to know? Would it hurt to smile?"

"Maybe."

"What about your CIA friends? Doesn't one of them have access to someone in the White House who could help?"

"Paul Ramsey. He's deputy director of the CIA and went to school with the president. I called him from Johns Hopkins and told him what I suspected."

"Is he going to do something?"

"Not yet. I told him that I needed more time. I didn't get an argument. He doesn't want to have to tell the president how little we can do. He said to contact him if I needed him."

"We do need him."

"I've every intention of calling him to tell him Ed confirmed the anthrax."

"And to do something official about it."

He stared at her impassively. "Have a cup of coffee."

"I don't want your damn coffee." She

wanted to strangle him. She drew a deep breath and tried to steady her voice. "Call this Ramsey and tell him to call the White House. I won't carry around this kind of responsibiiity."

"Then ignore it. I'll carry it." He finished his coffee in two swallows. "I've done it for a long time. A few more days won't hurt."

"Then I'll call someone."

"You will not," he said with clear precision. "Not even if I have to tie and gag you. I've seen too many operations bungled by bureaucrats through leaks or sheer stupidity."

"You won't use force on me."

"You weren't too sure a moment ago."

"You won't do it."

"You're right, I won't. So you have me defenseless."

She looked at him, startled. "Like a tiger. I doubt if you've ever been defenseless in your life."

"Not if I could help it." He added simply, "I can't help it. This means too much. Tenajo wasn't a complete success, but it was close. We're running out of time. I have to do anything I can to keep from triggering this thing, and I need you to help me."

"You mean you need my silence."

"That's a big help. I may ask you for more help later."

"It's wrong."

"Maybe. But Esteban is too volatile. I can't risk him doing something crazy. Do you know what anthrax can do?" His lips twisted. "In 1942 the British set off an experimental anthrax bomb on an isolated island off the coast of Scotland. A day after the explosion the sheep began to die. Gruinard is still un-inhabitable today."

She shuddered. "And that's supposed to convince me to keep quiet? Besides, you said the mutated strain has a life of only a few hours."

"What if Esteban decides to use the un-mutated organisms?"

"Stop it. You're scaring me."

"You're not as scared as I am. I've seen it. I know what it is."

"Where did you—"

"Help me."

She gazed at him with frustration. She had learned how clever he could be and how fully capable he was of manipulating her feelings. But he meant every word he said, and the sheer force of his honesty was overwhelming. "Damn you."

"I need you."

She whirled away from him and moved across the room.

"I'm doing the right thing." His words followed her. "Believe me, Bess."

Just because he thought he was doing what was right didn't mean it was.

But what if it was? She'd had a taste of Esteban's venom. What if a leak triggered him to act? The mutated strain was hideous enough, but the unmutated bacteria was worse. Kaldak's story about Gruinard had shaken her.

Kaldak said, "You don't know what Esteban is capable—"

"Shut up, you've made your point. You're just like Emily. I'll make my own decision, dammit."

Kaldak fell silent.

The decision was already made, she realized. She turned to face him. "I'll wait . . . for a while." She held up a hand to stop him from speaking. "Until we get Emily away from Esteban. After that, I don't know. But I won't be some ventriloquist's dummy who speaks when you tell her to. Don't you dare close me out again. I want to know what you know. If I'm going to be responsible for some doomsday weapon going off, it's not going to be because I'm being kept in the dark."

He nodded slowly. "Anything else?"

"Yes." She came toward him. "Give me a cup of that blasted coffee. I need it now."

She glared at Kaldak as he moved around the kitchenette, tidying after supper. She was an idiot. If she had a brain in her head, she would call the FBI or CIA or . . . someone.

But she could see Kaldak's point about bureaucracy interfering. She had seen too many snafus in Somalia to believe in even the best-intentioned organizations.

"You're burning a hole in me," Kaldak said mildly. "Would you mind stopping your glaring?"

"Yes, I would. I enjoy glaring at you."

"Whatever makes you happy." He neatly hung up the dish towel.

"Tell me, is all this domesticity a ploy to disarm me? The contrast is just a little too blatant."

"Oh, you think I'm trying to distract you

from this gargoyle mug of mine?" He shook his head. "I know it doesn't work. The face always stays with you." He turned off the kitchen light and came around the bar. "So I live with it and sometimes use it."

"I suppose in your profession it could come in handy."

"My, my, you are trying to hurt me, aren't you?"

"Does honesty hurt? You do kill people. I saw you."

"Yeah, I kill people."

This was ridiculous. For some stupid reason, she was feeling guilty about accusing him of something she knew very well was the truth.

But truth wasn't always kind.

And, dammit, he was what he was.

Still, since when did she start looking at things in black and white? Kaldak was a very complicated man, and she had found that complicated people were usually capable of doing both evil and good.

"Well, have you made up your mind?" Kaldak's gaze was fixed on her face.

"About what?"

"Weren't you struggling against giving me the benefit of the doubt?" He suddenly smiled. "I think you've lost. You're too soft, you know. Life must be hard for you."

"Life's hard for everyone." But it was harder when you ran across someone who seemed able to read your thoughts.

"It's your face. It shows everything."

She wrinkled her nose. "I know. You'd be surprised what a detriment it's been to my career."

"Oh, I know about faces. Nothing surprises me."

No bitterness colored his voice, which surprised her. What had it been like growing up with that intimidating face?

Perhaps he hadn't grown up with it. Maybe as a child he had looked entirely normal. His blue eyes were perfectly fine and—

"What are you thinking?"

"That you have nice eyes," she blurted out, not thinking.

He blinked, disconcerted. "Oh." He quickly glanced away. "We've located a safe house for you in North Carolina. I'll drive you there tomorrow afternoon."

"Why not tomorrow morning?"

"We have to go to the CDC. I asked Ed to have the reports ready for me on the mutant strain. I may need documentation."

"Have you contacted Yael Nablett today?"

"I tried this morning before I left. I couldn't reach him."

She frowned. "Shouldn't we have heard . . . something?"

"I'll try him again tomorrow before we leave." He paused. "But you shouldn't worry too much. He'll be in the hills close to Tenajo and unreachable by phone."

"But you'll still try?"

"No problem," he said.

Gentleness? She had to be mistaken. She stood up and moved toward the stairs. "I called Dr. Kenwood this afternoon. Josie's doing fine."

"That's good."

"You bet it is. I'll see you in the morning."

She could feel his gaze on her back as she climbed the stairs. It was strange how comfortable she was becoming with him. Well, anybody would probably become comfortable with a tiger if caged with the tiger for any length of time. That didn't mean she should trust Kaldak.

But she did trust him or she wouldn't have let him talk her into remaining silent. Dear God, she was tired of arguing with herself as well as Kaldak. She had made a decision. Now she had to stop questioning and teetering back and forth. She had done enough of that all her life. She couldn't afford not to act with sureness and authority now.

Emily, who had never needed anyone, needed her. She had to clear her mind of everything but that one important truth. To hell with Kaldak's safe house. She would give Yael Nablett one more day. If he didn't call with word of Emily, she would go back.

Kaldak could save the world. She would concentrate on saving Emily.

"Anthrax," Ramsey repeated. "Christ, I can't keep this under wraps, Kaldak."

"Go ahead. Tell the president. See what he does about it with no hard documentation. He's great on documentation. Even if we show him the CDC report, there's no proof Tenajo could happen here."

"Shit."

"Right."

"It may be too late by the time we get proof, and then it's the Company's ass on the line again. Politicians will sidestep quicker than you can blink. How much time do you think we have?"

"God knows. We may be on borrowed time already. I think he's almost ready to go." He paused. "But he's waiting for something."

"What?"

"I'm not sure. Have you managed to tap his phone?"

"Not his cellular. Only the one in his office."

"What have you found out about Morrisey?"

"Nothing much. He's evidently in Esteban's pay. We got the impression he was looking for someone for him. He's called Esteban several times lately from different cities in the U.S. Is he important?"

Kaldak had the uneasy feeling that he was very important. "He may be. Galvez said he's been faxing and phoning Esteban for a long time. Find him."

"You think we haven't been trying?"

"Try harder. What about the lab in Iowa?"

"You told me about it just the day before yesterday, for God's sake. I had to pull the FBI into it. They have more domestic contacts."

"What about the Cheyenne connection?"

"Nothing yet. No sign of any counterfeiting activity. No cases of anthrax reported."

"There probably won't be any cases reported in advance of the strike this time. Esteban is almost through experimenting. What about De Salmo? Heard anything more?"

"Only that he's dropped out of sight." There was a pause. Then Ramsey added, "I want Bess Grady, Kaldak."

He'd known that was coming. "The CDC is the only place Esteban would trace me to, and I made sure I wasn't followed. I'm heading for a safe house tomorrow. You can't have her."

"I could take her."

"That's what you'd have to do." He added softly, "And do you really want to piss me off that much, Ramsey?"

"Don't give me that shit. Remember, I made you what you are."

Ramsey was actually proud of the assassin he had created. Kaldak had never realized that. "The hell you did. You gave me the tools and showed me how to use them. Nakoa made me what I am."

Another silence. "You're lucky that you're in a unique position in this operation. I'll allow you to have your way . . . for now. Keep me posted." Ramsey hung up.

Lucky? Kaldak wearily leaned back on the couch. No one connected with this mess was lucky. Not him, not those people in Tenajo, and most certainly not Bess Grady.

He just hoped to hell De Salmo was on his way to Timbuktu and not Atlanta.

Bess did not dream of Emily that night. She dreamed of Danzar.

She woke in the middle of the night with tears streaming down her cheeks.

And Kaldak standing over her in the darkness.

She jerked upright in bed, her heart pounding furiously. For a moment she thought she was back in that hospital room in San Andreas.

"I heard you crying out," he said quietly. "I thought you'd want me to wake you."

She wiped her cheeks with the backs of her hands. "Thank you."

He shrugged. "We have enough nightmares to face every day without tolerating them at night." He turned and moved toward the stairs. "Good night."

"Good night."

No questions. No conversation. Just that single act of understanding.

She lay back down. She had thought she was getting better. She hadn't dreamed of Danzar for nearly three weeks. She *was* better. She wouldn't accept anything else.

She closed her eyes and took deep, steadying breaths. That usually helped.

It didn't this time. She started to shake. After several minutes she got out of bed and headed for the bathroom. She took an aspirin and drank a glass of water. She was shaking so badly, she almost dropped the glass.

Why wouldn't it go away? She sank down on the tile floor and hunched there, linking her arms over her knees. Think of something else. Think of Tyngate. Think of Julie or Emily or—

"Okay?" Kaldak was squatting beside her.

Oh, God, she didn't want anyone to see her like this. "No, I'm not okay. Go away."

"I tried to do that. It didn't work." He sat down and crossed his legs. "So I have to do something about it."

"Why? It's none of your business. I'll be fine."

"Is it Tenajo?"

"Do you feel guilty? No, it's not Tenajo."

"Esteban?"

"Do you think I'd let that son of a bitch do this to me?" She blinked furiously to keep back the tears. "Will you please go away?"

"No, neither of us will sleep if you keep on like this. You're shaking so bad, you're going to break your tailbone on that hard tile." He pushed back her hair from her forehead in a gentle gesture. It reminded her of the way he touched Josie. "I think you have to talk to me, Bess."

"The hell I do."

"Talk to me about Danzar."

She stiffened. "What?"

"Danzar. That's what you were muttering when I woke you."

She moistened her lips. "Then why did you ask about Tenajo?"

"A process of elimination."

"How analytical."

"Sorry, that's the way I am." He glanced around the brightly lit bathroom. "And my analysis of the situation tells me that this isn't the spot to get you to relax." He stood up, leaned down, and lifted her to her feet. "Bed."

"What?"

"Don't worry, I meant what I said. Relaxation." He carried her to the bed and set her down. "Not sex."

She looked at him in astonishment. "I didn't think you meant anything else."

"I know. I just thought I'd throw in something that would distract you." He tucked the blanket around her. "I realize I'm not what you'd call a sex object. Unless you get off on Dracula. Actually, there are some women who do." He got up and turned off the bathroom light.

The bedroom was plunged into darkness.

He sat down beside her and touched her arm. "You're still shaking, but not as much."

"Then you can go away."

"Not after I've gone to all this trouble. I don't want it to happen again tonight. I need my sleep. Talk to me. I won't go away until you do. Is Danzar in Croatia?"

"Yes."

"How long since you were in Croatia?"

"Three months."

"I've never heard of Danzar."

"It was only a tiny village."

"Was?"

"I guess it's still there."

"You don't know?"

"They didn't burn it."

"What did they do to it?"

The babies . . .

"What did they do, Bess?"

"I don't want to talk about it."

"Pretend I'm Emily."

"I didn't talk to Emily about Danzar." She hadn't told those details to anyone. Not even that shrink in the hospital in Sarajevo. Why should she talk to Kaldak?

"Because I don't care. I'm almost a stranger to you." He read her thoughts again. "It would be like talking to yourself. What did they do, Bess?"

Blood. So much blood . . .

"What?" Kaldak repeated.

"The babies . . ."

"What babies?"

"There was an . . . orphanage. I was doing a photo essay on the orphans of war, and I went to Danzar. The orphanage was crowded, but the kids . . . It always amazes me how kids can be happy in almost any circumstance. Give them a little food, a bed, companionship, and they'll smile at you. There was one little boy. Niko. He couldn't have been more than three. He followed me around while I was taking pictures. He was so—" She stopped, and it was a moment before she could continue. "I kept going back. At first I thought it was the story, and then I thought I was just being a good guy. So many couples in America can't have kids, and if they saw the photos . . . But then I realized it was Niko. I didn't have any business trying to adopt him. It was all wrong. I was single, I was always traveling, but I knew I had to have him with me. He was mine. I started the paperwork."

The dogs howling.

"And did you adopt him, Bess?"

"No."

"Why not?"

What are you? Some sort of ghoul?

"Why not, Bess?"

"He died," she whispered. "They all died."

"How?"

"The guerrillas. A truce was supposed to be in effect, but there were still attacks. I was sixty miles away from Danzar on another story when we heard about it. I made my driver turn around and go back to Danzar. The guerrillas had already pulled out but the dogs were howling. They kept howling and howling. . . . I went to the orphanage. The children were dead, butchered. Niko was in the kitchen. Who would kill a baby? Monsters. They had to be monsters."

"Yes."

"I went through the orphanage and took more pictures. I knew that they'd deny it once peace came. It would be covered up and forgotten. That's the way it always is. I couldn't let that happen. I had to show—" She could barely talk. She was trying to stop the sobs. "I couldn't let it—"

"Shh, I know."

"No, you don't. You weren't there."

He was silent a moment and then stood up. "I'd like to comfort you, but you don't want that from me. You don't want me here right now at all. You're afraid I'll think you're not as tough as you should be." His hand touched her hair with the same gentleness he had displayed in the bathroom. "You're wrong. I'll be right back."

He was gone. She heard his steps on the staircase.

She lay there with the tears running down her face. The sobs soon stopped, but the tears still came.

The babies . . .

What had she done? She felt as if her insides had been torn out. Once she had started, the words tumbled out and couldn't be stopped. Why spit out all those memories and pain to Kaldak?

It's like talking to yourself.

In a way it had been like that. He'd removed himself, stepped away and let the words pour out into the darkness. And then he'd left her so that she'd have no loss of dignity. Why had—

"Is it okay if I turn on the light?" Kaldak was back, a huge silhouette at the top of the stairs.

"Sure." She took a deep breath and hurriedly wiped her eyes with the blanket. "But why ask now? I don't remember you asking permission to turn it off."

"Different strokes for different games." He crossed to the bathroom and switched on the light there. "The situation isn't the same." He came back to her. "Drink this."

He was holding a glass of milk.

"Good heavens, warm milk?" she asked. "Is that one of your mother's remedies?"

"Cold milk." He smiled faintly. "If I went to all the trouble of heating it, you'd think it was another domestic ploy."

She looked at him over the rim of the glass as she took a sip. He didn't seem at all domestic. For the first time she realized that he was barefoot and bare-chested and his dark hair was rumpled. He looked muscular, powerful.

And she probably looked like a mess. Thank God, he'd turned on only the bathroom light. She felt vulnerable enough as it was. Was that why he hadn't turned on the more revealing overhead light?

"Drink all of it."

She took another sip and handed the glass back to him. "That's enough."

"Okay." He stood looking at her. "Do you mind if I ask what happened to the pictures you took at Danzar?"

"The film was confiscated."

"What?"

"You heard me. When I got back to army headquarters, the colonel confiscated the film. He said it was inflammatory and that publishing it would be detrimental to the peace process. I showed him inflammatory. I nearly went crazy. I screamed and ranted. I notified every politician I knew. None of it did any good. The army doctors said I was having a breakdown and stuck me in a hospital in Sarajevo. They kept me there for weeks. When I got out, the massacre had been neatly covered up." She smiled bitterly. "So even we cover up when it suits us. It made me sick. Christ, I hate lies."

"You have a right." He paused. "I'm sorry it was so rough on you. Do you think you can sleep now?"

Sleep? She felt ready to collapse. "Yes."

"Good, then maybe I can too. Good night."

"Good night."

He turned off the light and left, all brusque, abrupt, cool, as if that moment of intimacy had never happened. Intimacy? He was a stranger.

But he wasn't a stranger. Already, he was more familiar to her than many people she had known for years. She knew the terse, crisp way he spoke, the intensity masked by impassiveness. She had even seen through his menacing demeanor and detected a measure of humor and gentleness. Good God, it was like bonding with Jack the Ripper.

No, Kaldak killed out of necessity, not for pleasure. He had shown her violence, but he had not been wantonly brutal.

In another minute she'd be putting a halo over his head. She smiled. Not bloody likely.

What on earth had possessed him to bring her ice-cold milk? He hadn't answered her question about his mother's remedies. It was odd to think of Kaldak with a mother who taught him household tasks and manners. It was odd to think of him with a mother, period.

I didn't crawl out from under a rock.

He was obviously accustomed to people thinking of him as something other than human.

And that's exactly what she was doing.

Yet he was her companion now and had been her savior at San Andreas and guardian on that journey through the hills. In some way she was making contact with him.

And, yes, his presence was becoming almost comforting.

NINE

It was nearly nine-thirty in the morning when De Salmo got off the plane at Hartsfield Airport and close to ten by the time he drove his black Saturn rental car out of the lot.

He checked the city map and then got on the I-75 highway heading north.

It was raining hard, but the traffic was moving smoothly. He should be at the CDC within a half hour. If he was lucky, this might be a very quick job.

It took Kaldak and Bess almost an hour on I-75 South to make it to the CDC headquarters. Kaldak pulled into the parking lot and shut off the engine.

"Aren't we going inside?" Bess asked when he made no move to get out of the car.

Kaldak shook his head. "Ed is going to meet us here. He's a cautious man."

"If he was cautious, he wouldn't be involved with you." She tried to peer out the windshield. "And he's going to be very wet."

"Which will only make him worse-tempered." He nodded at a tall, gangly man in a trench coat springing across the parking lot. "Here he comes."

Ed Katz was in his early forties, with receding brown hair and a thin, freckled face. He opened the back door of the car, dove in, and slammed the door. "It's a bad sign."

"The rain?" Kaldak asked.

Katz nodded gloomily. "It's a bad sign." He stiffened when he saw Bess. "Who is she?"

"A friend."

"Oh, great. Why don't you invite the whole world, Kaldak?"

"She's safe."

"Until they ask her to testify against me."

"No one's going to testify against you."

"Yeah, sure. If this goes down, everyone's going to take a fall." He thrust the briefcase he was carrying at Kaldak. "Take this and let me get out of here."

"Thanks, Ed."

"Just don't ask me to do anything else. You know you could probably have done a better job than me. This was nasty stuff."

"Did you do a double check on the test?"

"I'm almost sure it was positive, but there was too much deterioration of the sample. We'd need a lot more to do the job."

"I know. I'll see to it."

"Make it quick. And I don't want to hear from you until then."

Kaldak nodded. "I won't bother you if I can help it."

"Find a way to help it." He got out of the car. "We're even, Kaldak." He hesitated, raindrops pouring down his face as he stared at Kaldak. "It's real nasty. You going to be able to do anything about it?"

"With a little help from my friends."

"I'm not your friend. Do you hear me, Kaldak? I'm not your friend. Don't you bring this back to me unless you have a way of stopping it."

"Not unless it's necessary." Kaldak started to back out of the parking space and then slammed on his brakes to avoid hitting a black Saturn that was whipping through the parking lot. "I'll call you."

"Don't."

The black Saturn was out of the way and searching for a parking spot in the next row. Kaldak backed out and headed for the exit.

Bess looked over her shoulder and saw Katz still standing in the rain, looking after them. "He's scared."

"We're all scared, aren't we?"

But it had shaken her to realize an expert in the field was so terrified by the results of the tests. She suddenly remembered something Katz had said. "He said you could do the test yourself. Could you?"

"Given the right equipment."

"Then are you a doctor like Katz?"

"No one's like Katz."

"Don't sidestep. Are you?"

"Yes. A long time ago. Ed and I went to school together."

"Then why—"

"Did I give it up to kill people?" Kaldak finished. "It takes time for a man to find his true vocation. Katz leads such a dull life."

It was clear Kaldak had no intention of telling her anything more. At least she had that little morsel Katz had thrown out. It put a whole new light on Kaldak.

Or did it? He had been an enigma since the moment she had met him.

"Don't worry about it." Kaldak shot her a sly glance as he negotiated his way through the traffic toward the freeway. "I didn't mean to overwhelm you with my myriad qualifications. Just treat me as your run-of-the-mill hit man. I'm sure you prefer it."

Damn him.

She changed the subject. "Will he help us if we need him?"

"He'll help us."

"He deals with dangerous germs every day. Why did the anthrax frighten him so much?"

"It comes packaged with money. He sees the potential. Money is alive."

She shook her head. "Money is just paper."

"Is it? Take a twenty-dollar bill out of your wallet."

"What?"

"Do it."

"This is stupid." She flipped open her purse, took out her wallet, and extracted a twenty-dollar bill. "It's just paper."

"Tear it up."

Her hand instinctively tightened on the bill. "Don't be ridiculous. We might need it."

"You see, it's not just paper, it's alive. That twenty-dollar bill could send your kids to college, pay for your house, free you from a job you hate, buy you a heroin hit to keep your body from screaming with pain. Who's going to refuse it even if there's a danger of it being contaminated? Most people think bad things are going to happen only to the other guy."

"I can tear it up."

"Then do it."

She ripped the twenty-dollar bill in two.

"Congratulations." Then he smiled. "But what are you doing?"

"Just putting the pieces back in my wallet."

"So that you can tape them together later."

Her eyes widened as she realized that's exactly what she had intended to do. "It would be stupid to lose the money for a silly experiment."

"Right." He swung onto the freeway. "They say self-preservation is the first law. Wouldn't you say that twenty-dollar bill has just preserved itself?"

Alive. The idea was ludicrous. No, it was frightening. Because she now understood what it meant. Money was not only currency, it was knit into the fabric of people's lives and dreams. Esteban couldn't have chosen a more irresistible siren to deliver the bacteria. "Diabolical."

"Yes."

"But if people knew, surely they'd reject it."

"Maybe. But when we see them tearing up or burning money, we'll know we're really in trouble. What emotional response do you think it would take to trigger an act like that?"

Despair. Frustration. Fury.

"There would be anarchy. Just the situation Habin wants. It was his idea to use the money. He planned and worked for over seven years to steal those plates from Denver."

"Where are they making the counterfeit money?"

"They made the pesos in an underground installation in Libya. I think they moved the operation earlier this year when they started making the U.S. currency."

"Where?"

"Somewhere in the U.S. is a good bet."

"You don't know?"

He shook his head. "But it would make sense not to have to transport the anthrax all over the world."

"My God, what do you know?"

He was silent for a few moments. Then, "I found references to Waterloo, Iowa."

"How?"

"Esteban had a lieutenant removed when he became overly curious about what was happening at Tenajo. I searched his belongings afterward."

After Kaldak had killed the lieutenant himself. It was too easy to make the connection.

"Yes." He answered her unspoken question. "And if I hadn't done away with Galvez, I wouldn't have had enough information to take the chance of getting you out of San Andreas."

"I didn't say anything. I just wish it had been Esteban."

"My, how fierce we're getting."

"Waterloo, Iowa." She shook her head. She could imagine the hidden laboratory in Libya or even Mexico but not in the heartland of America. "So the lab and the counterfeiting operation are both in Iowa?"

"Probably. It's more than likely that they transferred the counterfeiting operation to the same installation as the lab."

Everything in place, ready to move. "Where is the target?" she murmured. "And how do we find out?"

She saw a flicker of expression on his face. "Were you lying to me? Do you know where the strike is going to be?"

"I didn't lie to you. I'm not sure."

"But you do have an idea?"

"Galvez had a fax from Morrisey, who's evidently some kind of advance scout. The fax said his next stop was going to be Cheyenne."

"You aren't going to warn them?"

"It was mentioned in passing. No clear threat. Should I panic an entire city when it could be nothing?"

"Yes."

"And when Esteban learns of it, he'll just shift the target and we'll have no chance of intercepting them."

"I don't care about catching them. I just don't want another Tenajo."

His lips tightened. "Trust me. There won't be another Tenajo. Not if there's any way on earth I can help it."

But what if he couldn't help it? She leaned back, listening to the heavy pounding of rain on the roof of the car.

Bad sign, Katz had said.

She hoped he was wrong. They didn't need any more bad omens staring them in the face.

"I missed them," De Salmo said. "I was too late."

"There was always that possibility," Esteban said.

"Should I stick around?"

"No, get on a plane to New Orleans."

"Is that where she's going?"

Esteban smiled. "Oh, yes, that's where she's going."

"Where is this safe house?" she asked as she gazed out the window. The rain had lessened as they drove east, but it was still a steady downpour. "We're in North Carolina now, aren't we?"

"About twenty minutes ago. We'll be at the house soon. It's in Northrup, a little town a bit south of here."

"I want you to call Yael as soon as we get there."

He nodded. "Whatever you say. Though I told you he might not have—"

Kaldak's portable phone rang. He pulled it out of his jacket and punched the answer button.

"Shit."

There was nothing impassive about his expression now as he listened. His mouth twisted, and a vein pounded in his temple. "Are you certain, Ramsey?" he asked. "When?"

Something was wrong, she thought. The anthrax? Had Esteban set off—

"Bullshit. I can't do that. I *won't* do it." He disconnected the phone and his foot pressed down hard on the accelerator.

"What's wrong? What happened?"

"In a minute." He pulled off the highway onto a small road. He shut off the engine.

"Is it the anthrax?" she asked.

"No." He looked straight ahead. He grasped the steering wheel so tightly his knuckles were white. "There's been a development in New Orleans."

"A development?"

"An announcement in this morning's *Times-Picayune*."

"What are you talking about?"

"An obituary for Emily Grady Corelli, who will be buried two days from now."

Shock froze her. She couldn't breathe. Then she shook her head. "No, it's not true. It's crazy. It's just some vicious trick of Esteban's."

He shook his head.

"Don't tell me no." Her voice was shaking. "It can't be true. Emily was in Mexico. How would she— It's a lie."

"I wish it were." His voice was thick. "I wish to God it were, Bess. It was confirmed. She's at the Duples Funeral Home on First Street. The body was delivered last night by an air freight service with forged health department certifications, cash, and instructions for the funeral."

"It's a lie. He told me before that she was dead and in the morgue, but it was Rico. It wasn't Emily, it was Rico."

"It's Emily this time. They took fingerprints and—"

"I don't believe it. You said Yael was going to find her, that he was going to bring her—"

"She's dead, Bess."

She wouldn't believe it. If she believed it, then it might come true. "No, I'll show you. I'm going to New Orleans and I'll go to the funeral home and I'll prove—"

"No." He suddenly turned and drew her into his arms. "I'm sorry. God, I'm sorry."

He was trying to comfort her, she thought dully. But she couldn't accept it. Accepting comfort would be the same as admitting Emily was dead. "I'm going to see her."

"It's a trap. Why do you think Esteban sent her to New Orleans? It's where you live. He knew we'd be monitoring everything that went on there. He wanted to draw you there."

"So he killed her?"

He didn't answer for a moment. "He didn't have to kill her. She's been dead for a long time. We think she died of anthrax that first night in Tenajo."

"No, she wasn't sick. And she wasn't at San Andreas. It was Rico. It was Ric——"

"Shh." His fingers buried in her hair and his voice was uneven. "I can't take it. Christ, I never thought it would be like this."

"I have to go. She's not dead. I know it. She's not—"

"Bess. She's dead and Esteban wants you dead too. I can't let you go to New Orleans."

She pushed him away. "You can't keep me from going to her."

"Look, Ramsey's rushing the DNA test. They'll have absolute proof within a day or so."

"Screw their proof. It's not true." It was all lies. "Start this car. Take me to an airport, any airport."

"No." He looked away from her. "I can't do that."

"You *have* to do it. I'm not going to any safe house. You can do without your damn witness."

He shook his head.

"Don't you tell me no. It's my life."

"No, it's not. Not entirely."

What was he saying?

"There's a very good possibility you have an immunity to the mutated anthrax," he said.

She looked at him in bewilderment. "Immunity."

"You should have died at Tenajo. Everyone else did."

"You said the anthrax dissipated too soon."

He shook his head. "It had weakened, but it was still potent enough to do the job. It killed Rico. It killed your sister."

"It didn't kill Emily. Esteban—"

"It killed them, Bess." A muscle in his cheek jerked. "You survived. Why do you think Esteban didn't kill you right away? He couldn't understand why you didn't die, and he wanted to run blood tests."

"I don't remember—" The Band-Aid covering the needle marks. Not all sedative injections as she had thought. "Blood tests."

"Esteban didn't broadcast what he was doing, but I knew he didn't like what he found."

"What . . . did he find?"

"Immune antibodies."

"You can't know that."

"Yes, I can. I stole one of the blood samples from the hospital lab before I took you out of San Andreas. Ed ran a test last night. There was too much deterioration for it to be useful, but it tested positive for immunity. Do you know what that means? It may cut the time for developing a serum from nearly a year to weeks or even days." He paused. "That's why you can't take any risks. You're the answer, Bess. We'll need to take frequent blood samples from you so the CDC can work on a cure that will stop Esteban in his tracks."

The answer. She didn't want to be the answer to anything. She just wanted everything to be as it was before Tenajo. She just wanted Emily to be alive and well.

And Emily *was* alive. She had almost let Kaldak convince her that her sister was dead, that she was in that funeral home in New Orleans. "I'm going to see her."

"They'll be waiting for you."

"So you need to protect your precious blood supply. I'm sorry to inconvenience you, but you'll have to take a new sample in New Orleans." She added bitterly, "Unless you want to follow in Esteban's footsteps and lock me up and keep me under sedation."

"That option has been suggested." When she stiffened, he added roughly, "Do you think I'd let them do that to you? I'm just telling you so you'll realize how important this is. Ramsey didn't even want me to tell you about your sister's death."

"She's not dead," she said woodenly.

"If you believe that, why run the risk of walking into Esteban's trap?"

Because she had to know, she had to be

sure. "If I'm immune, then Emily is too. She's my sister, and she's always been healthier than me. I'm the one who always caught the colds and the—"

"It doesn't work like that," he said gently.

"And Josie," she said desperately. "What about Josie? Josie didn't die. Josie has to be immune too."

He shook his head. "Josie has no immune antibodies. Esteban lost interest in her almost immediately. She was just lucky enough not to have been exposed to the money by actual physical contact. Your sister and you were going from house to house and had to come into contact with the money at some point."

The cantina, the general store—she couldn't remember all the places. They hadn't put on the gloves and masks until after they had examined the bodies in the cantina. Had she and Emily touched the pesos, pushed them aside as they tried to help—

She was becoming frightened. Kaldak's logic was too convincing and she had to shut it out. "It's not true. It's not her. Take me to New Orleans and let me show you."

He didn't move.

Her hands clenched at her sides. "Please, Kaldak," she whispered. "Please."

"*Goddammit.*" He turned on the ignition. "It's faster to go back to Atlanta. We can get a direct flight to New Orleans from there."

Relief flooded her. "Thank you, Kaldak."

"For what?" He entered the highway with a violence that caused the tires to squeal. "Being stupid? Taking a chance that may get you killed? Taking a chance that could kill a city?" He picked up the telephone and dialed a number. "We're coming, Ramsey." He listened for a moment and then said, "I don't give a damn. We're coming. So pull out the stops on security." He pressed the end button and dialed again. "Meet us at the Atlanta airport at the Hertz check-in desk in an hour, Ed. I'll have the sample for you." He hung up again. "When we get to the airport, I need to take blood from you and give it to Ed Katz."

"How are—"

"I told Ed to include a kit in the briefcase he gave me this morning. I knew I'd have to get a sample to him as soon as possible."

"So you were prepared," she said slowly. "When were you going to tell me?"

"After I had you safe. But I wanted to tell you right away."

"Then why didn't you?"

"I couldn't risk it. You couldn't think of anything but your sister. If you knew how valuable you were to Esteban, you might have tried to arrange a swap for Emily."

"And you couldn't permit that."

"I couldn't permit that," he said grimly. "Any more than I can take you to New Orleans without getting that sample. It will give Ed a small chance even if Esteban kills you."

The bluntness of his words should have unnerved her, but it didn't. She had to retain control, or she would fly into a thousand pieces. She had to hold herself together until she got to Em——

Oh, God, it couldn't be Emily.

Emily was safe, hiding somewhere in those hills in Mexico. There were so many places to hide. She and Josie had found caves and hollows and—

It wasn't Emily.

TEN

The Duples Funeral Home was a large white building. The paint was starting to peel and the lawn was yellowing in patches. A statue of a winged angel with a trumpet was balanced on a pedestal beside the front door.

Was the angel supposed to be Gabriel? Bess wondered dully. Emily would have hated this place. She always liked things neat and well kept.

Kaldak's grasp tightened on her elbow. "You can change your mind."

She shook her head and quickened her pace up the walk. Just get it over with, she told herself. Find out they'd made a huge mistake and then get out of there.

"You've gone too far, Kaldak." A tall, gray-haired man stepped out from an alcove. "My God, do you *want* them to put her down?"

"It's your job to see that they don't, Ramsey. Have you checked out the funeral home?"

"Yes. Get her out of here."

Kaldak glanced at the row of houses across the street. "What about those?"

Ramsey nodded curtly. "We went through them. No snipers. I had to tell them we were having a presidential visit. They'll probably call their congressman. Why the hell would the president come here?"

Kaldak's gaze went beyond him to the foyer. "Where is she?"

"First room on the left." Ramsey's glance moved to Bess. "It's a waste of time, Ms. Grady. You don't want to do this. It's a closed casket."

"Why?"

Ramsey shifted uneasily. "She died in the hills and was buried there. It was hot and conditions weren't conducive to—"

"You're saying Esteban dug up her body and sent her here?" Callous and hideous. As hideous as digging a hole and tossing a woman in it in the first place.

But it hadn't happened to Emily. It was someone else in that room.

She opened the door and went inside. First room on the left. An oak casket in the center. Candles burning at either end. No flowers. Where were the flowers?

Her chest was constricting. She couldn't breathe.

"Bess." Kaldak was beside her.

She moistened her lips. "Open it."

"No."

"Open it, Kaldak."

"You heard Ramsey. You don't want to see—"

"I have to see. I have to know. Open it, or I'll do it myself."

He muttered a curse and stepped forward. He threw open the lid of the coffin.

She would take just one look and she would know they were wrong.

Just one look and it would be over.

Oh, Jesus!

Kaldak caught her when she fell.

"Emily."

"Hush." Kaldak was carrying her, climbing stairs, she realized vaguely. The stairs leading to her apartment. How had they gotten there? "Don't think. Just try to sleep."

"I didn't believe—"

"I know."

"Was she in pain?"

"Not for long."

"They just threw her in the ground, Kaldak. They just tossed her away." Her fingers were digging into his shoulders. "No one deserves— Emily was so bright and warm and— I didn't say good-bye. I just gave her Josie and ran out the door. I should have said good-bye."

"She would have understood."

"But I should have—"

"Please stop crying."

Was she crying? She couldn't feel the tears. Her entire body ached like an open wound. "I'm sorry."

"I didn't mean—" He sat down in a chair and held her on his lap. "Cry. Hit me. Do whatever you like. Just don't—" He was rocking her back and forth. "Don't *hurt* like this."

"I can't help it. She's . . . dead. Emily's dead." The truth was tearing her apart. Emily was lying in that shiny oak box at the funeral home. Emily would never laugh or smile or boss her around ever.

"It will be all right." Kaldak's low voice was agonized. "It will get better. I promise, it will get better."

How could it get better?

Emily was dead.

Kaldak carefully put Bess down on the bed and drew the coverlet over her. He hoped she wouldn't wake up right away. It had taken hours for her to fall asleep. He left her bedroom and gently closed the door.

He dropped into an easy chair and leaned his head back. He never wanted to go through anything like that again. He had felt her pain and her loss as if they were his own. The loss did belong to him, the loss and the responsibility and the guilt. Oh, God, yes, the guilt.

Stop thinking about it. It was over. Now he had to find a way to protect Bess, to keep her from suffering ever again.

Yeah, sure.

His gaze wandered around the small living room of the apartment. The furniture was simple and clean-lined except for the beige and burgundy striped chair and couch. The photographs on the wall were striking: one little black girl with enormous wistful eyes, Jimmy Carter in shirtsleeves at a Habitat site, the Somalian bandit he had mentioned to Bess. On the end table were family pictures: a much younger Emily in shorts and T-shirt on a swing beside a river. Emily in a wedding gown standing beside a tall man in a tuxedo. Emily and a little red-haired girl with bold, curious eyes. All Emily.

He glanced away to the Persian rug covering the oak floor and then to the plants that filled the room.

Plants.

He touched the African violets on the table beside him. Real.

He reached for his telephone and dialed Ramsey.

"You told me the apartment was safe," he said when Ramsey answered. "Bess is out of the country most of the time. Who has a key to get in to water her plants?"

"It is safe. Her landlord comes in twice a week. He hasn't been approached by anyone. Someone does know their job besides you, Kaldak."

"Sorry."

"How is she?"

"How do you think she is?"

"I told you that you shouldn't have brought her."

"No sign of Esteban?"

"Not yet. But you know he has someone here."

Yes, he knew it. Esteban would have had a man at the funeral home and he knew exactly where Bess was right now. "Did you check on the air freight service?"

"They were just doing a job. Maybe a little too willing to accept forged papers, but that's all." Ramsey paused. "We need to talk."

"Later. I'm not leaving her."

"What about the blood test?"

"We think it's positive. I'm calling Ed Katz to verify the results on the new sample."

"Positive?" Ramsey swore softly. "And you still let her come here? Are you nuts?"

"Probably." He changed the subject. "Has Yael checked in?"

"Not since yesterday, but he's on his way here. When are you taking her to the safe house?"

"Why don't you worry about finding that counterfeiting center and lab in Iowa and let me worry about Bess?"

"Because you're not worrying enough about her. You're going to get her killed and then where will we be if Esteban moves ahead with—"

"I'll call you back." Kaldak hung up the phone. He didn't need Ramsey to tell him how reckless he was acting. He dialed Ed Katz in Atlanta.

"It's a definite." Ed's excited words tumbled over one another. "We can work with it. But we need more, much more."

"What do you want me to do? Drain her veins?"

"No, no, of course not. But it wouldn't hurt to get me another sample right away."

"I'll get it when I can."

"Right away."

"She just saw her sister dead in a coffin."

"Oh." Ed paused. "Too bad. But maybe you could explain to her how important it is to—"

"Good-bye, Ed."

"Wait. She's upset?"

"Of course she's upset."

"Don't give her a sedative. It would compromise the results of the next batch that you—"

"I'll give her whatever she needs. If I have to knock her out for the next twenty-four hours, I'll do it."

"You don't need to get testy. It's your ball game. Just send me something as soon as you can."

Kaldak slid the phone back into his pocket.

It's your ball game.

Yes, it was his game and he was being permitted to call the shots. A dubious honor given him only because nobody else wanted to stick his neck out. Too many things could go wrong. Hell, too many things had already gone wrong. So far only one thing in the entire unholy mess had gone right, Bess's immunity factor.

So he was supposed to treat Bess as if she were a lab animal. To hell with what she felt or thought. To hell with individual freedom, think of the public good. Use her.

It made him sick. It was a nightmare that had gone on too long.

He was afraid that he couldn't do it any longer.

And he was more afraid that he could.

"She took the bait?" Esteban felt a rush of pleasure.

"She's there?"

"She collapsed at the funeral home," Marco De Salmo said. "She's at her apartment now. Kaldak is with her."

"Any way of getting to her?"

"Security is tight, real tight. I didn't have a chance at the funeral home."

"But you've been hired to get around it, Marco," Esteban said softly. "I'm sure you'll be successful. We don't have much time. They'll whisk her away and hide her as soon as they can. I can't tell you how displeased I'd be if that happened after I've gone to all this trouble."

"I've bugged the phone. And I'm watching the apartment. We won't lose her again."

"I hope not. Every minute she's alive is a dangerous minute. For you as well as for her."

There was a silence. "I'll find a way."

"I have every confidence." He hung up the phone. He did have a certain amount of confidence in De Salmo. He'd found him very efficient if a little lacking in imagination. Imagination was a great asset in an assassin. Kaldak had imagination, and it was one of his most valuable qualities.

"It's a call from Mr. Morrisey on your portable phone." Perez was standing in the doorway. "You said you'd take his calls any-time."

Morrisey. Eagerness shot through Este-ban as he reached for the phone. Of course he wanted to talk to him. He'd been waiting on pins and needles for weeks. It had taken Morrisey too long already to locate the right man. "You've found him?"

"Cody Jeffers. Twenty-one. A loner. Starstruck. Brags a lot. He's a minor driver in the demolition derby here. He's been hang-ing around the track for the past couple of weeks and bothering the headliners. He came in third and fourth in a couple of minor derbies, but he gambles the prize money away as fast as he gets it. Sound like the man you want?"

Excitement was soaring through Este-ban. "Exactly."

"Do you want me to approach him for you?"

"No, I'll do it myself." This part of his plan was too crucial to be handled by underlings. Jeffers was to be the linchpin and must be absolutely right. "Where is he?"

"Here in Cheyenne, Wyoming. Majestic Hotel. A fleabag near the track."

"Meet me at the airport. I'll be there tomorrow morning. Perez will call and let you know the flight number."

He hung up the phone and leaned back in his chair. The Grady woman would soon be dead and the linchpin had been found.

Things were moving forward very satisfactorily.

Light was streaming through the lace curtains at the window. Bess had always loved that misty, patterned look. She'd bought the lace in Amsterdam, framed it with striped wool draperies, and made sure the curtains hung straight, with no fussy flounces. She'd bought a length for Emily too, and Emily had ordered curtains made for Julie's room. Emily had laughed and said that she would have never dreamed Bess liked lace, that it didn't suit her personality at—

Emily.

Pain tore through Bess and she closed her eyes tightly, blocking out the thought of her sister.

"Don't go back to sleep."

Her eyes opened, and she saw Kaldak sitting beside the bed.

"You've been asleep for ten hours," he said quietly. "You need to eat now."

She shook her head.

"Yes." He stood up. "I'll go fix you soup and a sandwich."

"I'm not hungry."

"You have to eat anyway. Go take a shower and dress." He left the room.

He was back to being cool and decisive, she realized. Yet last night he had held her in his arms for hours and rocked her and agonized with her as if Emily had been his sister too.

Emily.

"Get up," he called from the kitchen.

To hell with him. She didn't want to get up. She wanted to go back to sleep and forget the sight of Emily in that coffin. Oh, Jesus.

He returned, lifted her to her feet, and pushed her gently toward the bathroom. "I'll give you ten minutes. If you're not out of the shower, I'll come in and finish the job."

She wanted to hit him.

"Life goes on, Bess. You don't heal lying in bed. You heal doing something about it."

"Stop preaching to me. You don't know how—"

He was gone.

She slammed the bathroom door and leaned against it. She was crying again. "Dammit," she whispered. "Damn you, Kaldak."

And damn Esteban, who had killed Emily and had her thrown in a hole in the ground as if she were nothing. Monster. Crawling out from under the rock and tearing, hurting—

"Five minutes, Bess."

Why wouldn't he stop nagging her? she thought as she stripped off her clothes. He was just like Emily and the way—

Was everything going to remind her of Emily? Kaldak wasn't like Emily. No one was like her.

She turned on the shower and stepped beneath the spray.

Emily had been bright and loyal and loving. And that monster had killed her.

Show them the monsters.

But they all knew who the monster was, and Emily had still died. The monster was walking around, breathing air, eating food, laughing and talking, and Emily was dead.

And Bess was standing there weeping and wailing because "they" had done nothing. It was always "they." They had done nothing at Tenajo. They had done nothing at Danzar either.

She had done nothing.

Emily was dead and she was doing nothing.

"Bess?"

Kaldak was standing outside the shower stall. She could see his large frame through the mist on the glass.

"Go away, Kaldak."

"Come out, your lunch is ready."

"Go away."

"You've been in there long enough." He started to slide the shower door open.

"Get *out*." She slammed the shower door shut. "I'll come out when I'm good and ready. Just leave me alone right now."

He stood there, startled at the fury in her voice.

She was startled too. She hadn't realized how fast and high her anger had soared. Her fists were clenched so hard, her fingernails were digging into her palms. Wave after wave of anger and hate washed over her.

Esteban.

"Your robe's on the hook on the door." The door shut and she was alone.

No, not alone.

The memory of Emily as she had seen her in the funeral home remained with her. Would she ever see her sister any other way? Would every memory of the past be burned away but that one?

Push it aside, block it. She would only cry again, and that weakened her. She had to think and plan. She couldn't be weak now. She had to be as strong as Emily would have been in her place.

Because, at last, she'd learned that it did no good to just show the monsters.

You had to kill them.

She didn't come out of the bathroom for almost an hour.

Kaldak looked up when she came into the kitchen. "Your soup's cold." He rose to his feet and picked up the bowl. "I'll put it in the microwave for a minute."

"You're feeding me in the kitchen?" She gave him a ghost of a smile. "Your mother wouldn't approve."

"She understood emergencies. Sit down."

"Okay." She sat at the table and said haltingly, "I'm sorry . . . I yelled . . . at you. You were only doing what you thought best."

"No problem."

"And you were very kind to me last night. Thank you."

"For God's sake, I don't want you to thank me." His gaze raked her face. "Are you okay?"

No, she wasn't okay. Emily was dead and Esteban was not. "I'm fine."

"The hell you are. You're pale as a sheet and look like you're holding on by a hair."

"I'm fine," she repeated.

"I called Dr. Kenwood this morning. Josie's doing well."

"Does he know when they're going to operate?"

"He won't commit yet." He set the soup down in front of her. "He said she needs to build more blood."

Blood Esteban had taken from her.

"Has anyone notified Tom and Julie about Emily?"

"Not yet. They can't be reached. They're still in Canada."

"I don't want you to try to find them. I don't want them to know."

"Why?"

"They'd come down here and it would be dangerous for them. You said they might be targets."

He nodded. "We'll continue to keep a watch on the ranger station and their house."

"I don't want them to see Emily . . . the way I did." She had to stop a minute to steady her voice. "Tom and Julie wouldn't believe she's dead any more than I did. They'd open the casket and see— I can't let them do that. I want her to be buried with dignity and respect. I want you to arrange a quiet funeral for tomorrow. When we tell them, I need to be able to show Julie that her mother is in a place that—"

"You're not the next of kin. Tom Corelli has the right to make that decision, Bess."

"I'm taking the right." She picked up the spoon. Her hand was shaking only a little. "You can fix it. You're the CIA. If you can forge papers and kill people, you can do this. I won't let Tom and Julie see Emily like that. I want them to remember her as she was before Esteban— Do it, Kaldak."

He nodded slowly. "I'll make the arrangements. But the burial should be done today. The sooner we get out of here, the better."

"Tomorrow." She would be ready tomorrow. She wasn't strong enough yet. She forced herself to start eating the soup. Eat the soup, the sandwich. Try to sleep tonight. Get strong. "Tomorrow, Kaldak."

"I don't like— Okay." He sat watching her eat. "But now I have a favor to ask you. Ed says he can work with the sample we gave him, but he needs more."

Blood. She had almost forgotten. She shouldn't forget. It had to be entered into the equation. "Then take it."

"I can wait awhile."

"Take it."

He got up from the table and disappeared into the living room. He came back with the black leather kit he had used in the parking lot in Atlanta. When the needle entered her arm, she barely felt it. "You're very good at that."

"Stay still." His expression was intent as he drew the blood. "There." He put a Band-Aid on her arm. "I'll be right back. I have to get these tubes packed in ice and ready to go. They need to reach Ed by tonight. His team is working around the clock."

"Then there is a big hurry. You said you could wait."

"You were out for a long time." He smiled

crookedly. "And I was trying to be humane. Couldn't you tell?"

"Yes." He had been kind. He had held her and tried to keep away the darkness. For a while he had done it, but now it was back and must be dealt with. "I could tell."

He was gone again, to get the blood ready for the CDC. It didn't seem right she was immune to the disease and Emily had died. Emily was a doctor and had a family. Did God just randomly choose?

She stood up and moved toward the window overlooking the rooftops and wrought-iron balconies of the French Quarter. She had always loved this city. When Emily had come down to visit, she had disliked it and tried to convince Bess to get an apartment in Detroit. New Orleans was too whimsical for practical Emily.

"I've called Ramsey and told him to send a courier for the package," Kaldak said when he came back into the kitchen. "I'll answer the door when we hear the bell."

"Are you afraid someone's going to show up with a machine gun and blow me away?" she asked wearily.

"No, not a machine gun. There are quieter and more competent ways." He set the package on the chest by the door. "And I doubt if they'll come to the front door. They'll wait until you go out."

She looked back out at the window. "You think they're waiting?"

"Yes, I told you they would be. That's what this is all about."

She didn't take her gaze away from the Quarter. "It's all about the blood, isn't it? You want the blood and Esteban wants me dead before I give you enough to spoil his neat little plan."

"Yes."

"How much is enough, Kaldak?"

"We don't know."

"Then I seem to be a very valuable asset."

Kaldak was silent, watching her.

"Do you think Esteban is here?"

"I doubt it. He wouldn't risk it. But he's sent someone."

"I'm sure that was a disappointment to him. I remember his face in the hospital when he told me Emily was dead. Why did he lie to me about Emily being in the morgue?"

"He wanted to hurt you. You might not have believed him if he'd told you he'd buried her in the hills. You'd have thought he was lying and that Emily had gotten away from him."

"I did think that when we found Rico. I hoped she had—" Even that hope was painful to remember. "How did Ramsey know she'd been buried in the hills?"

"Yael."

She turned to look at him. "Yael?"

"I told him to look for a grave."

She stiffened. "What?"

"I called him back that day on the aircraft carrier and told him to look for a grave."

"You thought she was dead even then?" she whispered.

"I hoped she wasn't. I prayed she wasn't. But I knew there was a good possibility."

"Why?"

"She wasn't brought to the hospital with Josie. From what you told me about your sister, I didn't think she would allow herself to be separated from the baby." He paused. "If she was alive."

Bess had thought the same thing, but she hadn't allowed herself to accept it. "There was a chance she was still alive. There was a chance."

"But a greater one that she was dead."

His lips lifted in a faint smile. "My analytical mind. I had to play the odds. I told Yael while he was searching to also be on the lookout for a shallow grave."

"And he found it. When?"

"Three days ago. He spotted a suspect site in the foothills about ten miles from Tenajo. He verified and was on his way back to report to me, when Esteban's men came and began to exhume."

"You mean dig her up," she said bitterly. *Exhume.* Such a smooth, clean word for an ugly violation.

He nodded.

"You didn't tell me. You let me hope."

"There was a chance I was wrong. And would you have believed me if I'd told you Emily was probably dead?"

No, she wouldn't have believed him. She hadn't let herself believe it until she had actually seen Emily's body.

Veer away. Don't think of that moment. Keep controlled and steady. "I'm . . . tired. I'm going back to my bedroom. Let me know when you've made arrangements for Emily's funeral."

"If you feel up to it, you might start packing. We should leave immediately after the funeral."

She went into her bedroom and shut the door, closing him out. She had started to shake, but she didn't think he had seen. She had shown him too much weakness already and she couldn't afford to have him perceive her as anything but strong and decisive.

She drew a deep, steadying breath. That was better. Just a little more time and she would be fine.

She was so finely balanced, Kaldak had expected her to shatter at any moment.

It might be better if she had. That careful control could be more dangerous than the wild despair of last night. Her manner today was not what he had expected. He was usually able to read her, but he hadn't known what she was thinking today.

That was not going to be a problem though. He had an idea she would make her thoughts and needs known soon enough.

Cheyenne, Wyoming

"Yeah, you're a real Evel Knievel, Jeffers. A real, rootin'-tootin' cowboy," Randall said solemnly. "I guess I'd better watch out." He cast a sly glance at his wife sitting next to him at the bar.

He was snickering, laughing at him, Cody Jeffers realized. He didn't believe Cody's story.

Snooty son of a bitch. So he'd exaggerated a little. Who did Randall think he was? Just because he'd won a few derbies—

Cody got off the stool, jammed his Stetson on his head, and strode out of the bar. So he hadn't won any big events. He was still young. He'd make it. He'd be a headliner when Randall was cavorting around in a wheelchair instead of that monster truck.

He jammed his fists into the pockets of his sheepskin jacket and started down the street.

Randall wouldn't laugh tomorrow night when one of the big tires came off his vehicle while he was performing. Everybody would be laughing at him instead. All it would take would be a few turns of a wrench to loosen the nuts, and boom, crash. He'd done it once a couple of years before when that bastard in Denver had—

"Mr. Jeffers?"

He turned.

"My name is Esteban." The man came toward him. "I was told you might be here. I've heard what a promising young man you are, and I may have a proposition for you. Could we go somewhere and talk?"

ELEVEN

Kaldak and Bess left her apartment the next morning when it was still dark. They slipped down the back staircase to a waiting car and drove to the old St. Nicholas's Cemetery in Metairie, just outside New Orleans.

Emily was interred in an ancient moss-stained crypt overlooking a small, quiet pond. It wasn't dawn yet when the clergyman closed his Bible, nodded politely, and hurried out of the crypt.

Poor man, Bess thought numbly. Dragged from his bed and brought to a cemetery that resembled something out of an Anne Rice novel.

"We should go too," Kaldak said gently.

Bess looked down at the smooth stone sarcophagus in which Emily's coffin had been enclosed. *Good-bye, Emily. I love you. You'll always be with me.*

"Bess."

She nodded, turned, and walked out of the crypt. The air was damp and fresh. She took a deep breath, watching the cemetery custodian lock the iron gates of the crypt. Weak gray rays of light were now filtering through the cypress trees and illuminated the inscription on the tomb.

Cartier.

Kaldak's gaze followed hers. "I borrowed a place for Emily from an Étienne Cartier. It's their family crypt. Everyone has to be buried above ground here."

She knew that. But she hadn't thought even Kaldak would be able to persuade someone to relinquish his final resting place. "Borrowed?"

"I thought it likely that Tom Corelli would eventually want to take her home."

Take her home. The words were sweet and melancholy at the same time. *Take Emily home.*

"In the meantime, she'll be safe here."

Safe in that tomb. Weren't the dead al-

ways safe? They didn't care, they weren't afraid or angry. . . .

"Is that okay?" Kaldak asked.

She nodded. "I guess I didn't think. Emily wouldn't have wanted to stay here forever. She didn't really like New Orleans. She would have wanted to go home." She turned and walked away. Don't think about her. Don't look back. You're not leaving her alone. She'll always be with you.

Kaldak immediately caught up with her, and they walked in silence down the gravel path lined with crypts.

"How did you get them to let us into the cemetery this early?" she asked as they neared the gates.

"Oh, Ramsey has his ways."

"Are we trying to avoid a hit man? Is that why we're creeping around burying my sister in the dark?"

"Do you think she'd prefer it if you were an easy daylight target?"

"No."

"I don't either. That's why we're here at this time in the morning and eight agents are stationed behind those crypts."

Her gaze went to the row of crypts. "I didn't see them."

"You weren't supposed to."

She wouldn't have noticed anything on that journey from the car to the crypt. She'd closed everything out but the thought of Emily.

But it was done. All that was over now.

Kaldak stopped her as she started for the tan Lexus rental car parked at the curb. "Wait a minute." He glanced at a man in a checked sports coat climbing out of a sedan parked down the street.

She stiffened.

"It's okay. He's one of ours. He was watching the car."

The man was nodding, and Kaldak opened the passenger door for her.

"You were afraid of a bomb or something?"

"I'm afraid of anything and everything," he said as he got behind the wheel. "You name it."

"Is Ramsey in that car?"

"Probably."

"What kind of man is he?"

He looked at her in surprise. "What do you mean?"

"He seemed very angry and impatient at the funeral home."

"He likes to be in charge."

"So do you." Her gaze returned to the sedan. "Do you trust him?"

"Up to a point. I've known him to step on a few people on his climb to the top of the agency. He's good at his job, but he's ambitious, and that always colors a man's actions."

"Yes, it does." Her gaze went to the east. "The sun's rising."

"Which means we'd better get going. I'll be glad to get you away from this town. We're driving straight out of the city from here. I'll have someone pick up your suitcases from the apartment and deliver them to—"

"No."

He went still and then slowly turned to face her. "What?"

"We're not leaving. At least, not yet. Drive me back to the apartment."

"No way."

"Drive me back to the apartment and send for Ramsey. I want to talk to him."

"I'll let you talk to him on the phone."

"Face-to-face. I want everything very clear. Do you remember I told you once that was how I had to have everything?"

He was silent a moment. "I remember."

"Then take me back to the apartment. Or I'll get out and walk, Kaldak. Do you want to have to trail after me?"

"I could just knock you out and take off."

"You've been there, done that," she said. "It would be trite to repeat yourself. If you want to keep me safe, take me back to the apartment, where I have four walls around me." Her voice hardened. "Because I'm not going anywhere else, Kaldak."

"Don't do this, Bess."

She reached for the handle of the door.

"All *right,*" he said through his teeth. He turned the ignition and stomped on the accelerator. The car jumped forward, pressing her back against the seat.

She had won the first battle.

"What the hell are you still doing here?" Ramsey slammed the apartment door shut. "You're supposed to be halfway to Shreveport to board that flight to Atlanta. Kaldak, for God's sake, I won't stand for—"

"Kaldak had no choice," Bess said. "And I'd appreciate it if you'd talk to me, Mr. Ramsey. I'm a little tired of being treated as if I have all the intelligence of a prize cow."

Ramsey glanced warily at Kaldak sitting in the easy chair across the room.

Kaldak shrugged.

Ramsey turned back to Bess. "No one intends to treat you with anything but respect, Ms. Grady. We're all very sympathetic toward your loss. I understand Dr. Corelli was a fine woman and a—"

"Emily is dead. So what kind of woman she was doesn't matter to anyone but the people who loved her. I didn't bring you here to mouth condolences to me."

"Then why did you bring me here?"

"Information. I need to be clear on a few points. Are you going to go into Mexico to get Esteban?"

"We can't. That would cause a diplomatic incident. We have no proof."

"You have my sister's body."

"And a confrontation now might trigger another incident. Be patient."

"I'm not patient." She paused. "I need another piece of information. I need to know about Kaldak. I decided to go to you, since I've noticed he tells me only what he wants me to know."

Ramsey looked uneasily at Kaldak.

Kaldak said, "Tell her."

"You're his boss?" Bess asked.

"In a manner of speaking."

"Which means you're not his boss? It has to be one way or the other."

"Kaldak has been working with us for a number of years. He has special qualifications that make him invaluable to us."

"Qualifications in killing people or in germ warfare? He's a scientist, isn't he?"

"He told you?" Ramsey hesitated. "Then you know about Nakoa?"

"No, she doesn't." Kaldak's gaze had narrowed on her face. "What are you getting at, Bess?"

"I want to know how much power you have with these people. You seem to be able to call on them at will, but I have to know how far it goes."

"We cut Kaldak more slack than we ordinarily would," Ramsey said. "Due to the unusual circumstances surrounding the—"

"They use me," Kaldak said bluntly. "Everyone's scared to death of this thing. I'm convenient because I'm there to blame if anything goes wrong." He smiled sardonically at Ramsey. "And I use them."

"You're not scared?" Bess asked.

"Hell, yes. I just can't let that get in the way."

No, Kaldak wouldn't let anything get in his way. "So everybody uses everybody."

"It's the way of the world, Ms. Grady," Ramsey said. "But you can be assured that we're doing everything we can to stop Esteban."

"I'm not assured. I don't trust you."

"You think we'd let a national disaster occur?" Ramsey asked impatiently. "We appreciate your concern, but it's idiotic to suggest—"

"Listen to her," Kaldak said. "She wants something."

Bess nodded. "Oh, yes."

"What?" Ramsey asked.

"Not what, who. Kaldak."

Though she was looking at Ramsey, she could sense Kaldak's sudden tension.

"I'm not sure what you mean," Ramsey said cautiously.

"Everybody uses everybody. I want to use Kaldak."

"In what fashion?"

"To keep me alive. To help me find Esteban." She looked at Kaldak and added deliberately, "To help me kill Esteban."

"Ah, there we are," Kaldak murmured. "The crux of the matter."

"You don't understand," Ramsey said. "It's not so simple. The picture is much bigger than—"

"I don't care about the big picture. You worry about the anthrax. Just give me Kaldak and make sure he has the authority to do what has to be done."

"Do you prefer me with or without gift wrapping?" Kaldak asked.

She ignored him, concentrating on Ramsey. "I want Kaldak."

"I can understand you're hurt and angry, but our efforts have to be focused on stopping Esteban from causing another Tenajo."

"Then we agree. I've every intention of stopping Esteban."

"If you'd listen to reason, I'm sure that—"

"*You* listen." Her voice vibrated with intensity. "I don't trust your 'reason.' I've seen too many deals made under the table, too many cover-ups. It's not going to happen again. No one's going to make a deal with Esteban and watch him walk away from this. No way."

"No one's going to make a deal."

She whirled on Kaldak. "Could it hap-pen?"

He slowly nodded.

"Damn you, Kaldak," Ramsey said through his teeth. "You're not making this any easier."

"I'm too interested in all of this to lie for you, Ramsey. I've never been on the slave block before."

Ramsey shot him a poisonous glance before saying gently, "Ms. Grady, we've done everything we can to make sure you're safe. Now we need your cooperation."

"Stop patronizing me. Let's be very clear. You need not only my cooperation, you need my blood. Give me Kaldak and you can have it."

"Bingo," Kaldak said.

Ramsey froze. "You'd refuse? But it could mean thousands of lives."

"Then I'm sure the White House would be very upset with you for antagonizing me and making me walk away. Give me Kaldak."

"Suppose I promise you that after this is over, Kaldak will be sent after Esteban. Will you go to a safe house and let us handle things?"

"No safe houses. I'm staying here."

"My God, do you want to die? You're a target."

"No, I don't want to die. Kaldak is going to keep me alive and you're going to help him. Right here in the open. If I hide, there's not going to be any way of drawing Esteban."

"Esteban will send a hit man. He won't come himself."

"Not at first. But I think he's going to get more and more frustrated the longer I stay alive."

Ramsey shook his head. "You're too valuable to use as bait and you have no conception of what you're asking."

"I'm not asking. I'm not giving you a choice. That's the way it's going to be. Esteban's going to pay for Emily. There's nothing more to say. Good-bye, Mr. Ramsey."

Ramsey stared at her with frustration. Then he started toward the door. "I need to talk to you, Kaldak."

"I thought you would." Kaldak rose to his feet. "I'll be back in a few minutes, Bess. We won't go any farther than the hall."

Bess walked into the bedroom. Second battle. She was glad to have it over but she didn't fool herself that Kaldak would be as easy as Ramsey. He had sat there, watching her, adding, subtracting, analyzing. She had been aware of him every second she had been fighting with Ramsey.

She changed quickly from a black suit into jeans and a shirt. Before she could fasten the last button, she heard the front door close. She braced herself and went back into the living room.

Kaldak was again sitting in the easy chair. "You won." He tapped his chest. "I'm yours."

"Are you?"

"As far as Ramsey's concerned. Of course, he suggested that we go back to his first proposal and keep you doped up while we take the blood we need. But when I wouldn't go along, he caved."

"Do you see a certain similarity to Esteban's methods?"

"Maybe. Actually, you handled Ramsey very well. He didn't realize you were bluffing."

"I wasn't bluffing."

"I think you were, but at any rate, it was too dangerous to call your bluff. The blood is essential."

"You'll get it."

"I know. I intend to make sure of it." He

paused. "And to do that I have to keep you alive. That means I'm with you every minute. You don't get in a car, you don't even answer the door without me."

"I'm not arguing."

"Let's go over the apartment, and I'll show you the security measures we've installed."

She followed him down the hall.

"Neither your bedroom nor this guest room has a fire escape or other entry. They were okay." He went to the door at the end of the hall. "The lock on this door leading down to the small courtyard was too flimsy. We replaced it with a dead bolt. The courtyard's enclosed by a wrought-iron fence and has a gate. There's a long walkway that leads to the side street so we've stationed a man in the courtyard as well as the front street entrance."

"Can they make themselves unobtrusive? I don't want to scare my neighbors."

"Peterson was on duty this morning when we came back from the cemetery. He was standing across the street in the shop alcove. Did you notice him?"

"No."

"Then I guess he's unobtrusive." He

opened the next door. "And this is your dark-room. Turn on the light."

She turned on the switch beside the door and the room was illuminated by a dim red glow.

His gaze went to the window. "You had installed shutters, that's good."

"I didn't do it for protection. I did it to block out the light. That's why they're specially sealed." She frowned. "You've nailed boards across them. Was that necessary?"

"Yes." He grimaced. "Lord, it stinks in here. Chemicals?"

"I like the smell."

"Weird."

"Maybe. But it's a good thing I do like it, since I spend a good portion of my time in this room."

"Then you must not suffer from claustrophobia."

She shook her head. "I like it. I always feel safer here."

He looked at her inquiringly.

"I don't know why." She shrugged. "Or maybe I do. I guess it's because when I develop a print in that pan over there, it's going to show the world as it really is. Not what I want it to be, not what someone else tries to tell me it is. The truth. It cuts through the bullshit."

"You have an interesting idea of a security blanket." He flipped off the light, went back into the hall, and opened the next door. "As I said, the guest room is secure. I'll occupy this room. It's close enough to your bedroom for me to hear anything. Leave your door cracked open at night." He glanced at her. "Any objection?"

"No, why should there be? You're keeping me safe. That's why I wanted you."

"Not really. I'm a means to an end. You want Esteban dead and you want me to help you get him. All the rest is secondary." He paused. "You want to be bait? Okay, but it will be my way. You want Esteban? I'll deliver him but I'm not going to get either one of us killed in the process."

"I don't want you to deliver him. I just want you to help me get to him."

"Do you know how many bodyguards he keeps around him? You couldn't get near him."

"It won't always be that way. No one's protected all the time. I could do it, if you help me."

"And then Habin might panic and go

ahead with the strike on his own. Is that what you want?"

"No, find a way to get around it."

"Do you think I can work miracles?"

She had thought it was a miracle when he had found the aircraft carrier for Josie. "You're smart and you get things done. That's miracle enough. I'm not stupid enough to think I can do this alone. I need you."

He was silent a moment. "So you're really going to use me?"

She flinched. "Yes."

"You're already having trouble with the thought."

"I'll get over it." Her hand went to the Band-Aid on her left arm. "You're not the only one being used. I'm not asking for your blood."

"You might be." He studied her. "But not at the moment. So, like a true loyal serf, I'll make myself handy in other ways. What do you want for lunch?"

Relief surged through her. She hadn't been sure until that moment that he'd go along with her. "I'm not hungry."

"You'll have to eat anyway. You're like Josie. It's necessary to build the blood supply."

"Then give me anything."

He nodded and started for the kitchen.

"Kaldak." She hesitated when he glanced over his shoulder. "I couldn't see any other way. Everyone knows what Esteban is but no one's stopping him. I don't want anything to happen to you, but you're the only one I can trust."

"You trust me?" he asked slowly.

"Yes."

"Don't, Bess." He disappeared into the kitchen.

Third battle. She supposed she should consider it a victory, but she did not. Kaldak had temporarily conceded, not surrendered. She had sensed the anger and frustration in him seething just below the surface, and it had upset her. It must have been that same anger that had caused him to say she couldn't trust him. She could trust him. She *did* trust him. She didn't always know what he was thinking, he was sometimes rough and brutally frank, but almost from the start he had been beside her, helping her.

I'll take care of you.

She didn't need anyone to take care of her but it had been good not to be alone.

And right now she felt very much alone.

. . .

"Steak?" She looked at her plate dubiously. "I can't eat all that. Not for lunch."

"Sure you can." He sat down opposite her. "It's good for you."

She shrugged and picked up her fork. "I'll try."

"I'm glad to see you're cooperating."

"We made a deal. I keep my promises."

"As I recall, it was more like blackmail. But that's okay. Semantics don't matter. Not if you eat your steak." He took a bite of his own. "And I was a bit deceptive too. I've no intention of devoting my entire attention to serving you. I may have a few other things to do."

"What things?"

He didn't answer. "Don't worry, I won't leave you unprotected."

"What things?"

"I've been working for over two years to keep Esteban and Habin from turning that anthrax loose. I wasn't able to stop what happened at Tenajo. It's not going to happen here." He met her gaze. "I can understand why you want Esteban dead. Do you think I don't? I have my own reasons for wanting the bastard dead. There were times when I was working with him down in Mexico that I was barely able to hold myself back. Do you know how many opportunities I had? It would have taken just one twist of his neck. But I kept myself from killing him and I'll keep you from killing him until it's safe to do it."

She shook her head.

He shrugged. "I knew it wouldn't do any good to talk to you. The pain's too fresh. I wouldn't have listened either."

"You said you'd help me."

"I'll help you. I'm just trying to be honest with you. If killing him interferes, I'll see that you delay it." He glanced at her plate. "You've barely made a dent in that. Eat a little more."

"I don't think I can right now. Maybe we can stop at a restaurant while we're out."

He stared at her in shock. "Out?"

"We're going for a walk in the French Quarter. We'll go out every day but always at a different time and to a different destination. I hear it's always a mistake to show habit."

"We're not going anywhere outside this apartment."

"Yes, we are. I want Esteban to know I'm here and that I'm going to stay here."

"Bravado could get you killed."

"It's not bravado. I'm not safe here in the apartment either, am I?"

"You're a hell of a lot safer than on the street."

"Answer me."

He finally nodded. "There's always a way if you put your mind to it. An electrical charge, a poisonous snake in the shower drain." He shrugged. "If they want to get extreme, a small missile through that window over there."

"So much for security."

"Why do you think we want you out of here?"

"It's a question of relative safety, then. If we stay holed up, they'd only start figuring out how to get at me in here. If they think I'm going to be someplace where I'll be an easier target, they might wait."

"Maybe. Are you going to risk your life on it?"

"Yes. It's better than hiding and waiting for them to come and get me. I'd rather go after them."

"You don't have the advantage. They know what you look like."

"But I have you to protect me. That's how it's going to be, Kaldak."

"Great, just great," he said. "Anything else?"

"Yes, I want any calls from Ed Katz at the CDC to come over my regular line."

"That line is sure to be tapped."

"I want Esteban to know what we're doing. I want him to worry about it. I want to make him nervous."

"He's not the only one you're making nervous."

"You'll survive." Curious, she asked, "Have you ever put a snake in a drain?"

"Hell, no. I'm scared of them. But not everybody is as squeamish."

"Comforting."

"You asked me. If you want comfort, you'll let me take you to that safe house in North Carolina."

She shook her head.

"I didn't think so. So we show ourselves and let them see that it's not worth their while to target the apartment. Is there any place you particularly want to go?"

She said immediately, "Zontag's."

He gazed at her inquiringly.

"It's the best camera equipment store in town. I have to buy a new camera."

. . .

The camera in the window at Zontag's captured and held her attention.

"I wish you'd looked that way at the steak I made for lunch," Kaldak said. "Ravenous. Definitely ravenous."

She was. She could hardly wait to get her hands on it. "It's a good camera. All the bells and whistles."

"Is that the kind you had before?" Kaldak asked.

She shook her head. "That was a Hasselblad. Oh, I have other cameras too, but that was my favorite."

"Don't you want to replace it with the same model?"

"No, I can't replace it. I lived with that camera for eight years. It was like an old friend. You can't replace old friends just because they're not there anymore." Just as you couldn't replace a sister. The thought brought a rush of pain, but she quickly blocked it as she started for the shop entrance. "So you make a new friend with great qualities and hope for the best. I'll be right back."

He followed her. "Where you go, I go."

All the way from her apartment he had stayed glued to her. "I doubt if anyone's waiting inside to pounce on me."

"I would be. You're a photographer with no camera. This is the best camera shop in town. It's an ideal match." He opened the door for her and glanced inside. "No customers. If anyone comes in and gets close to you, step away. Don't let anyone touch you. It would take only a pinprick."

"Mardi Gras starts next week. It's going to be hard to avoid being touched in the French Quarter. You'd have to run interference for me like a Saints linebacker."

"Then that's what I'll do. But help me out, okay?"

"You can be sure of it," she said absently, looking back at the camera in the window. The familiar eagerness was surging through her, and she felt a moment of guilt. An obsession, Emily had called it, and she had buried Emily only that morning. Should she be feeling this—

"Would you rather go back to the apartment and curl up in a corner?" Kaldak asked roughly, his gaze on her face. "Is that what Emily would want for you?"

Emily would have wanted Bess to live

and enjoy life. Emily hadn't understood Bess's passion, but she would never have wanted Bess to do without anything that would make her happy. In fact, she would have fought anyone who tried to interfere with Bess. Not that she hadn't done plenty of interfering herself. She could almost hear her. . . .

She moved purposefully toward the counter. "No, that's not what Emily would want and that's not what I want either."

"You're stroking that camera as if it were a dog," Kaldak said as he held the shop door open for her.

"I'm just getting the feel of it. And it's feeling like a German shepherd. Definitely not a golden retriever. We had one when I was a kid, and Simon was lovable, but really dumb." She touched the camera hanging around her neck. "This camera is smart, very smart."

"A new friend?"

She shook her head. "Not yet. It's still just an acquaintance. But I think it will grow on me." It was already growing on her. She was feeling that solid sense of *rightness,* of completion. She raised the camera, focused on the balcony across the street, and took a quick shot. "It's a good camera."

"Then I'm glad you managed to find it." He took her elbow. "It's time we got back to the apartment. We've been on display long enough."

The tall clown with green hair juggling on the corner.

Focus.

Shoot.

The old bag lady with rouged cheeks and thick stockings sitting on the stool beside the alley.

Focus.

Shoot.

The musician dressed in overalls and checked shirt playing his fiddle in the middle of Royal Street.

Focus.

Shoot.

"If you keep stopping, we're not going to make it back to the apartment before morning," Kaldak said dryly.

"Well, I have to break it in." She took another shot of the clown. "And there's no place on earth more photogenic than New Orleans. That's one of the reasons I moved here. It has everything I want. You can go one block in any direction and find a picture that tells a story."

"Just so you're not the story." He kept an eye on the crowd around them. "And I've a hunch you're not taking pictures for the love of it."

"He could be here, couldn't he?"

"He probably is nearby."

"Then I may have a picture of him."

"Is that why you picked up the camera today?"

"No." She shot him a glance. "But I thought you'd approve of the reconnaissance."

"Sorry." Kaldak's gaze was on a trio of teenagers ahead. "I guess I'm a little edgy."

It would take a lot to make Kaldak edgy, she thought with a chill. "I don't think your hit man is one of those kids."

"Could be. Could be anyone. I'd bet he's here, watching. You never can tell."

"No, you can't tell." She had taken photographs of murderers before. In Somalia, in Croatia, that butcher of young boys in Chicago. But she had never taken a picture of anyone who wanted to murder her.

Show them.

Her hands were trembling a little as she lifted her camera.

Focus.

Shoot.

She had taken his picture.

De Salmo gazed after the Grady woman and Kaldak until they disappeared around the corner.

She had taken him by surprise. He hadn't expected her to be strolling around, shooting pictures. Security surrounding her was so tight, he'd thought they'd be keeping her under wraps. He had already started planning how to get inside the apartment.

That cocky bastard Kaldak evidently thought his presence was enough of a deterrent. Stupid. It wasn't going to be as difficult a hit as Esteban thought. Easy money.

But it bothered him that she had taken his picture.

TWELVE

A man was sitting on the stairs outside her apartment.

Kaldak saw her stiffen and said quickly, "It's okay. It's Yael. I told Ramsey to send him over as soon as he got to the States."

"Just out for a nice stroll?" Yael Nablett rose to his feet and held out a hand. He had just the hint of an accent. "It's no wonder Ramsey is having a cow."

Kaldak smiled as he shook Yael's hand. "Now, that's a sight I'd pay to see. I'm glad you're here. Bess Grady. Yael Nablett."

She murmured something polite. This was the man who had searched for Emily, the man who had found her grave in the hills.

Yael Nablett was nearing forty, with green eyes, short brown hair, and a lean, strong body.

"I wasn't sure you'd leave Mexico," Kaldak said. He unlocked the front door and let everyone inside.

"Not much left for me to do there. Esteban's dropped from view. He left a note officially requesting a medical leave of absence. We think he's left the country."

"Shit. When?"

"Yesterday." His gaze shifted to Bess and he said quietly, "I'm very sorry about your sister. I tried to get Kaldak to give you some warning, but Esteban was too fast. He had everything planned and set up before he sent the crew to exhume your sister."

"A warning wouldn't have helped." Nothing would have helped but it was kind of him to have tried. She got the impression he was usually kind. "Thank you, Mr. Nablett."

"Yael." He turned to Kaldak. "Do you think he's headed here?"

"Not yet. I almost wish he were. I'd bet he has other fish to fry."

Yael grimaced. "Let's hope not. How close is he?"

"Too close. The anthrax is almost at the

point where they want it. He could strike any-time. That may be why he's left Mexico. He wouldn't have done it without reason."

"He just disappeared?" Bess asked. "How could that happen? Weren't people watching him?"

"He's probably been planning it for a long time," Yael answered. "He went into a build-ing on the Paseo de la Reforma and never came out."

"That should never have happened," Kaldak said.

"I agree," Yael said. "But it did."

"And what did Ramsey say?"

"What didn't he say? He's foaming at the mouth. He sent a man to pick up Perez, Es-teban's secretary, and put pressure on him. But I doubt if he knows anything. Ramsey's not sure which way to turn." He smiled at Bess. "You've unsettled everyone by staying here, you know."

Bess didn't return the smile. "Too bad. It may be the only way to get Esteban. You couldn't even keep track of him when you had him in full view."

He flinched. "True." He turned to Kaldak. "Rescue me. Give her one of those intimi-dating glares."

"You're on your own. They don't faze her."

"No?" He looked back at Bess. "Interesting." He smiled again. "Then could I throw myself on your mercy and beg a cup of coffee? I came here straight from the airport."

She nodded. "I'll make some. If you promise me it's not an excuse to get me out of the room so you can talk to Kaldak."

"Well, actually it was."

He looked like a kid with his hand caught in the cookie jar, and this time she found herself smiling. "Then you can make your own coffee. No secrets."

"Okay, I was only trying to keep you from worrying." He glanced at Kaldak. "Ramsey thinks he knows who Esteban sent as hit man. The local police said one of their informants told them Marco De Salmo is in town."

"So it is De Salmo," Kaldak said. "I've heard of him."

"But you've never seen him?"

"Once. In Rome, from a distance."

"He's good?"

"Very good."

"You couldn't recognize him?" Bess asked.

"I don't think so," Kaldak replied, then

turned to Yael. "Can Ramsey get me a photograph?"

Yael shook his head. "De Salmo has no police record."

"How could that be?" Bess asked.

Yael shrugged. "He appeared out of nowhere three years ago. The name's probably false, but we can't verify. We have practically zero on this guy."

So the killer had a name, Bess thought. He might be faceless but he had a name. Marco De Salmo.

Yael turned to Kaldak. "You asked me to gather additional information on Esteban before I left Mexico, but I came up with nothing more than you know already."

"Damn," Kaldak said. "I was hoping for a break."

"And what do you know already, Kaldak?" Bess asked.

"He grew up in the slums of Mexico City as one of twelve children. His father was a laborer. We located a social worker, Señora Damirez, who covered the zone and was familiar with the family. She said there was never enough to eat and they were packed like sardines into a two-room hut. The area was overrun by rats, and when Esteban was eight, he was taken to the clinic twice in one month with severe bites."

"Only him? What about the other children?"

"No, evidently the rats liked little Esteban."

"Pleasant."

"But things got better for him. His brother, Domingo, died the next month and Esteban didn't have to sleep on the floor anymore. He took over his brother's cot. Then his oldest sister died and there was suddenly more food to go around."

"How did they die?"

"Food poisoning."

"Esteban?"

"Maybe. But the social worker said food poisoning was pretty common in the slums. When there's so little food, the kids eat anything in sight." He paused. "But even if he didn't do it, he might have recognized the advantages of being an only child."

"There were other deaths?"

"In the next five years three sisters and four brothers died."

"How?"

"More food poisoning, two drownings, two knifed in alleys."

"The social worker didn't suspect anything?"

"Not until we started investigating. In fact, she was a little indignant that we were asking questions about Esteban. Señora Damirez admires him. She described him as a polite, hardworking little boy. He hardly missed a day of school, which was extremely rare. He fought his way out of the gutter and joined the army when he was sixteen. A local success story. God knows, she couldn't have many."

"Are his parents still alive?"

"His father died in an earthquake when he was twelve. His mother was injured in the same quake but lived another three years."

"He has two surviving siblings?"

"One. Another brother died eight years ago. His sister Maria has been married to General Pedro Carmindar for five years. She's twenty-one and he's sixty-nine. Esteban introduced them while he was working under Carmindar."

"Did you try to contact her?"

"She wouldn't talk to anyone about Esteban. She's a scared little rabbit."

"Which probably keeps her alive."

"Do you want to try to use her?" Yael asked.

"Against Esteban?" Kaldak shook his head. "No ammunition there. Besides, she's survived this long. It would be a pity to rock her boat now."

"My God, do I actually hear a note of compassion? You must be getting soft, Kaldak." He turned to Bess. "No wonder he doesn't intimidate you. He's becoming a wuss."

"I wouldn't say that," she said dryly. "Now, if you're finished, I'll go make your coffee."

He held up his hand, palm forward. "I swear."

She went into the kitchen and opened the cabinet door.

Flesh-devouring rats . . . The image was terrifying, but the thought of a little boy committing fratricide was even more frightening. Cause and effect.

So that was how monsters were created.

"She seems to be taking it well." Yael's gaze was on the kitchen door through which Bess had disappeared. "Tough lady?"

"Sometimes," Kaldak said. "She's definitely a survivor."

"Not if she stays here."

"She won't leave."

"And you won't let Ramsey have his way."

"By God, I won't treat her like an animal," he said harshly. "She deserves better."

Yael's lips pursed in a soundless whistle. "You appear to have a problem. You're going to have a hell of a time keeping Ramsey from taking her."

"Do you think I don't know that? Ramsey's almost as big a threat as De Salmo. That's why I wanted you here." He paused. "I may have to leave her for periods of time. I need her protected."

"She's valuable. Ramsey will see to it."

"I don't trust Ramsey to do it right. All he's concerned about is making sure she's available to the CDC. I trust you."

Yael shook his head. "That's not why I was sent here. I have a job to do."

"Your job is Esteban. Esteban may come here."

"And he may not."

"She's the key. Even if we get Esteban and Habin, who's to say that someone else won't get hold of that mutated anthrax? She has to stay alive until we find a cure. You know damn well that your government is scared to death of that anthrax."

Yael nodded slowly. "Good argument."

"Good enough?"

"I'll stay around . . . for a while."

Kaldak felt a rush of relief.

"You like her." Yael was studying his expression. "It's not just that she's our ticket out of this mess."

"She didn't deserve this."

"Innocent bystanders get in the way, and things happen."

"She's had enough. I want her safe."

"Coffee." Bess entered carrying a tray. She frowned as she noticed the sudden silence. "You've been talking."

"Nothing you would have found interesting," Yael said. "I've just convinced Kaldak that since he's become a wuss, he's inadequate to the task of guarding you. Would you mind if I help him on occasion?"

"Not at all." She put the tray down on the table and poured coffee. "But it seems a pretty thankless job. He tells me I'm not safe even here." She shot Kaldak a look. "And he refuses to protect me from snakes in my shower drain. So what good is he?"

"Ah, yes, the old black-mamba-in-the-drain trick," Yael said solemnly as he reached for his cup. "I'm very good at taking care of that. Amazing what you can learn from watching James Bond movies."

"There are only two cups." Kaldak pointed.

"I don't want any coffee." She started across the room. "I'm going to my darkroom and develop the roll of film I took this afternoon." She raised her eyebrows. "Unless you want to check for a mamba in the drain."

"You do it yourself," Kaldak said evenly. "And if you find one, call for Yael."

The red glow of the darkroom light made the faces in the prints seem strange and sinister.

There were pictures of clowns and musicians and tourists. She had taken similar photographs in the French Quarter hundreds of times before and they hadn't made her uneasy.

But then one of these faces might belong to her murderer.

One of these faces might have watched her bury her sister that day.

Her eyes were suddenly burning with tears.

Shit. She had been fine, almost normal, and then the memory of Emily had come out of nowhere and ambushed her. Would it always be this way?

"What was the hurry?" Kaldak asked when she came out of the darkroom twenty minutes later. "What did you think was on that film?"

"Probably nothing. I don't like undeveloped film. I'm always afraid something is going to happen to it."

"Like Danzar?"

She nodded and glanced around the apartment. "Where's Yael?"

"He went to see if he could locate an apartment nearby."

"It's not likely with Mardi Gras so close."

"But Yael is very persuasive."

"Like you."

He shook his head. "Yael and I are nothing alike. He has a much more accepting and gentle nature."

"Accepting?"

"His wife got on the wrong bus in Tel Aviv

twelve years ago. She was going to visit her mother. It blew up before she got there. Palestinian terrorists."

"Terrible."

"Another innocent bystander. But the world seems to target innocent bystanders these days. They're easier to kill." He shrugged. "Yael was able to let it go. He married again six years ago. He has a son now."

"I like him."

"So do I." He looked at her. "But it didn't keep me from putting him between you and Esteban."

His sudden intensity made her uneasy. "Because of the blood samples."

"Sure." He glanced away from her. "Because of the blood."

Her uneasiness was increasing. "I'm going to bed. It's been a long day. I'd like to call Dr. Kenwood first. Could I use your portable phone?"

He handed it to her. "Let me know if there's a problem with her, okay?"

She nodded and started for the bedroom. She hoped there was no problem with Josie. Everything else was going wrong. Please, God, just let this one thing go right.

She stopped at the door. "Do you need to take a sample tonight?"

"No. Maybe tomorrow."

"Well, if you change your mind, let me—"

"I told you, I don't *need* it, dammit."

She threw up her hands in self-defense. "Okay. Okay." She closed the door behind her, shutting him out. All she needed now was an edgy Kaldak barking at her. She dug in her purse, got Dr. Kenwood's number, and quickly dialed it.

Ten minutes later she returned the phone to Kaldak. "I couldn't reach Dr. Kenwood, but I spoke to the head nurse. Josie's doing fine."

"Good. Now, where are those pictures you developed?"

"Still in the darkroom. Why?"

"I thought I'd study them and see if I recognize anyone."

"Do you think you might?"

"We assassins belong to a small and select group. There's a chance."

"Don't be stupid. You're not . . . like them."

"You're mistaken. Ask Ramsey. He trained me for eight long months to make sure I was a very good assassin." He moved toward the darkroom. "Go to bed. I promise I won't disturb anything."

"Why did he train you?"

"Because I asked him to do it."

"Why?"

"Does it matter?"

"Yes, it matters." She wasn't sure why, but it mattered very much to her. "He mentioned—" She searched her memory. "Nakoa. What's Nakoa?"

He was silent for a moment and she didn't think he was going to answer. But then he spoke. "Nakoa was another Tenajo. It was a U.S. biological research facility on a tiny island in the South Pacific whose purpose was to develop vaccines against possible germ warfare attack weapons. A rare virus escaped from one of the level 4 laboratories." His face was without expression. "Everyone died. No survivors."

She stared at him, sick. "Everyone?"

He nodded. "The virus entered the central air-conditioning system of the complex that serviced both the laboratories and private quarters of the scientists who worked there. Forty-three men, women, and children."

"And Esteban had something to do with it?"

"Oh, yes. We didn't know who was responsible at the time but we found out later that Esteban had one of the scientists on the island in his pay. Jennings smuggled out various bacteria to Esteban, who then sold them to Saddam Hussein. But Ramsey started sniffing out what was going on, so Esteban needed to destroy evidence and stop the investigation in its tracks. Jennings planted the virus before he took off and went into hiding. It was too dangerous for Ramsey to send anyone to the island to continue the investigation. Nakoa will be a wasteland for the next fifty years."

Men, women, children—they all died because of Esteban. "Why didn't I ever hear about it?"

"We covered it up. It wasn't too difficult. It was a top secret installation and nobody wanted to admit it existed anyway."

"A cover-up?"

"You're horrified? I know how you hate them. But I'd do it again. We didn't know who was responsible and we had to find out. It took me three years to make the connection to Esteban. I tracked Jennings until I found him in Libya. Before he died he led me to Esteban and Habin."

"Were you one of those scientists who worked on Nakoa?"

"Yes."

"But you lived."

"I was in Washington, giving a report. It was all over by the time I got back. Ramsey met me in Tahiti to break the news."

His voice was level, without emotion. He might have been talking about the stock report, but the indifference was a lie. She knew him better than that now. "I'm sorry."

"You don't have to be sorry. It was a long time ago. I was a different man."

"Bullshit."

He smiled faintly. "You don't believe me?"

"I believe you protect yourself by denial just like the rest of us."

"Maybe you're right," he said wearily. "I know it's getting harder all the time to know what's right and what's wrong. It used to be much simpler. Getting Esteban was right. Everything else was wrong." He looked into her eyes. "And that's the way you feel now, isn't it?"

"Yes, that's the way I feel."

"Let me give you a hypothetical question. If, in order to kill Esteban, Josie has to die too, would you let it happen?"

"Don't be crazy. You know I wouldn't."

"Then you're not nearly as bad as I was. At one time I would have let anyone on earth die to make sure I got Esteban."

She shook her head. "No, you wouldn't."

"Your faith is touching but misplaced. First, I was the devil incarnate and now—"

"Good God, I'm not saying you're an angel. You're just not a monster. And neither am I. Esteban is the monster."

"I hope you're right."

"Count on it."

She strode to her bedroom and shut the door behind her. She needed to shower and go to bed and close out everything. She hadn't needed Kaldak's story to cap off this horror of a day. But she had asked for it. No, she had demanded it. She had needed to know. Why had it been so important to her?

Probably simple curiosity. Kaldak was an important and integral part of her life just then. He was helping to keep her alive. Surely it was natural for her to want to know what made him tick.

- - -

Kaldak spread the photographs out on the table.

It was like trying to identify somebody at a masquerade ball.

A clown in full makeup, the musician with the wig and fiddle, the old bag lady with the thick veil. Even one of the teenagers was wearing a Darth Vader mask.

It could be one of them or none of them. How the hell was he to know?

Study them. A body position, an expression might trigger a fleeting memory.

He sat down at the table and began to study the pictures.

CDC, Atlanta

"Go take a nap, Ed."

Ed Katz looked up to see Donovan standing beside him. "I will. I just want to run one more test. I don't know what the hell is wrong. The anthrax should be overwhelmed by those antibodies, but it's not."

"You said the first test was promising."

He nodded. "But the second showed mega resistance."

"Let me run the test for you. You haven't had any sleep for the last twenty-four hours.

What good's a team if you don't use the teammates?"

"Soon."

"Marta called and told me to make you eat and rest. Do you want to get me in her bad graces?" Donovan glanced down at Ed's microscope. "And I have to admit I want to get my hands on this baby. It's interesting that they used cash to deliver the bacteria."

Interesting. Donovan was always objective. Ed had been like that once. Science for science's sake. It was a comfortable way to work. That comfort had gone down the drain when he'd been sent out in the field during those first years of HIV research. He had learned to put faces and voices to the death statistics. HIV had seemed to be everywhere. Those babies infected by an untested blood supply had nearly destroyed him. He and Marta had been trying to have a child for the last nine years and he had felt the pain of the parents of those babies. "Yeah, very interesting. How would you like a few of those twenties stuffed in your pay envelope?"

"Hey, don't give me a hard time just because you're beat. I didn't mutate this anthrax."

"Sorry."

"You should be. Call me if you need me." Donovan walked away.

Ed shouldn't have barked like that. Donovan was a good guy. He couldn't help being what he was. Ed was just frustrated because of the lack of progress.

No, because he was scared. What if the antibodies didn't work and this mutated strain had no cure? What if this was the Big One? Ever since HIV had appeared, he'd had nightmares about the Big One, the virus or bacteria that couldn't be stopped. Someday it would rear its ugly head in some rain forest or genetics lab. It was only a matter of time. It was out there somewhere.

He just hoped to hell it wasn't on this slide in front of him.

THIRTEEN

"Esteban went to Cheyenne. Perez said he got a call from Morrisey before he took off," Ramsey told Kaldak on the phone the next morning. "I've sent two extra agents to Cheyenne to see if they can track him down."

Morrisey again. "I doubt if Esteban's still there. He would never have left a loose thread like Perez hanging if he'd thought Perez could hurt him. Have you found out anything new about Morrisey?"

"We traced one of the calls he made five days ago to a motel in Jackson Hole, Wyoming. We sent an agent to see what we could find out and we got lucky. Morrisey charged the room to a credit card. We may be able to monitor his future actions."

"You weren't able to trace that last call?"

"No, it was on the portable."

Brick wall. Esteban was moving and they couldn't even find Morrisey.

"What do you hear from the CDC?" Ramsey asked.

"Progress."

"That's not enough. The only thing that may save our ass is an antidote. She should be made available to them."

"She is available to them. I'm sending them a sample every day."

"Which will stop if you get her killed. She was out on the street yesterday, for God's sake."

"And she'll be out today."

"How long do you think I'll permit this, Kaldak? She's too valuable for you to—"

"Call me when you hear about Morrisey." Kaldak hung up the phone.

"Morrisey?" Bess was standing in the doorway.

"Esteban took off after receiving a call from him. The last report we have is that he went to Cheyenne."

"Then what are we doing here?"

"He won't be there any longer. Our best bet is finding Morrisey and squeezing the information out of him."

"If he knows anything. You said Esteban seldom confided anything to anyone."

"Morrisey knows the job he was given. That's a start."

"Did you recognize anyone in those photos?"

He shook his head.

"Then I'm going to go out and take more."

"It may not do any good."

"And it may." She grimaced. "At least, I'll feel like I'm doing something. I hate just marking time."

"You don't find being bait entertaining? Ramsey's very interested in the entire process. He wants to put you in a nice sterile cell and throw away the key."

"Screw Ramsey."

"My thought exactly." He stood up. "Twenty minutes. You show yourself, you take a few photos, and then we come back."

"And I make sure that no one brushes against me."

"I'm not as worried about close quarters now that I know it's De Salmo. He prefers a knife or a gun, and a gun isn't subtle enough in these circumstances. I'd bet on the knife."

"How reassuring." She moved toward the darkroom. "I'm glad *you're* not worried. I'll be right back. I need to get more film."

Oh, no, he wasn't worried. He was terrified and had been every second of that trip to the camera store the previous day. He didn't know how much longer he could go on with this.

The streetlight cast shadows on the brick wall, shadows that looked vaguely like hunched gargoyles.

Interesting, Bess thought. She must have stared out this window across the street a hundred times. Why had she never noticed that effect before? Maybe she hadn't wanted to see gargoyles that close by.

She held the camera up to her eye and focused.

"What are you doing?" Kaldak asked from behind her. "Do you see someone?"

"A gargoyle."

"What?"

"Only a shadow across the street. But it's too good to miss."

"I told you never to stand directly in front of a window."

"I forgot." She stepped to one side.

"I would have thought you'd taken enough photos for one day. You were in the darkroom all afternoon."

"I have to do something or I'll go crazy."

"I can sympathize. I'm close to that point myself. You really missed that camera."

"Yes." She turned to look at Kaldak sitting in the easy chair across the room. He was in shirtsleeves, his long legs stretched before him. He should have looked relaxed, but he didn't. The edge was still there. She had never seen him really relaxed. "But no more than I would my eyes."

"Or an old friend."

She nodded.

"Don't you ever look at anything without seeing it through the lens of a camera?"

"Sometimes. Not often, I guess. Even when I don't have my camera, it's not un-usual for me to see things as if I were taking the shot. Emily said—" She stopped. So many things in her life led back to Emily. "She used to laugh and say I was obsessed."

"Are you?"

"Maybe. Okay, I guess I am. There are

times when it's worse than others." The gargoyles seemed taller now, more Gothic. Had the light changed? She took another shot. "I know I felt naked when I didn't have it."

"No armor?"

She looked at him. "What?"

"Doesn't taking the photos distance you from the situation? Keep the pain away?"

"Distance me?"

His gaze was fixed intently on her face. "When do you do it most often, Bess? When do you distance yourself?"

"I don't know."

"The bad times? Danzar? Tenajo?"

"Maybe." She frowned. "Back off, Kaldak. I don't need you to psychoanalyze me."

"Sorry, it's just habit. You're right, it's none of my business. And I didn't mean to intimate there was anything wrong with putting up barriers. We all do. I just found it interesting that you use a camera."

"And what do you use?"

"Anything I can. I improvise."

"It's not just a barrier. I *like* what I do."

"I know. Forget what I said. Actually, I envy you."

But she wouldn't forget what he had said. He was sharp and perceptive and annoyingly right too often. She had the sudden desire to disconcert him. She lifted the camera. "Smile, Kaldak."

She smiled herself as she caught the look of surprise on his face. It was deliciously satisfying to catch Kaldak off guard.

"Again."

Focus.

Shoot.

"May I ask what you're doing?"

"Taking your picture. You're a very interesting subject."

It was true. Through the lens of the camera his face was a fascinating mixture of boldness and subtlety. She wished she had the proper lighting to shadow those cheekbones.

"Because I'm so pretty? Or do you feel the need to compare gargoyles?" He smiled sardonically and waved his hand. "Be my guest, if you want to risk that new camera. I've been known to break them."

He was relaxing just a little; the tenseness flowed out of his muscles as she watched. It was odd. She had never been able to look at Kaldak with any objectivity before. From their first meeting, every moment had been colored with a wild range of emotion—anger, fear, frustration . . .

The hand he'd waved was big, well formed, she thought absently. Like the rest of him. Muscular thighs, narrow waist, broad shoulders.

Power and grace and sexuality.

She almost dropped the camera.

Sexuality? Where had that come from?

"Something wrong?" Kaldak's gaze had narrowed on her face.

"Nothing." She hurriedly lowered the camera, turned away, and headed for the darkroom.

She was feeling safe. So safe that she was even going out on the street, Esteban thought.

And De Salmo was doing nothing about it. He was only giving excuses.

She was trying to show him that her sister's death meant nothing to her. He knew it had affected her. She had collapsed at the funeral home. Yet there she was, going out, taking pictures, when she should be hiding, terrified. She was taunting him. The thought enraged him.

It wasn't to be tolerated.

The phone was ringing when Bess and Kaldak walked into the apartment the next day.

"Did you enjoy the funeral, Bess?"

Shock rippled through her. "Esteban."

Kaldak moved swiftly toward the kitchen.

"I'm sorry I missed it, but I was represented by one of my employees. He said you held up very well at the crypt."

"You son of a bitch." Her voice was shaking. "You killed her."

"I told you I did. You should have believed me. But then I'd have been cheated of the pleasure of presenting you with such an exquisite gift. Unfortunately she was a little worse for wear, wasn't she? What did you think when you saw—"

"Shut up."

"You're upset. But then, what can you expect from Mother Nature? It was hot. We know about that heat, don't we? You must have gotten very hot running through those hills."

"But we got away from you. You lost, you bastard."

"Not because of you. You're only a woman. I would have gotten you if it hadn't been for that helicopter. Are you listening in, Kaldak?"

"Yes," Kaldak said.

"I thought you would be. You're taking very good care of her. But it's not going to do you any good. I'll still get her. The bitch isn't going to stop me, but she has annoyed me. However, to show my forgiving nature I've sent her another present."

Bess's hand tightened on the receiver. "Why don't you come and give it to me yourself?"

"I'm otherwise occupied, and you're not that important."

"The hell I'm not. You wouldn't be calling if you weren't scared shitless."

"There's a trash can one block away. Your present is on top."

He hung up.

Kaldak was already out of the kitchen and heading for the front door. "Stay here. I'll get it."

"I'm going with you."

"He may be setting you up."

"Then you keep me safe, dammit. I'm going with you."

"You put one foot out that door and I swear I'll knock you down. I'll send an agent to get the damn thing."

He ran down the stairs, and the street door slammed behind him. He was back in seconds. "He'll be here in a couple of minutes. He's going to set the box inside and then go back to his post. Now, you stay put."

It was a long two minutes before the agent set the cardboard box inside the door.

She stared down at it.

"Don't touch it. Back away. I'll call the bomb squad," Kaldak said.

"It's not a bomb. He'd know that would be your first thought." She moistened her lips. "I made him angry. This isn't meant to kill me." She reached down for the box. "He wants to hurt me."

He knocked her hand aside. "I'll do it." He carefully lifted the lid.

Inside was a white cotton shirt, a child's shirt with a school insignia on the pocket. Julie's school. Bess had seen her wear that shirt many times. There was a dark red stain beneath the pocket.

Blood. Fear rocked through her. "Julie."

"Steady." Kaldak's hand was on her arm. "This is what he wants."

"That's Julie's shirt."

"But Julie wouldn't have taken a uniform shirt on a camping trip, would she?"

The relief that flooded her was so intense, her knees felt weak. "No. She never wore it except to school."

"Then he had someone go in and get it from Emily's house. He doesn't have her, Bess. He didn't hurt her."

Yet. Esteban's threat lay between them like a burning brand. First Emily, and now her daughter.

"She's out of his reach. And we have a man waiting at the ranger station. Esteban won't be able to get at her."

But how long would she remain out of his reach?

Kaldak was urging her gently away from the box. "I'll send the shirt out and get the stain analyzed. It's probably animal blood."

"No, it's human blood. He wouldn't make it that easy for me."

"It's not Julie, Bess. He just wanted to show you that you aren't out of his reach here. You could let me take you to that safe house and we'd—"

"I know what he wanted to do," she said. And he had succeeded. This latest obscenity had frightened and hurt her. "His damn ego is hurt because he can't manage to kill a 'mere' woman." Anger ripped at her. "Well, screw him."

"You won't go?"

"And let him win? Let him know that he scared me enough to make me run away? I'm glad I'm making him angry. Maybe if he gets annoyed enough, he'll come himself. You find out why that agent who's supposed to be guarding Emily's house let that shirt be taken. And make sure there's more than one of Ramsey's men at that ranger station."

"You didn't have to tell me that."

"Yes, I did. Nothing's going to happen to Julie and Tom." Oh, God, the blood on that shirt . . . "Do you hear me?"

"I hear you," he said quietly. "I'll call Ramsey and chew him out for letting this happen."

She nodded jerkily. "Be sure to tell him—"

"I know what to tell him."

Of course he did. "I'm sorry, it's just—"

"It's just that you're so damn stubborn, you won't let me take you away from this town even though you're scared to death," he said roughly.

She was scared. Until a few minutes before, anger and numbness had shielded her like armor. But Esteban had pierced that armor and let the fear come in.

"It's not Julie's blood," Yael said when he called the next morning. "We got her blood type from her doctor and it doesn't match."

She felt a burst of relief. "Thanks, Yael."

"It must have been an ugly surprise. Are you okay?"

"Just mad." And frightened. She was still frightened. "As you say, it was ugly." She hung up the phone and turned to Kaldak. "No match." She put on her jacket and reached for her camera. "Let's go."

"You're going back out there?"

"Nothing's changed."

He looked at her.

"He's not going to know that he upset me." She headed for the door. "I'm not going to give him that victory."

.   .   .

More pictures.

She hadn't singled him out, but she must have five or six photographs of him now.

It shouldn't matter. Who was going to recognize him?

It did matter. He had made sure no pictures had been taken of him since he had become Marco De Salmo. Photographs were dangerous. People remembered a face when they couldn't remember anything else, and all kinds of technical things could be done to photographs these days.

Would she ever stop taking those fucking pictures! He'd thought he'd be able to take her out sooner, but Kaldak was always there, watching. He hadn't been able to get near her, and Esteban was getting impatient. He should probably go back to his first plan and hit the apartment.

Regardless of where the hit was made, he couldn't leave those photographs behind. He'd have to go in and get them.

"Are you satisfied?" Kaldak said between his teeth as they walked down the street toward her apartment. "We've been out more than two hours. Did you want to make sure that they got a nice try at you?"

She didn't answer. She had known Kaldak was tense all the time they had been on the street.

He opened the street door. "Well?"

He wasn't going to let it go. She started up the stairs. "Nothing happened. He has to know he can't—"

Rats.

Dozens of rats. Huge rats.

On the stairs in front of her. And behind her too. Scurrying wildly up and down the steps.

She shuddered as one ran over her foot.

"Out." Kaldak grabbed her arm and pulled her down the steps and out onto the street.

The rats streamed out the door onto the sidewalk. Another rat brushed against her foot.

Agent Peterson ran across the street. "What happened?"

"How the hell did they get in there?" Kaldak asked.

"No one was in the building. I've been watching—"

"Get them off the stairs."

Peterson disappeared into the building.

"I hate rats. Filthy. . . ." She couldn't stop shaking. "Esteban?"

He nodded. "Considering his background, I'd bet on it. He wanted to give you his own worst nightmare."

She closed her eyes.

"Are you all right?"

"It was just the shock." She opened her eyes and moved toward the staircase. "I need to get upstairs. He'll call me. He's going to want to know what this did to me."

She passed the agent, who was struggling to shoo the rats down the stairs, and unlocked the apartment door.

Kaldak was right behind her and nudged her aside. "Let me check out the apartment first. That agent must have fouled up."

The phone rang as Kaldak was coming out of the darkroom. "Let me get it."

"No, he wants to talk to me. And I want to talk to him."

"Ah, you've come home at last. This is the third time I've called," Esteban said when she picked up. "Did you like my little surprise?"

"It was a pretty weak attempt. I knew you didn't have Julie," she said. Be calm. Don't show him the fear and revulsion. "As for those rats . . . they didn't bother me. I like them. I had a pet rat when I was a kid."

There was a silence. "You lie."

"He was a white rat and his name was Herman. He had a cage with a treadmill and a little—"

He hung up on her.

"Did you really have a rat when you were a kid?" Kaldak asked.

"Don't be crazy. I can't *stand* them." She let her breath out. "But I think he believed me."

"If he did, he'll hate you even more. You're now in league with his nemesis."

There was a knock on the door and Kaldak opened it. It was Peterson, and Kaldak said to Bess over his shoulder, "I'll be right back. I need to check something out."

She was glad he was gone. She hadn't wanted him to see how unsettled that latest attack had made her. She needed a moment to recover. Hell, she needed a year to recover.

First, the mental attack with Julie's shirt, and then the physical one with the rats.

"There's a hole drilled in the wall that borders the alley," Kaldak said as he came back into the apartment. "It could have been done anytime and Peterson wouldn't have seen him from across the street." His lips tightened. "From now on there will be a guard in the alley too."

"That's the way they came in?"

He nodded. "A length of tunnel tubing was inserted. We went out, the rats were let in to wait for us."

"De Salmo?"

"Or one of Esteban's other men. De Salmo's a specialist and this is small stuff."

It hadn't seemed small stuff to her. It was the stuff of which nightmares were made.

"If you don't like it, you know what you can do."

"Shut up, Kaldak. I'm not going any-where."

"Except out in the Quarter tomorrow."

"Yes."

"Bright," he muttered. "Very bright."

The next afternoon she tossed the new batch of photographs on the coffee table in front of him. "Here they are. See what you can make of them."

He leafed through the prints. "You took enough."

"Four rolls. I wanted to make sure I got him if he was out there." She plopped down in a chair. "Well?"

"Nothing so far. I'll have to study them."

"We could go out again," she said, disappointed.

"No!" He quickly looked down at the photos again. "The streets are starting to get too busy. We may not be able to go out again."

"The hell we won't."

"The hell we will," he said curtly. "It's not safe, dammit. We'll stay here."

Don't get angry. Try to keep it light. "And what about the missile through the window and the mamba in the drain?"

"I'll take care of them."

"We agreed the risk wasn't that much greater." She leaned forward, frowning. "You're not making sense, Kaldak."

"I never agreed to anything, and I'm making perfect sense. You wanted me to keep you alive. I'm doing it."

"We've been out on the street every day and nothing's happened so far."

"We're not going out again."

"Why are you objecting now? What's different?"

"I thought he'd make a move and I could take care of him. But he's playing cat and mouse."

"Then we'll play too. And in the meantime, I'll keep on taking photos and you can—"

"No, it's too risky."

"You didn't think it was too risky before."

"Goddammit, I do now." He swept the photographs to the floor. "Just do what I tell you."

He had erupted like a volcano, taking her completely by surprise, shocking her. She had seen him violent before, but the violence had been cold and controlled. There was nothing cold about this outburst. The man standing in front of her was nothing like the Kaldak she had come to know. "What's wrong, Kaldak?"

"What's not wrong? Esteban's trying to feed you to the rats, the strike can come at any time, Ramsey hasn't been able to find Morrisey or Esteban, and De Salmo is out there just waiting for me to make a wrong move so he can take you out."

"Maybe he's not even here. Maybe the informant was wrong."

"He's here." He nodded jerkily at the photos on the floor. "I just can't recognize the bastard."

"You only saw him from a distance once."

"There should be something . . . some way."

She knelt down to gather the photos, and he was immediately beside her. "I did it. I'll pick them up."

"Is that another one of your mother's rules?"

"It's my rule. You break something, you fix it." He set the photos on the coffee table. "At least, you try. Sometimes you can't put Humpty Dumpty together again."

"Well, this particular Humpty Dumpty wasn't irreparably damaged."

He wouldn't look at her. "I'm sorry."

Before she could respond, he vanished into the kitchen.

FOURTEEN

Bess had never seen Kaldak like this. He was practically pacing. She could almost feel his intensity charging the room.

All evening she'd tried to keep her eyes on the pages of her book, but she was scarcely aware of what she was reading.

She finally gave up and tossed down the novel. "Anne Rice isn't holding me tonight. I think I'll go to bed."

He glanced at the book. "She writes about vampires, doesn't she?"

"Yes, and about New Orleans. I'm a big fan."

He smiled crookedly. "I can see why you'd want to avoid vampires at the moment.

It's got to be overkill when you're living with one."

"You may take my blood but you're too scientific to be a vampire," she said lightly.

"Am I?"

She looked hurriedly away from him. "You'd know if you ever read Rice. Lestat is definitely not scientific. He's a very complex vampire with—"

The phone rang and she automatically tensed. She picked up the receiver. "Hello."

"Kaldak. I need to talk to Kaldak."

Not Esteban. She tried to mask her relief with a shrug as she handed Kaldak the phone. "I vaguely recall a time when I actually got normal telephone calls. I think it's Ed Katz. Talk about vampires . . ."

She stood up and wandered over to the window. The shadow gargoyle seemed smaller tonight. She wondered what it looked like just before the streetlights went off in the morning. Maybe she should set her alarm and see.

"I have to take a sample."

She turned to see Kaldak hanging up the phone. "Why? You sent one off this morning."

"The closer to a breakthrough he gets, the greedier he gets."

"And how close is he getting?"

"It's hard to tell. In developing any anti-dote, it's usually one step forward, two steps back."

"He sounded excited."

"Well, he thinks maybe he took a step and a half forward on the last test." He paused. "You don't have to do it. I can wait until morning."

She shrugged. "Give it to him." She sat down at the dining room table and rolled up her left sleeve. "It doesn't matter."

"It matters." He took the kit out of the desk drawer. "Do you think I'd put you through this if it didn't matter to a lot of people."

"I didn't mean—" She gave it up. "Just take the sample and let me go to bed, Kaldak."

"That's what I'm doing."

She always hated to watch the blood enter the tube, so she fastened her gaze on his dark head. The muscles at the sides of his neck were rigid as he carefully inserted the needle.

"Did I hurt you?" he asked in a low voice.

"You never hurt me."

"Yes, I do." His gaze never left the needle. "But maybe not this time." He took out the needle and put it on the table. "I'm sorry. It's over now."

"Why are you apologizing? It's no big deal. I gave more at the last Red Cross blood drive."

"But I wasn't the one who took it." He held her arm while he applied pressure, then dabbed at the tiny drop of blood at the puncture site. "I don't like to—" He stopped, staring down at her arm.

"Something wrong?"

"Yes," he said thickly. "Something's wrong." He slowly lifted her arm and pressed his lips to the wound.

She couldn't breathe. She couldn't move. She wasn't supposed to feel this lust. But it was there.

Crazy. Not now. Not with Kaldak. Never with Kaldak.

He lifted his head and looked at her. "That's what's wrong."

"No," she whispered.

"Yes." His lips slid down her forearm to the veins of her wrist. A wave of heat moved through her. "I want it. I've wanted it for a long time. Sometimes just the smell of you makes me hard." He pressed his lips to her palm. "I know I'm no sex object, but you won't be disappointed. Ugly men have to know more. I can make you—"

"Stop it," she whispered. "I can't—Emily."

"Would Emily want you to stop living? Would you love her less because you went to bed with me?"

"Of course I wouldn't."

"And you want it."

God, yes, she wanted it. She wanted *him*. He was scarcely touching her and her body was responding. "It would . . . interfere."

"It's already interfering. It can't get much worse. I can't—" He stopped, his gaze on her face. "No?" He slowly released her arm. "You're sure?"

She wasn't sure about anything. She was confused and uncertain and . . . aroused. Oh, yes, definitely aroused.

He stood up and picked up the needle and kit. "Don't worry, I'm not going to push," he said jerkily. "I want to. You don't know how much. But I won't. I've already taken too much from you." He moved toward the kitchen. "I'll get this sample ready for Ed."

She closed her eyes and leaned back in her chair. She wanted him. She wanted him to touch her. She wanted him inside her. Christ, she hadn't felt like this since those first heady weeks with Matt. No, she couldn't compare Matt to Kaldak. She couldn't compare anyone to Kaldak.

"I told you not to worry about it."

She opened her eyes to see Kaldak standing by the front door with the familiar sample package in his hand. "If you don't want me, you don't want me, but don't feel guilty. This has nothing to do with what happened to Emily. Sex has a way of ambushing us while we're in the middle of a crisis. It probably has something to do with preservation of the species." He opened the front door. "I'm going to go downstairs and give this to Agent Peterson to ship tonight. You go on to bed."

Don't feel guilty.

Go on to bed.

He was always telling her what to do, dammit. He always thought he knew best. From the very beginning he had tried to guide her down the path he wanted her to go.

Except tonight. He'd backed away. He'd given her a choice.

. . .

The lights were out when Kaldak came back into the apartment twenty minutes later.

Bess had gone to bed.

Or maybe she was just hiding out in her room, trying to pretend what had happened between them didn't happen, trying to pretend that he didn't exist.

He was a fool. He knew all about discipline. He had learned it in the hardest school. Why hadn't he used it tonight? Why had he put her on the spot? It was the wrong time. Not that any time would be right. Not for him. Not for them. Too much had happened that—

"Are you going to stand there all night, Kaldak?" Bess called out. "For God's sake, come to bed."

He went rigid. He slowly turned toward her bedroom. "Bess?"

"Who do you think it is? There are only two of us in the apartment." She paused, and when she spoke again her voice was unsteady. "And one of us is scared to death about this."

He moved toward the door, his heart pounding like thunder.

"Two of us, Bess," he whispered. "Two of us."

New Orleans was suiting Marco extremely well. The crowded streets, always convenient to his profession, reminded him of Rome.

The man was right ahead of him. Gray suit, no tie, balding head.

Marco dodged a drunken couple coming out of a bar. His pace quickened. He couldn't lose this quarry. Esteban was up-set, but this should pacify the bastard.

The man in the gray suit was heading down Bourbon toward Canal Street. His car was probably parked in one of the lots on Canal.

Marco cut down to Royal, then ran at full speed before doubling back to Bourbon.

He was breathing heavily as he stepped into the alley.

He waited.

A woman in a short skirt and leopard-patterned high heels passed the alley.

He waited.

Gray suit, bald head.

There.

The pencil-slim blade of his knife cut through the gray suit straight to the heart even as he dragged the man into the alley.

"Kaldak."

He moved closer, his mouth closing over her nipple. "What?"

"I want my camera."

He raised his head. "I beg your pardon?"

"Will you get me my camera?"

"I will not. I'm otherwise occupied."

"I want to take your picture."

"Later." He suddenly chuckled. "Though I'm sure you discovered something stunning about me that you want to commemorate."

"Braggart." She *had* found out something stunning about him. Sex with Kaldak was glorious fun. After the first intense, passionate release he had become almost playful. It had been totally unexpected. "I want to take a picture of the vainest man I know."

"And the best lover."

"I don't remember." She gasped as he reached between them and massaged her. "Well, close."

"The best?"

"I don't know if I should pander to your van—"

She couldn't talk anymore. Her climax was mounting.

"Pander to me, Bess," he whispered. "I need it. I need you."

She nestled closer, staring dreamily into the darkness. She felt small and fragile curled up next to Kaldak's big, muscular frame. Strange that she didn't resent it. It felt . . . cozy, nice. "What time is it?"

Kaldak looked at the luminous dial of the clock on the nightstand. "Four thirty-five." He brushed a kiss on her temple. "Why? Do you have another appointment?"

"Don't be so flip. It's not as if I'm not a busy woman. You're just lucky you happened to catch me between jobs."

"Hallelujah. That's the only lucky thing that's happened to me lately."

A little of her contentment ebbed away as memory intruded. No, there hadn't been good luck in her life lately either.

"Shh, don't think about it." He drew her closer. "This moment is damn magnificent. To hell with—"

"What's your name, Kaldak?"

"What?"

"Well, Kaldak couldn't be your real name. Esteban would probably have recognized it from Nakoa. I think every woman who sleeps with a man should know his real name."

"How conservative of you."

"Is it Deuteronomy? Rumpelstiltskin?"

"It's David."

"David what?"

"Gardiner."

"David Gardiner." She shook her head. "It will take some getting used to."

"Don't get used to it. I told you, he doesn't exist anymore."

"Haven't you ever been tempted to resurrect him? I'd think that you'd—"

The phone on the bedside table rang.

She stiffened.

He reached over and picked up the receiver. "Hello." Then he sighed, sat up, and turned on the light. "For God's sake, Ed, this better be good news. Do you know what time it is?"

Ed Katz? The man had to be a fanatic. Bess sat up and leaned against the headboard.

"What do you mean? I sent it. It should

have reached you by one at the latest. . . . How do I know? . . . Okay, okay, I'll call Ramsey." Kaldak hung up. "Ed didn't get the sample. We may have to take another one. I'll check with Ramsey to see what the holdup is."

"Great." She made a face as she got out of bed and reached for her robe. "Just what I need to crown the evening. I'll go get a snack."

Kaldak came into the kitchen a couple of minutes later.

"Well, do I have to shed more blood, or did they find the—" She broke off when she registered the look on his face. "What's wrong?"

"Ramsey didn't know anything about the sample. Peterson never notified him. As far as he knew, Peterson was still on guard outside the apartment. They're looking for him now."

She swallowed. "Maybe it's just some small mistake."

"Maybe."

"But you don't think so." She hesitated. "I don't understand. It doesn't—"

She jumped when the digital phone in Kaldak's hand rang.

Kaldak punched a button and identified

himself. He hung up a few moments later. "They found Peterson in an alley five blocks from here. He's dead."

She stared at him in bewilderment. "Dead?"

"A stiletto in the back. No sample on him."

A stiletto. "De Salmo?"

Kaldak nodded.

"But it doesn't make sense. Why would he kill over the sample? He must know we'd just take another one."

"Maybe De Salmo thought a delay would please Esteban."

And she had been the one who had insisted that all CDC calls come in on her regular phone. Peterson might be alive still if De Salmo hadn't been able to monitor her phone.

"Stop it," Kaldak told her roughly. "Peterson was an agent. Risk goes with the job. And his death might not have had anything to do with the call. It could be that Esteban just wanted to give you another scare."

"Then why take the sample?" She crossed her arms over her chest to keep them from trembling. "It was my fault, dammit."

"Okay, it was your fault. But not because of anything you did. It's because of the immunity factor. Esteban and De Salmo are getting desperate because, for once, time may be on our side."

"Maybe. Katz isn't sure. You're not sure."

"Pull yourself together. You'll need it. Ramsey's on his way over."

"Why?"

"To hit you at your weakest point. He knows he can't budge *me,* so he'll try to persuade you to change your mind about staying here."

"I won't change my mind." She felt a sudden rush of anger. Not only were De Salmo and Esteban trying to kill her, but Ramsey was coming to bully her. "Ramsey can just do his job and catch the bastard."

He smiled. "You tell him that."

"I will." She sat down at the table and pushed up the sleeve of her robe. "Now, get that damn kit and take another sample."

"It was sheer stupidity," Esteban said coldly. "Did you think such a small delay was going to help me? It's the woman I need dead. You're a grave disappointment to me, Marco."

"It will be accomplished, but when I heard how close—"

"You heard what they wanted you to hear. Do you think Kaldak would permit such carelessness?"

"He's always with her. It's going to take more time than I—"

"I don't *have* time." Esteban tried to control his anger. "Do you hear me? I don't have time. That's what this is all about."

"A few more days."

In a few more days, that Katz at the CDC might come up with the antidote, Esteban thought with frustration. And then his entire plan would go down the tubes.

Think.

There had to be a way.

Yael arrived at the apartment before Ramsey got there.

"She's all right?" he asked Kaldak.

"I'm fine," Bess called from across the room. "Does everybody in the world think I'm going to fall apart because of this?"

"Well, Ramsey's hoping," Yael answered. "I got the impression he wouldn't mind losing Peterson if it would push you into his camp."

"That can't be true," she said, repulsed. "What kind of man is he? Is that the type the CIA produces?"

"Don't blame the organization for Ramsey," Kaldak said. "He's an ambitious man with his back against the wall. A strike by Esteban could ruin his political ambitions."

"And forget the people who could die." Bess stood up and moved toward the bedroom. If she was going to do battle with Ramsey, she didn't want the disadvantage of a bathrobe and mussed hair. "I'm going to shower and get dressed. Call me when Ramsey gets here."

It was only a little before six, she realized as she walked into the bathroom. It seemed impossible that merely an hour and a half earlier she had been lying in bed with Kaldak. Yet the evidence of intimacy was still there: the rumpled covers, the impression of their heads on the pillows.

Not only sex, but intimacy, she thought as she stepped into the shower. The fact was shocking. What would have happened if she hadn't been so abruptly jarred out of that crazy euphoria? It was probably for the best. He had proved to be a great lover, but she was too vulnerable just then. She couldn't handle a relationship with a man as complicated and tormented as Kaldak.

Not when she was tormented by the same demons.

"Ms. Grady."

Jesus, Ramsey was knocking on her bathroom door.

"I'm sorry. But I'm limited for time and I need to talk to you."

She turned off the shower. "I'll be out in a minute. I hope you won't mind if I dry off first."

"I know it's an inconvenience." A pause. "I'll wait in the living room."

She was surprised he hadn't invaded the bathroom and jerked her out of the shower. The more she came in contact with Ramsey, the more he annoyed her.

She ran a hand through her damp hair as she strode into the living room a few minutes later.

"Sorry," Kaldak said. "Short of breaking his neck, I couldn't keep him from trying to hurry you."

Breaking his neck wouldn't have been

such a bad idea. "Did you give him the new sample?"

Kaldak nodded. "But he's not satisfied with the milk, he wants the cow."

"What a way with words," Yael murmured. "You don't resemble a cow in the slightest, Bess. Well, maybe your name. Wasn't there a commercial with Bessie the cow or some such—"

"You must see by now that you can't go on like this," Ramsey cut in. "It's not safe for you and it's not safe for the public either. Not to mention my own men. Peterson had a family. Do you want to be the one to tell them that—"

"Stop right there," Kaldak said.

"It's okay. No, I don't want to tell them," Bess said unevenly. "I feel terrible about him. But it doesn't change the fact that my staying here is still the best way to get to Esteban. Unless you can show me that you have a better way, I'm staying."

Ramsey whirled on Kaldak. "For God's sake, tell her to get out of here. You must have some influence with her."

Kaldak shook his head.

"Damn you." Ramsey's voice was shaking with anger. "It's your fault, Kaldak. Do you think I don't know you're just using her so you can get Esteban? You don't give a shit that I'm going to be crucified. I won't let you do it. No way."

He stormed out, slamming the door behind him.

"I think he's a little upset." Yael shook his head reprovingly. "Really, Kaldak, setting up a poor, defenseless woman like Bess. It's deplorable."

"I'm surprised he thinks I could manipulate you," Kaldak told Bess. "We've all been dancing on your strings."

"I can see why he does." She glanced at the bedroom. Ramsey might be a selfish bastard, but he wasn't stupid. He had been in her bedroom and had seen that the bed had obviously been occupied by two people. He clearly thought Kaldak was using a sexual relationship to influence her. "But he's mistaken."

"Yes, he is." Kaldak's gaze was on her face. "Completely."

"I think this is the time I offer to furnish breakfast." Yael rose to his feet. "And since I can't cook, I'll go down to the Café Du Monde and get a bag of beignets to go." He checked his watch. "I walk very slowly, but I should be back in an hour or so."

"You don't have to leave," Bess said.

But he was already gone.

"Last night wasn't about trying to use you, Bess," Kaldak said quietly.

"Don't be stupid." She walked over to the window. "I know that."

"Then why aren't you looking at me?"

"I feel . . . awkward. I don't have one-night stands."

"For God's sake, this isn't a one-night stand."

She said haltingly, "It can't be anything else. It's crazy to think the two of us could have any kind of sane relationship."

There was a silence behind her. "Oh, then you've chalked me up as another one of your mistakes? Like that philandering husband?"

Had she hurt him? Oh, God, she didn't want to hurt him.

"I wouldn't be a mistake for you, Bess. We'd be good together."

She shook her head.

"Look at me, dammit."

"It's not your fault. I was lonely and I needed—"

"*This* is the mistake."

"Don't make this difficult for me, Kaldak," she said shakily.

A silence.

"We'll go to bed again, you know," he said. "We're living too close and now we know how good it is. You don't have to worry about me jumping you, but I won't try to stop it when it happens." She heard him move away. "I'm going to take a shower. I still smell of you, and it's driving me crazy."

The tension didn't leave her even after he'd disappeared. His last words had brought the night tumbling back to her. Close it out. She had done the right thing. She couldn't afford to have her focus blurred. She couldn't think about Kaldak.

She had to remember Emily.

"Are you sure he's competent?" Habin's voice was edged. "I still think one of my own men would have been better. Their loyalty can't be bought."

Esteban's hand tightened on the receiver. That loyalty was just the quality Esteban wanted to avoid. The reason he'd wasted so much time on finding Jeffers was that he'd known he couldn't control any of Habin's men. Bribery and threats worked beautifully on everyone but a fanatic. "Jeffers is quite brilliant and your men are too valuable to waste on his task. You're wanted by the authorities here in the U.S. and you need them for protection. I hope you've found a safe location?"

"A farm outside Kansas City. And you should worry about yourself. You move from motel to motel with no guards to watch your back."

"I'm accustomed to taking care of myself. I prefer not to risk betrayal. That's always a possibility."

"And the woman. If my men had gone after her, she would not still be alive."

Esteban's smile faded. "Kaldak knew all your men. And they knew him. It would have presented problems." Kaldak would have gathered them up and squeezed everything they knew from them. De Salmo had not proved effective, but at least he had not been caught. "And you'll be glad to know I've arranged to personally supervise the matter myself."

"I can't move yet. I need three more days."

"You'll get them." He hung up the phone.

Three days.

Esteban could feel the tightness in his shoulders and shrugged to loosen them. He mustn't let the pressure get to him. He had planned too long for the moment at hand. Nothing must go wrong. He could not permit anything to stop him now.

The woman was just another barrier to overcome.

And if you couldn't attack a barrier from the front, you just went around and attacked from the rear.

Three days . . .

FIFTEEN

"I suppose you won't be going to Alison's bat mitzvah tonight." Marta Katz made a face. "You just don't want to dress up in a suit and tie."

"Yeah, I arranged for Kaldak to drop this mess in my lap so I could get out of going to a party." Ed gulped down the last of his orange juice.

"Just because you don't like my sister is no reason to slight her daughter."

"I'll give Alison a terrific present."

"But you don't like my sister, do you?"

Ed was too tired to deny it. "Leslie's a snob. She thinks you married beneath you. Which means she's also stupid."

"Maybe. At times like this I tend to doubt it. You haven't been home for three days."

He leered at her. "But I was home last night."

"For four hours, and only because it was my fertile time."

He stood up and gave her a kiss on the nose. "I think we hit the jackpot. Did I perform like a prize stud or what? Nine months from now we'll be changing diapers."

"*I'll* be changing diapers. You'll probably still be at the center playing with your nasty little bugs." She watched him grab his briefcase and head for the door. "Just look at you. Why couldn't you have left that work for the little time you came home?"

"Sorry. I wanted to check some results in the car back to the office."

"Just drop in for an hour at the bat mitzvah?"

"I can't, babe. I'm too close."

"What about Donovan? Can't he carry on without you?"

"Maybe. But speed's important right now.

You know I wouldn't miss Alison's party if I could help it."

She nodded resignedly and followed him. "Okay, I'll make your excuses." She grabbed him as he started out the door. "Come back here." She cradled his face in her hands. "Definitely a stud." She kissed him. "Now, don't work so damn hard. I don't want you having a stroke before the kid gets here."

"No chance. We're almost there." He hugged her and then started down the porch steps. "Hell, maybe I'll even get to the bat mitzvah."

"Fat chance." She frowned as she saw the gray Ford parked at the curb. "I was going to take those policemen some coffee. I forgot."

"We can stop at McDonald's on the way. Paul likes their french fries."

"Paul does the driving, right?"

"Jim does the driving. Paul is his partner."

"Why the policemen, Ed? Why aren't you driving yourself? Is it Ebola or something?"

He shook his head. "I told you, I'm a very important man. The president, the mayor, and I all need police escorts." He winked at her. "When this is all over, we'll have to be sure and tell your sister."

She smiled. "Leslie's okay. She just doesn't understand."

"Go on inside. It's chilly out here."

"My robe's warm. The air feels good."

Ed could feel her gaze on him as he walked toward the car. He shouldn't have told her he might make the bat mitzvah, but he'd felt guilty. Marta put up with a hell of a lot. Maybe next month he'd take her away for a vacation. With any luck, the antidote would be ready in less than a week. The last test had proved very promising. Promising, hell, it had sent him over the moon with excitement. It wasn't often that a scientist got a chance to stop a disease in its tracks.

"Hi, guys." He hopped into the backseat of the car and slammed the door. "We'll have to stop at McDonald's. I forgot to bring you coffee. Marta was—"

No response. Jim and Paul were both looking straight ahead. A thin line of blood welled slowly from the back of Paul's collar.

"Christ."

Ed reached for the door handle.

He never heard Marta's scream.

"You're sure?"

Bess froze in her chair. She had never seen such a look of pain on Kaldak's face.

"Yeah, I'll go. You're right. It's my job." He hung up the phone.

"Ramsey?"

He nodded. "I've got to go to Atlanta."

"Why?"

"Ed Katz is dead."

"What?" she whispered.

"His car blew up. He and two officers were killed in the blast." His fist crashed down on the arm of the chair. "Son of a *bitch*."

"He was your friend."

"We went to college together. I went to his wedding. Oh, yes, some friend I am," he said bitterly. "I bulldozed him into taking on the project. I didn't think he'd be a target. Not if Ramsey arranged security for him."

"De Salmo?"

"I don't know. He likes a knife, but he's used explosives before. It might be De Salmo or one of Habin's people."

"How does this affect the research?"

"It's got to set it back. It was a team

project, but Ed was team leader." He stood up and strode toward the door. "So Esteban's got a delay. The bastard couldn't get you, so he went after Ed."

She flinched. "I wish there was something I could do. I'm sorry, Kaldak."

"That you're still alive? Don't worry, I'm sure Esteban has plans to change that. Well, he's not going to get you. I'll be back tonight. I have to check out the situation with the research and see Ed's wife. Ramsey's called Yael and he'll be over in five minutes. I'll wait for him downstairs, but I won't leave until he gets here."

"You can go. It's only a few minutes."

"It took less than a minute for them to incinerate Ed." He looked over his shoulder. "If you want to help me, you'll stay inside the apartment today."

She nodded. "Whatever you say."

"Yeah, sure. Whatever I say." The door closed behind him.

She had met Ed Katz only once, but she had a vivid memory of looking back at him as he stood in the rain in the parking lot. He had been frightened, but that hadn't stopped him.

And now he was dead. Esteban had

killed him as he had killed Emily and all those other—

A knock on the door.

"Just a minute." She got up and moved across the room. She paused with her hand on the lock. "Yael?"

"Ramsey."

Great. He always seemed to be hovering over her like a vulture when something bad happened. She opened the door. "Where's Yael?"

He smiled. "He'll be here shortly. I intercepted him and asked him to wait downstairs while we had a talk."

"I don't want to talk. We've said everything there is to say."

He came into the apartment and closed the door. "Katz's death is the final straw. We can't delay much longer. You have to trust me to take care of you."

"I don't have to do any such thing. I don't trust you. I trust myself."

"And Kaldak."

She gazed directly into his eyes. "And Kaldak."

"You feel safe with him?"

"Will you leave, Mr. Ramsey?"

"You shouldn't feel safe. He's a dangerous man. He's using you. He's using all of us. He's used Ed Katz, and you know how that turned out."

"I didn't hear you object to Kaldak using Ed Katz."

"But Kaldak is a driven man. Sometimes I think he's unbalanced."

"We're a good match. I'm driven too."

"Then let me help you. You don't need Kaldak. Believe me, you don't want Kaldak." He smiled persuasively as he stepped closer. "Just be patient and hear me out."

"I nagged him," Marta whispered. "I wanted him to go to a bat mitzvah. I knew how tired he was, and I still nagged him."

Kaldak's hand closed on hers.

"I thought it was important." Tears were running down her face. "I thought a damn bat mitzvah was important."

"It was important," Kaldak said.

"I should have— Oh, shit." She buried her face in his chest. "Why didn't I keep my mouth shut?"

Christ, this was killing him. "You had sixteen good years. Ed loved you. He didn't care about—"

"I wanted a kid. That's why he came home last night. It was my fertile period. He should have stayed at the center. He would have been safe." She raised her head. "It's crazy. None of it makes sense. He was a scientist. No one blows up scientists. That happens to politicians or evangelists or Mafia bosses. Not to men like Ed."

"Has someone called your family?"

"I told my sister not to come. She and Ed didn't get along."

"Someone else?"

"My mother's flying in from Rhode Island." She pushed him away and sat up straight. "I'm sorry, I'm embarrassing you. You don't know what to do. Hell, I don't know what to do either."

"You're not embarrassing me."

"Sure I am. You never did know how to handle—" She hesitated. "It was what he was working on, wasn't it? It was the stuff you gave him to do."

"Yes."

"And it killed him."

"Yes."

"He was your friend," she whispered. "Why?"

"It was important."

"Important enough for him to die?"

Her every word was like a whiplash. "I thought he'd be safe, Marta."

"He wasn't safe." She was rocking back and forth. "He wasn't safe. It was a mistake. You made a mistake."

"I know," he said hoarsely. "I know I did."

"And I did too. I made a terrible mistake."

"You didn't make a mistake. He wouldn't have thought you were nagging him about that bat mitzvah."

"No, not about that. The baby. Oh, God, what if I have a baby?" Her eyes were swimming with tears as she whispered, "I couldn't stand it. It would kill me. I couldn't stand to have a baby without Ed here."

"What about the project?" Ramsey demanded when Kaldak answered his phone on the way to the Atlanta airport.

"The team is in shock, but everyone's scrambling to regroup. Donovan will take over, but some of the papers were destroyed in the blast."

"How long are they set back?"

"I don't know. But Donovan's a good man and he seems confident."

He wished he could say something more positive. This was Ramsey's cue to push for moving Bess, and he braced himself for the battle.

No battle. Ramsey changed the subject. "I just heard from my man who's tracking Morrisey. A week ago the Majestic Hotel in Cheyenne requested a guarantee on his credit card. We checked with the hotel and they still have a John Morrisey registered."

Excitement flared through Kaldak.

"You could fly straight from Atlanta," Ramsey continued. "I thought you'd want to go get him yourself."

He did want to go. Hell, he was desperately eager to go. Morrisey might be the key to Esteban, and he was afraid that any one of Ramsey's men might let him slip through his fingers.

But that would mean Bess . . .

"I can't leave Bess right now. When I get to New Orleans, I'll ask Yael to go get Morrisey."

There was a silence. "Well, if you change your mind, let me know."

"I won't change my mind." He hung up the phone. Ramsey's mildness had been unusual. Ordinarily, Kaldak could predict which way Ramsey was going to jump, but Ramsey surprised him this time.

He didn't like it.

"You look like hell," Yael said when Kaldak walked into the apartment. "Bad?"

"It couldn't have been much worse."

"You know how sorry I am."

Yeah, he knew. The whole world was sorry, but it didn't bring Ed back. Kaldak's gaze went to the bedroom. "Where's Bess? Is she in her room?"

Yael shook his head. "I wish she were. She's been in her darkroom since I got to the apartment."

"Her darkroom? Has she been working?"

Yael shook his head. "I don't think so. Ramsey came to see her."

Kaldak stiffened. "And he upset her?"

"Whatever he said must have been a knockout punch."

I feel safe there.

He remembered what she had said about her darkroom. Whatever Ramsey had told her had sent her fleeing for safety.

He should have expected it. Ramsey had stepped in the minute he'd seen his opportunity. Everything else was toppling down around him. Why not this too?

"Should I leave?" Yael asked.

"No, stay." He started down the hall. "I'll go see her."

He stopped outside the darkroom. Do it. Face her. He braced himself and then knocked on the door. "May I come in, Bess? We have to talk."

"You bet we do." She threw open the door. Her eyes blazing, she drew back a hand and slapped him. "You son of a bitch."

"Bess, I didn't mean—"

"The *hell* you didn't." She slapped him again. "You son of a bitch." Tears were suddenly running down her cheeks. "You did this. None of this should have happened. Emily shouldn't have died." She hit him again. "Why couldn't you have just left us alone?"

"I'm sorry," Kaldak said. "I never meant to hurt you. I thought it was safe."

"You sent me to Tenajo. You let me take my sister. Do you know how guilty I've been feeling since she died? You did it all, you bastard." She was sobbing so hard, she could barely get the words out. "Emily died. . . ."

"She wasn't supposed to go with you. You were on assignment. You were supposed to go alone."

"And you arranged it. Ramsey said you pulled strings at the magazine and mapped out the assignment. You wanted me to go to Tenajo."

A muscle jerked in his left cheek. "Yes."

"Why?"

"Didn't Ramsey tell you?"

"All he could talk about was how you set me up and how I should trust only him." She took a step closer and said between her teeth, "You tell me, Kaldak. You tell me why you wanted me dead."

"I didn't want you dead. I knew there was a good chance you'd survive."

"You couldn't know that I'd—" Her eyes widened. "You *did* know. My God, you knew about the immunity. But how could you?"

"Danzar."

She stared at him, stunned.

"You got a very low dose of the mutated anthrax in Danzar. It was much weaker than the strain Esteban used in Tenajo." He added grimly, "But it was strong enough to kill everyone in the village."

"You're saying Danzar was another testing ground?"

"The first. It was a perfect scheme for Esteban. He supplied the anthrax to the guerrillas, and they sent it into the village in a food shipment."

She shook her head. "No, it's not true. Everyone was butchered. I was there. I saw it."

"It was part of the deal. The guerrillas went in later and made it look like a massacre."

"It *was* a massacre."

He shook his head.

"You knew about it?" she whispered. "You knew about the babies?"

"No, I was with Habin at the time. Danzar was strictly Esteban's show. But I found out about it later."

"And you did nothing?"

"What do you want me to say?" he asked harshly. "All right, I did nothing. Just as I did nothing after Nakoa. Because there was no proof." He paused. "But after Danzar I thought we might have an edge. When you were in the hospital in Sarajevo, I had them take blood tests. You'd developed immune antibodies to the weaker strain of anthrax Esteban used in Danzar."

"You were there at the hospital in Sarajevo?"

"I had to know. I had to be sure."

"You were there all the time."

"Yes."

"My driver survived too."

"We checked him out. He wasn't immune. You must have had more contact with the bacteria as you moved from room to room at the orphanage. You were our only hope."

"If you knew I was immune, why didn't you do something about it? Why didn't you take some damn blood and try to save Tenajo?"

"Esteban considered Danzar a failure and continued mutating the strain. But we didn't know what those new mutations were. So developing an antidote beforehand would have been useless."

"So you sent me to Tenajo."

"You had to be exposed. I had to make sure you were immune."

"And one more death didn't make any difference."

"Hell, yes, it made a difference. But I couldn't let it stop me."

"You killed Emily."

"You were the only one supposed to go to Tenajo. Dammit, I had no intention of exposing your sister."

"You killed her."

"All right, I killed her. It was my fault."

"You killed her and you lied to me and you fucked me." She stared at him in disgust. "And I let you. I let you do it all."

"I didn't fuck you. I made love to you." He took a step toward her. "Bess, it wasn't—"

"Don't you *touch* me." She backed away. "No wonder you were so protective and kind to me. You were feeling guilty. Jesus, I want to kill you. I want to cut your heart out."

"You'll have to stand in line," he said wearily.

"Get out of my apartment, you son of a bitch."

"De Salmo is still out there."

"I don't care."

"I care." He paused. "Are you going to let Ramsey take you to—"

"I'm not letting Ramsey take me anywhere. I don't trust him any more than I do you. Get out." Her voice was shaking. "I can't even stand looking at you."

"Bess, this is just what De Salmo and Esteban want."

"Get *out*."

She slammed the door of the darkroom in his face.

His hands clenched into fists at his sides. It was what he expected. He had always known she would eventually find out. But he hadn't known it would hurt so much.

He strode back into the living room.

"Ramsey blew the whistle?" Yael asked. "She knows about the setup?"

"She knows everything. She wants me out." He went to the guest bedroom and took out his suitcase. "Which means you're in. She can't be left alone."

Yael followed him. "I didn't promise I'd be in this for the long haul, Kaldak."

He threw his clothes into the suitcase. "Do you want her dead?"

"Ramsey will—"

"You keep her away from Ramsey. He was supposed to be protecting Ed Katz, and Ed Katz is dead. Do you think Ramsey will keep her any safer?"

"What are you going to do?"

"The only thing I can do." He slammed the suitcase shut. "I'm going to Cheyenne after Morrisey. Ramsey finally tracked him down. Call Ramsey and tell him I'm on my way." Not that he needed to be told. He had known Bess would not let Kaldak within a mile of her after what he'd told her. He wanted to break the interfering bastard's neck. "I just hope to hell it's not a wild-goose chase." He paused. "Will you stay, Yael? Will you take care of her? We need her. She's . . . valuable."

"In more ways than one, evidently." Yael slowly nodded his head. "I'll take care of her."

God, it hurt.

Bess huddled in the corner of the darkroom, her arms wrapped around herself.

Why had she trusted him? She knew he didn't care about anything or anyone but getting Esteban. He had even warned her not to trust him.

But she hadn't listened. And she had let him use her as he used everyone else. He had sent her to Tenajo and Emily had died.

She felt as if she were bleeding inside. She hadn't been stupid enough to actually let him mean anything to her. So why was she curled up like a wounded animal in the dark?

It was the shock. She would be better soon. She would stay here for just a little while longer and let herself heal. Then she would go out and function perfectly well.

Just a little longer.

Kaldak was gone.

It was the best chance Marco might have. He wasn't worried about the guards downstairs. He could dispose of them with no problem. Esteban had been very pleased about his deftness with those policemen in Atlanta. It was Kaldak who had been the big stumbling block, and Kaldak had left.

The window of opportunity couldn't stay open long.

But it might be long enough.

Over two hours later Yael was sitting in front of the television set, watching a basketball game, when Bess came into the living room.

"Would you like some dinner?" Yael

snapped off the set. "It's after nine and you haven't had anything to eat all day."

She shook her head. "I'm going to bed. I'm tired."

"I can see why."

She looked at him. "You knew about it."

Yael nodded. "Most of it. I learned the rest from Ramsey after I got here."

"It seems everyone knew but me. I find that as unforgivable as the rest."

"You'd be surprised what you can forgive." He held up his hand. "I'm not trying to persuade you that Kaldak was right."

"There's no way you could."

"I'm just saying we all have our priorities. Kaldak isn't all black and he does care whether you live or die."

"That's why he sent me to Tenajo."

Yael sighed. "This obviously isn't the time for me to talk to you." He stood up. "I have to go downstairs and ask one of the guards to go to my flat and pack a suitcase for me. I'll stand his duty downstairs until he gets back. I shouldn't be long."

"You don't have to move in here. I'll be all right."

"I promised Kaldak. And my apartment was getting lonely anyway. I miss my wife and son." He paused as he opened the door. "Are you going to drag me out on the street tomorrow?"

"Yes."

"Would it do any good to tell you to lie low for a few days?"

"No, it wouldn't."

"I was afraid of that."

"Yael." She had just thought of something. "I'll need to send a blood sample by tomorrow morning. Kaldak usually took it."

"I'm sorry, I'm not qualified. I'd probably butcher you." He paused. "Katz's death has probably thrown everything into turmoil anyway. It may take a little while to regroup."

"They can't do anything without the blood samples. The sooner they get it, the better."

He nodded. "There's got to be an agent who can take blood. I'll have Ramsey send someone over."

"Thanks."

"Thank you. You're the one who's doing us the favor."

"It's not a favor." Esteban had killed Ed Katz just to cause a delay. She'd be damned if she'd give him more. "Have the agent come early. I want that sample in Atlanta by noon."

Yael saluted. "Yes, ma'am."

"Oh, and could I borrow your portable phone? I always used Kaldak's and I don't want to use the apartment phone when I call to check on Josie."

"No problem." He handed her the phone. "I'd much rather supply you with this than rob you of your blood."

She moved toward the bedroom. After she showered she'd call the hospital and check on Josie. Then she'd go to bed and try to sleep.

Who was she fooling? She was exhausted but there was no way she was going to be able to sleep. Her nerves were as raw as when Kaldak had left.

So don't waste the time.

She went back to the darkroom and gathered all the pictures she'd taken since she'd returned to New Orleans. Kaldak had not recognized anyone, but maybe she'd get lucky and catch . . . something.

Twenty minutes later she wearily stacked the photos on the nightstand. Nothing. There was no use staring at the faces any longer. Everything was blurring before her eyes. Hell, some of the shots had been a little blurry too. She must have—

Why would they be blurred? She couldn't remember any unusual circumstances to account for blurring.

She riffled through the pictures. Only four shots had any blurring.

The clown. The tall clown with green hair and a white-painted face. In each shot he was moving away from the camera at the exact moment she had taken the photograph.

Coincidence? Or had he been trying to avoid the camera? Even with a disguise, had he felt uneasy?

She ran to the darkroom, got her magnifying glass, placed it over the clown's face.

"Bess." Yael was knocking on the front door.

She ran to open it. "I've found De Salmo. I think I know who he is."

Yael set down his suitcase and took the photos she was handing him. "The clown?"

"He's been there every day. The shot from the first day doesn't have any blurring, but every day after that he tried to avoid being photographed."

"Possible." He smiled. "Very possible. It's worth having Ramsey pick him up."

She watched him as he talked to Ramsey. They would pick up the suspect, and if she was right, she wouldn't have to worry about a murderer on her doorstep. She should feel safer, but she didn't. Esteban would only send someone else.

Or maybe he would come himself. Maybe this would be the trigger.

Yael ended the call. "Done. Now we simply wait to hear more." He sat down and looked at her. "Tell me how your Josie is."

Josie. She had forgotten to call Dr. Kenwood.

She reached for Yael's phone and quickly dialed. A short time later she was connected with Dr. Kenwood.

"You just caught me, Ms. Grady." He sounded tired. "I was about to leave."

"How's Josie?"

"Better. Much better. I'm planning on operating tomorrow morning."

Her heart jumped. "What time?"

"Eight o'clock. Can you be here for her?"

God, she wanted to be.

"We'll take good care of her, even if you can't make it."

But Josie would be sick and in pain and among strangers. "When will you know if she's—" She wouldn't say the word *paralyzed*. "If the operation was a success?"

"We'll have a good idea by tomorrow evening. You could call then."

"Yes, I could do that." She could do phone calls and prayers just as she'd done ever since she delivered Josie to the hospital. To hell with it. She was tired of this long-distance caretaking. "I'll be there tomorrow morning."

He chuckled. "To keep an eye on me?"

"You bet. I'll see you tomorrow, Dr. Kenwood."

She hung up the phone, feeling Yael's eyes on her.

"How is she?" he asked.

"Better. They're operating tomorrow."

"I see."

"And I'm going to be there."

"I want to argue with you, but I won't," he said quietly. "I'd do the same. Children are tough to fight."

"Ramsey will try to stop me from going. Will you help me?"

"Suppose you go get your overnight case packed while I work out a strategy." He looked down at his suitcase. "I seem to be ready to go. Do you think I'm psychic?"

"I think you're a very nice man."

He smiled. "But that goes without saying."

Cheyenne, Wyoming
Majestic Hotel
11:45 P.M.

The hotel was old and shabby. Not even the snow could disguise its run-down state. Inside, the chipped and discolored reception desk was manned by a pimple-faced kid in jeans and a plaid shirt who was reading *USA Today*.

"I'm here for John Morrisey," Kaldak said. "Which room?"

The kid didn't look up. "You'll have to call him. We don't give out that information."

"Which room?"

"I said we—" The kid glanced up and stiffened as he met Kaldak's gaze. "It's against the rules."

"I won't tell anybody. Which room?"

"Two thirty-four."

"Has anyone been here to see him?"

"Only Cody."

"Cody?"

"Cody Jeffers."

"You know this Jeffers?"

"Sure. He lives here in the hotel. Cody's cool." The kid nibbled on his lower lip. "You with the police or something?"

Kaldak nodded and showed his ID.

"CIA? Cool."

"No older man has been around? Graying hair, hooked nose?"

The kid shook his head. "Haven't seen him. But I work the night shift. I haven't even seen Morrisey for a couple of days."

"But he's still registered?"

He nodded.

"How long has Morrisey been here?"

"Two weeks." He frowned. "Cody's not in trouble, is he? He's clean. He drinks a little, but he told me that no performer with any sense does drugs."

"Performer?"

"Cody drives in the demolition derby." He pointed his thumb to the right. "You can see his name on the poster on the stadium two blocks down. It's in real little letters, but Cody told me the management thinks he's hot stuff and next year they're going to feature him. He's going to be a star."

What the hell could Esteban want with

Cody Jeffers? Kaldak wondered. He turned and walked toward the elevator. "Don't call Morrisey and tell him I'm coming."

Two minutes later he was standing in front of Morrisey's door. A Do Not Disturb sign hung on the knob. He knocked. No answer. He carefully turned the knob. Locked. Morrisey might have already flown the coop. The kid had said he hadn't seen him for a few days.

He knocked again. No answer.

He suddenly noticed the door was ice-cold.

He kicked in the door.

The window across the room was wide open and snow covered the carpet beneath it. A man was lying on the bed, a fistful of money clutched in his hand.

Shit.

Kaldak backed away and slammed the door shut. He took out his phone and dialed Ramsey. "Get a crew over here right away. Morrisey's dead and there's money all over the bed. Room 234."

Ramsey cursed. "Anthrax?"

"Probably. Tell your men to be careful but to go over everything with a fine-tooth comb," Kaldak continued. "See if we can come up with any leads." Not that he had any hope they would. Esteban wasn't care- less.

"They'll be there in thirty minutes."

"Tell them to come in the back way. That may save us from the five o'clock news."

He hung up the phone and returned to the lobby. The clerk straightened apprehen- sively when he saw Kaldak approach.

"I didn't call him. If he wasn't there, it's not my fault."

"I know you didn't call him." He placed his elbows on the desk. "What's your name?"

"Don Sloburn."

"My name is Kaldak. I need your help. I need you to try to remember if you ever saw Morrisey with anyone except Jeffers. Anyone at all."

Sloburn shook his head. "No one except the guys at the track. He was a real fan, like me. He used to go down to Shea's bar at the corner and sit around and talk to the per- formers. But I never saw him deal any drugs or nothing."

"He talked to performers other than Jef- fers?"

"Yeah, sure, but he and Cody really hit it off." He hesitated. "Cody's in trouble too?"

"Maybe. Can you tell me where to find him?"

He shook his head.

Kaldak couldn't be sure if the kid was telling the truth. Time to shake him up a little. "Morrisey's dead. Murdered. He's been dead for days."

Sloburn's eyes widened in shock. "Cody did it?"

"No, I don't think so, but Jeffers may know something." He added, "Or he may be in danger himself if he saw something he shouldn't have. We have to find him."

"Drugs? Mafia?"

"Possibly. Where's Cody Jeffers?"

"I don't know. I haven't seen him in a couple of days. I thought maybe he went down to see his mother in Kansas."

"He hasn't been in the show or down at the bar?"

He shook his head.

"Do you know where his mother lives?"

"I don't remember." He frowned. "Some suburb that sounds like— Northern Lights, maybe."

"Northern Lights?"

He shrugged. "I don't remember."

"Does he have a girl?"

"Not here. He always said a performer had to devote himself to his work if he wanted to be a headliner."

"Do you have a photograph of him?"

"No." He thought about it. "Dunston might have one. They take a lot of publicity pictures."

"Dunston?"

"Irwin Dunston. He runs the demolition derby."

"Where can I find him?"

"The derby was over at eleven. He's probably down at Shea's bar with everyone else."

"Thanks." He leaned closer. "Now, I want you to listen very carefully. No one's to go into Morrisey's room. This has to be handled discreetly. A group of technicians will be here shortly to take the body and clean up the room."

"Technicians?"

"We're not sure what killed him. There are all kinds of gases and powders the mob uses these days. I'm sure the hotel manager wouldn't appreciate having anyone know the room might be contaminated."

"No."

"Good. Then you'll cooperate and keep this from the media."

Sloburn was frowning uncertainly. "I watched the O.J. trial. This isn't how things are done. You're disturbing evidence."

Christ, everyone in the world had watched that trial and thought they were experts. "Oh, am I?"

"Yes, and how do I know that ID isn't forged or something? You might not be CIA. You could be anyone."

"Yes, I could be anyone." He gazed directly into Sloburn's eyes and said softly, "There's a dead man upstairs who was killed by the mob. Now, if I'm not one of the good guys, who could I be?"

Sloburn swallowed hard. "No one. You're legit. Of course, you're legit."

"And you'll cooperate with the men who want to save your manager a major headache?"

He nodded.

"And you don't know anything more about Cody Jeffers?"

"I told you everything."

Which wasn't much. "The lock's broken on the door. Go on up and stand guard until the technicians get there."

"I shouldn't leave the desk."

Kaldak looked at him.

Sloburn nodded quickly and started around the desk. "I guess this is a more urgent matter."

"Very urgent."

So urgent it was scaring the pants off him, Kaldak thought as he headed for the exit. Morrisey's death could have been another experiment.

Or Esteban could be throwing down the gauntlet.

SIXTEEN

Kaldak was on his way to Shea's bar when he got the call from Yael.

"Bess is leaving New Orleans. I thought you should know."

"What?"

"She's in the bedroom, packing. She's going to Johns Hopkins. The kid is being operated on tomorrow morning."

Murphy's Law. He should have known the one event that would draw Bess into the open would happen when he was hundreds of miles away. "You're going with her?"

"I seem to be. Since I was rash enough

to make you a promise. But protecting her is escalating in difficulty. One good thing is that we may have zeroed in on De Salmo."

"How?"

Yael explained. "Ramsey's ordered him picked up for questioning."

"Does he know you're leaving town?"

"Not yet. Should I tell him?"

"After the fact. So he won't be able to do anything about it except make sure she's protected at the hospital."

"That's my reading too."

"Take her down the courtyard staircase and out the back way. Do you have a car?"

"It's parked on Canal Street. And how am I supposed to get past Ramsey's guard in the courtyard?"

"How the hell do I know? Improvise. You usually don't have any trouble."

"Thanks a lot."

"Buy a ticket to Milwaukee by way of Chicago. When you get to Chicago, make sure you're not followed and then take a flight to Baltimore."

"Any other orders?"

"Sorry." Yael had a perfect right to be sarcastic. Kaldak was trying to control the situation long-distance. He just felt so damn helpless. He wanted to *be* there. And he was so scared, he was sick to his stomach.

"No problem." Yael paused. "Did you find Morrisey?"

"Dead."

"Shit."

"Yes, but I may have a lead. I'll fill you in later. Call me when you get to the hospital."

"When I can do it discreetly. Bess won't like seeing me report to you. She may toss me out on my ear and you wouldn't like that."

"As soon as you can, then." He hung up the phone. Just try to locate Cody Jeffers, he told himself. Don't think about Bess. There was nothing else he could do. Yael was smart and careful. He would take care of her.

Just don't think about Bess.

Yael was talking on the phone. Bess couldn't hear what he was saying, but she'd bet she knew who was on the other end of the line. She didn't give a damn that Kaldak knew where she was going, but she didn't like the fact that Yael had waited until she was in her bedroom to call him.

She put on her jacket, looped the strap of

her camera around her neck, and strode back into the living room. "I'm ready to go. I hope Kaldak gave you a good suggestion as to how we should get out of here."

"Oops." Yael stood up and grabbed her suitcase and his own. "I was only trying to be discreet."

"I'd rather you be honest than discreet. Which way are we leaving?"

"The courtyard." He moved down the hallway and unlocked the door. "You stay here at the head of the stairs and I'll go down and talk to Ramsey's man, see what I can do about getting him out of there."

"What if you can't?"

"I guess I knock him very gently and carefully on the head."

"I don't think you can knock anyone gently on the head. Ramsey will be very upset with you."

"Why should I be different?" Yael started down the stone steps. "Stay here."

The courtyard had no lights and Yael seemed to disappear into a black hole. Bess strained to see, but she couldn't make out either Yael or the guard.

She was suddenly uneasy. She should

be hearing footsteps. Yael's voice. Something . . .

Silence.

"Bess," Yael called out.

She jumped.

"Come on. Hurry."

She ran down the stairs and Yael led her across the courtyard.

"How did you get rid of him?"

"I didn't," he muttered. "He wasn't there."

"What?"

"He wasn't there." She could sense his tension. "And I don't like it, dammit. Ramsey wouldn't have called him off the job."

"The other guard, Peterson . . ." Peterson had died. Peterson had been murdered.

Yael didn't answer, but his grasp tightened on her arm.

The walkway leading to the street loomed dark and ominous.

"Stay a few paces behind. I'm going on ahead." Yael disappeared into the darkness.

Alone. Fear iced through her. Someone was watching. She could *feel* it.

Not on the walk where Yael had gone. Behind her.

She glanced over her shoulder and saw

only gargoyles. Shadows on shadows. Then
movement.

Oh, God.

She raced down the long walkway after
Yael. She could see the lights of the street
and Yael's silhouette. "Yael!"

"Bess, what's—"

A hand closed on her hair, jerking her to
a stop.

She looked over her shoulder. A white-
painted face gleaming in the darkness.
A skull. It looked like a skull. Something else
was gleaming, the blade in his hand.

"Run, Bess." Yael tore her from De Salmo
with a force that threw her against the brick
wall.

She couldn't run away. She couldn't
leave Yael. Where was he? She could barely
see the two figures struggling in the darkness. It lasted only a moment, and then one
of the men was getting to his feet, coming toward her.

Yael?

De Salmo?

She turned and ran.

He was right behind her.

He grabbed her arm. "Bess!"

She went limp with relief. "Yael. I thought—I wasn't sure—"

"I wasn't either for a minute." He was breathing hard. "He was very good."

"De Salmo?"

"I assume. I don't know anyone else with green hair, do you?"

"What did you do to him?"

"He won't bother you again."

"He's dead?"

"Exceptionally. I'm very good too."

They were out of the walkway, on the street. Lights. Beautiful lights. Thank God.

"What are you going to do about him?" Bess asked.

"Unless you've changed your mind about going to Baltimore, we'll leave him for Ramsey. I doubt if he'd be entertaining company on our trip."

"I haven't changed my mind."

"I didn't think you would." He urged her down the street. "Then let's see if we can get out of the Quarter without running into Ramsey or one of his men."

Cheyenne
1:40 A.M.

The lighting in the demolition derby stadium office was soft and diffused, and Kaldak had to step closer to study the group photo on the desk.

"This is Jeffers. Second row, third from the left." Dunston pointed at a man in a cowboy hat. "I told him not to wear that hat, but he put it on anyway. He's a real hot dog."

Jeffers was in his early twenties with a wide face and deep-set, light eyes. "Is he good?"

"Not bad but not as good as he thinks he is."

The cowboy hat almost entirely hid Jeffers's hair. "What color is his hair?"

"Light brown, sort of sandy."

"Short?"

Dunston nodded. "And curly. He was always combing it down."

"I can't tell what color his eyes are."

"Blue."

"Do you have a personnel record on Jeffers?"

"Sure. Do you think the IRS would let me run a business without records out the wazoo?" Dunston went to the file cabinet and riffled through the folders. "Jeffers." He handed the file to Kaldak. "You know, this doesn't surprise me. I always knew Cody would end up in trouble."

He opened the folder. "Why?"

Dunston shrugged. "Nothing I can point a finger at. Bad things happen when he's around. Most of the time to people Cody doesn't like."

Jeffers's mother was divorced and lived in Aurora, Kansas, a suburb of Kansas City. No other relatives listed. Northern Lights, the clerk at the hotel had said. Aurora Borealis? "Do you know anything about Jeffers's mother?"

"I know he visited her pretty frequently. She came here last month and I gave her a complimentary ticket to the show. He was preening and showing off for her like a peacock." He made a face. "She was a real pushy bitch. She had the nerve to ask me why I wasn't starring sonny boy. I almost felt sorry for him. It was pretty clear Cody couldn't measure up in her eyes unless he was top of the heap."

"Did he ask for a leave of absence when he took off?"

Dunston shook his head. "One night he was here, the next he no-showed."

"May I have this folder and the picture?"

"As long as I get the folder back. I don't want the IRS saying I claimed an employee who doesn't exist."

He took a marker and drew a circle around Jeffers's face on the photo. "You'll get it back."

"Can I lock up and go back to the bar now?" Dunston asked. "This isn't how I planned to spend my evening, you know."

Kaldak nodded. "Thanks for your time. Call me at that number I gave you if you hear from Jeffers."

"It's not likely, is it? You wouldn't be here if he hadn't done something pretty bad."

"You never can tell." Kaldak left the office and headed for the exit. He doubted that Dunston would hear from Jeffers ever again. Esteban had plucked the young man from this world for his own purpose, and he would make sure Jeffers remained cut off.

But Kaldak might have gotten a break. It was hard to cut off a man from his mother, particularly a dominant woman like the one Dunston had described. He would fax the picture and file to Ramsey and then catch the next flight to Kansas City.

Kaldak was becoming more uneasy the more he learned. Jeffers sounded reckless, volatile, and vain. He would be a piece of cake for Esteban to manipulate.

Bad things happen when he's around.

He hoped to hell Dunston's words weren't prophetic.

Des Moines, Iowa
6:50 A.M.

Cody checked his wristwatch. Time to make the run to Waterloo. Esteban liked everything to go like clockwork and precisely to his orders. Well, he was forking out the money.

Cody would give him what he wanted.

8:30 A.M.

De Salmo was dead.

Esteban hung up the phone. Inconvenient.

Or maybe not. He would have had to dispose of De Salmo eventually anyway, and De Salmo hadn't proved efficient where the woman was concerned. Not that Esteban could worry about the woman just then.

He was coming so close. Cody Jeffers should be in Waterloo already.

After all this time, after all his planning, the countdown was about to start.

Waterloo, Iowa
10:05 A.M

Cody yawned as he leaned against the truck's front fender.

This waiting around was boring. But it looked like they were almost done.

He climbed back into the driver's seat. It was all too easy. No excitement. Even the extra little job Esteban had given him had gone off without a hitch. Those Arabs hadn't even gone with him when he'd said he'd had to take a leak.

He watched them swarming over the truck. If this was his truck, he wouldn't be letting those foreigners touch it. You couldn't trust anybody but good, white Americans. Everybody knew that.

They were through now, waving him imperiously out of the barn. Arrogant sons of bitches. Just like those smirking Japs in that old John Wayne movie.

But John Wayne had shown them.

Just as Cody Jeffers would show them.

Johns Hopkins
11:20 A.M.

"Why is she still in the operating room?" Bess said worriedly. "It shouldn't be taking this long."

"Oh?" Yael said. "I didn't know you were a surgeon. Maybe you should go in and take over for Dr. Kenwood."

"Shut up, Yael. I'm scared to death. She's so little. . . ."

"I know," Yael said gently. "That's probably why it takes so long. It must be a very delicate operation."

He was right, she realized with relief. Maybe nothing had gone wrong. It was good that Yael was there with her and not Kaldak. "I suppose you called Kaldak when we got here."

He nodded. "While you were talking to

Dr. Kenwood before the operation." He let a couple of seconds go by, then said, "I also called Ramsey."

She stiffened.

"I had to do it. You couldn't stay here without a lot more protection."

"Just so he doesn't try to make me leave Josie."

"He probably will, but we'll stave him off for a while."

"Did you find out what happened to the guard in the courtyard?"

Yael grimaced.

"Dead?"

"They found him underneath the courtyard staircase. De Salmo was evidently trying to get into the apartment."

She smiled with effort. "A mamba in the drain?"

"I doubt if De Salmo was clever enough to appreciate James Bond. Don't worry about it now. You're here and safe."

"You shouldn't have told Ramsey I was here. I'd bet it was Kaldak's idea."

"Well, I agreed with him. I knew he had Josie's and your welfare at heart."

"Bullshit. He doesn't care about us."

"You know better than that. He cares. He

just couldn't let it get in the way. He waited a long time to get this close."

"He was wrong. I can imagine how upset he was about his colleagues dying on Nakoa, but that doesn't excuse—"

"His colleagues?" Yael asked. "Is that what he told you?"

"Yes." His reaction puzzled her.

"His mother and father were scientists and they were both on Nakoa. His mother headed up the project. They were the ones who brought Kaldak into the project. His wife, Lea, was a lab assistant. They had a four-year-old son."

Shock jolted through her. "And they all died on Nakoa?"

Yael nodded. "I'd say that's enough to make someone a little obsessive."

"He didn't tell me."

"He didn't tell me either. I had to find out for myself."

"Why?" she murmured. "Why did he keep it a secret from me?"

"I couldn't tell you. I'm not Kaldak."

Who *was* Kaldak? He had recounted the story of Nakoa with all the emotion of a robot. He had said he was no longer the man who had lived through that horror. But his pain was evidently still so intense, he couldn't talk about his loss even after all these years.

"It doesn't make what he did any more forgivable."

"I'm not defending, merely explaining." He smiled. "And perhaps I wanted to distract you a little. I don't like to see you this—"

"Here they come." She jumped up as the operating room doors opened and a wave of nurses and doctors flowed out. In their midst was a gurney with Josie on it.

Dr. Kenwood pulled down his mask and smiled at Bess. "Josie's doing very well. She's stable."

"Is that all?"

"That's pretty good for an operation of that length. You'll be glad to know I did a brilliant job."

"I *am* glad. But I'd be happier if you told me Josie's prospects are just as brilliant."

He shook his head. "I can't say that. I wish I could. She's doing well now. We won't know more until later."

Disappointment flooded Bess. That's what he had told her before, but she had hoped—

"I promise you'll know as soon as I do." Dr. Kenwood moved down the hall.

Yael's hand comfortingly grasped her shoulder. "She survived the operation. Five minutes ago you would have been happy with just that."

"I know. I only wish—" She wanted desperately to know Josie was going to completely recover and it was hard to wait. "I'm going to find someone to take a blood sample for you to send to Atlanta. Then I'm going to Recovery to wait for Josie to wake up."

"I'll go with you." Yael fell into step with her as she hurried in the direction they'd taken Josie.

Aurora, Kansas
3:50 P.M.

The Jeffers home was a small, neat clapboard house like a half- dozen others on the same block.

The woman who opened the door was slipping into a brown coat. "Yes?" she said impatiently.

"Mrs. Jeffers?" Kaldak asked.

"Are you a salesman? For God's sake, I was just walking out the door." Donna Jeffers was probably in her fifties, but she looked younger. Her blond hair was stylishly coiffed, her makeup perfect. She wore a tweed suit and the short flip skirt revealed shapely, slightly muscular legs. "And I'm late for an appointment."

"I'm not a salesman. I'm looking for your son, Cody."

Her lips thinned and she looked him up and down. "Why? Are you a bill collector?"

He shook his head. "I'm thinking of opening a demolition track in town and I'd like to offer him a job."

"Cody has a job."

"Perhaps I can up the ante for him. Can you tell me where I can find him?"

"Cody doesn't live here anymore."

"But you must be in contact with him."

"Why must I? We've been estranged for some time." She checked her watch. "And I have thirty minutes to get to the other side of town to show a house."

"You're a real estate agent?"

"Does that interest you?" She moved past him toward an Oldsmobile parked in the driveway. "Maybe you want to offer me a job too."

"I'd really appreciate your help if—"

"I can't help you, Mr. . . . ?"

"Breen. Larry Breen."

"You'll have to find Cody on your own, Mr. Breen. I've no idea where he is. We've lost touch over the years."

Kaldak watched her back out of the driveway before he strode toward his rental car at the curb.

He'd done his job. He'd disturbed Donna Jeffers and made her suspicious. All he could do now was wait and see if Ramsey had done his in tapping her home and car phones.

If she knew where her son could be reached, he doubted that she could resist contacting him. The big if.

He drove four blocks and pulled into a supermarket parking lot to wait for the call from Ramsey.

8:15 P.M.

Dr. Kenwood was coming down the corridor toward her.

Bess tensed. Oh, God, he wasn't smiling. He just looked . . . abstracted.

He stopped beside her. And he smiled.

"She's going to be fine," he said. "She still

has a long haul, but there should be a full recovery."

"Thank God."

"Amen," Yael said.

Dr. Kenwood frowned sternly. "Now, will
you go get some sleep? Your friend here has
arranged a bed in the room next to Josie's.
How, I don't know. This floor was supposed
to be full."

Bless Yael. Bless Dr. Kenwood. Bless
everyone in the whole damn world. "Soon. I
want to go and sit with Josie for a while."

"She's still under sedation."

"I don't care."

Dr. Kenwood grinned. "I did good, huh?"

"Dynamite." She headed down the hall
toward Josie's room. "You're right, you're totally brilliant."

9:30 P.M.

"Des Moines," Ramsey said when Kaldak
picked up the phone. "1523 Jasper Street."

"She called him?"

"He called her. She evidently doesn't
have his number because she tried to get it
when he called. He put her off and she didn't

like it. He didn't like your visit to his mother either. I'm arranging transport for you, but I'm also sending men in from St. Louis in case you don't move fast enough."

"Do you expect me to argue? I'd tell you to have the local police pick him up if I wasn't afraid they'd blow it. I'm on my way to the airport." He pulled out of the supermarket parking lot.

There was a chance Jeffers might already be gone before anyone got there. Making him uneasy was a risk Kaldak had had to take when he'd contacted the mother. Uneasy enough to contact Esteban or make a move himself?

He hoped not. He had an idea time was running out.

11:10 P.M.

"Will you please go to bed? It's almost midnight." Yael was squatting beside her chair. "This isn't doing Josie any good."

"I know." She leaned back in the rocking chair, her gaze fixed on Josie's face. "I guess I'm afraid to leave her." She smiled. "She opened her eyes about five minutes ago. I think she recognized me."

"That's good."

"This is a nice room, isn't it? All children's rooms should have rocking chairs. They're very comfortable."

"I suppose they put it here for rocking sick babies."

"I wish I could rock Josie. Look at her. She's in a straitjacket."

"I believe the correct term is *body cast*. I guess they have to keep her from moving."

"Did you call Kaldak and tell him she's going to be all right?"

"You think he'd be interested? A cold, cruel man like Kaldak?"

"Shut up, Yael. He's all of those things, but he liked Josie. Who could help but like Josie?" Sitting there, she'd been remembering that night on the *Montana* when Kaldak had stayed with her until they'd known Josie would live. He hadn't been pretending that night. He'd been genuinely concerned about Josie.

Yael nodded, his gaze on the baby's face. "She reminds me of my son. It's been a long time since he was this young. They grow up so quickly."

"How old is he?"

"Four." He paused. "The age Kaldak's son was when he died."

"I don't want to talk about Kaldak's son. I asked about yours."

"Just a comment. Can I talk you into going to bed now?"

She shook her head. "I'm comfortable. I want to be here in case she wakes again."

"You really should go to—" Yael stopped. "I can't convince you, can I?"

"No, you use the bed."

"I wouldn't be so ungentlemanly." He sat down on an upright chair across the room. "I'll stay here in case you change your mind."

There was a comfortable silence in the room.

"Yael, call Kaldak and tell him about Josie."

"He already knows. He called me."

"He did?"

"He was on his way to the airport in Kansas City. He was very relieved about Josie."

"Kansas City?"

"He's been tracking down a man who might lead him to Esteban."

Esteban. She had been on such an emotional roller-coaster ride about Josie that she hadn't had time to dwell on Esteban. But Kaldak had not forgotten him. He was as driven as he'd always been. Could she blame him? When Emily had died, she had almost gone crazy. How would she have reacted if her entire family had been killed?

My God, she was making excuses for him when there was no excuse. Kaldak couldn't have been more wrong. He had used her and manipulated the situation to suit—

As she had done after Emily's funeral. She'd had no compunction about using Kaldak. She would have used anyone to get Esteban. Monsters should not be allowed to live.

Show them the monsters.

No, not now. The hatred and the passion for revenge would come again, but that night she didn't want to think of Esteban or Kaldak or anything disturbing. She just wanted to relax and enjoy this moment of thanksgiving. Josie was alive and someday she was going to run and play like other children.

Surely it would be safe to forget about monsters for a little while longer.

SEVENTEEN

DAY THREE
Des Moines, Iowa
3:30 A.M.

When Kaldak arrived, three cars were parked in the driveway at 1523 Jasper Street and the house was blazing with lights.

Not good.

A short, heavyset man dressed in a suit and tie came out the front door. "Kaldak?"

"Too late?"

He nodded.

"Shit."

"I'm Harvey Best. Jeffers was already gone by the time we got here."

"Have you searched the place?"

"Clean. We woke up some of his neighbors. They didn't know much about him. He moved in only a few days ago. He drove a truck."

"What kind of truck?"

"Big, strong van type. *Iowa's Pride Cleaning Service* painted on the sides. One of the teenagers next door said she saw the truck get on the freeway heading south."

"South." As if that were a help. Jeffers could have changed direction at any point. He dialed Ramsey. "It's time to pull out the stops. We can't wait any longer. I want you to call the president."

"Aren't you panicking? We don't have proof that Cody Jeffers is actively involved."

"Hell, yes, I'm panicking."

"Not yet," Ramsey said. "Let's see if we can do some damage control. We'll find Jeffers and then—"

"Then find him. Quick," Kaldak said harshly. "I've got a bad feeling about this, Ramsey."

"I'm not calling the White House and putting my ass on the line because you have a hunch."

"Look, put it together. Esteban sent Morrisey to find a man with Cody Jeffers's qualifications. He found him. Cody Jeffers goes to Iowa, where we suspect the counterfeiting installation is."

"It's still speculation."

Kaldak's hand tightened on the phone. He wished it were Ramsey's throat. "If you won't call the White House, then call the highway patrol, okay? Ask them to pull over Jeffers's truck." He paused. "But not to search it."

"You think he's carrying the currency?"

"He's either got it or he's going to pick it up. Wouldn't bet on either one."

"Another hunch?" Ramsey asked sourly. "Okay, okay, I'll contact the patrol. Stay where you are until I find out something. What direction was he going?"

"South." He hoped he was telling the truth.

Collinsville, Illinois
1:40 P.M.

Cody Jeffers picked up the phone on the first ring. "Esteban?"

"You made it with no trouble?"

"I breezed through without the highway patrol giving me a second look. I parked outside Des Moines and just peeled off that cleaner truck lettering like you told me."

"And the currency?"

"All loaded and ready to go."

"What about the extra boxes?"

"I dropped them off at the mill."

"And the little extra job?"

"Done."

"Excellent. Then go ahead," Esteban said. "I want it done by three P.M."

"Same plan?"

"No diversion." Esteban paused. "Don't take any of the cash yourself. You'll be paid later, as arranged, when I meet you tomorrow at Springfield."

"Right."

"You've filled the gas tank on the getaway car so you won't have to stop?"

"Yes."

"On no account do I want you to stop where anyone will see you. If you grow tired, find a secluded place to rest."

"You've told me that before."

"No other questions?"

"You're not paying me to ask questions. I'm not dumb enough to think that's real money. It would pass anywhere though. It looks real good."

"Thank you," Esteban said dryly.

"It's all pretty weird, but it's your business."

"That's right, it is."

Eagerness flooded Jeffers as he hung up the phone. This was the chance of a lifetime. Big time. He was going big-time.

He jumped to his feet, buttoned his gray shirt, and strapped on his holster. He liked the gun. It made him feel like John Wayne. He crouched and whipped the gun from his holster. "Pow. Gotcha."

It felt good. He did it again.

He reluctantly slid the gun back in the holster. He sat down on the bed and reached for his boots. Esteban had told him to wear plain black shoes, but screw him. He'd had to go along with the uniform, but the boots were important. Would John Wayne or Evel Knievel have worn plain black shoes?

"All set, Habin." Esteban strode to the helicopter, where Habin was waiting. "In a few
hours it will be over and all we'll have to do
is issue our demands."

"I've been thinking," Habin said. "It would
be better to cut down the monetary demand
and put more emphasis on the release of
the prisoners."

"Cut down?" Esteban repeated. "How
much?"

"We're asking fifty million dollars. If we go
for twenty-five, it would—"

"Fine. As long as you take it out of your
share."

"Don't be ridiculous. That would leave me
with nothing."

Which was what the pompous idiot deserved. "Nothing but your political ideals.
Isn't that what's important to you?"

"The decision on the money should be
mine. You wouldn't have been able to get
anywhere without me. I set up the counterfeiting operation, I supplied the men and the
money."

Esteban judged he had protested

enough. Maybe just a little more reluctance. "Let me think about it. We still have a few hours before we can issue the demand. I'll call you at the farm after the strike." He shut the helicopter door and strode back to his car.

Too bad he'd had to restrain himself even then. He would really have enjoyed seeing that arrogant son of a bitch humbled. But a wise man never indulged himself if it might cause complications.

He started his car, watching as the helicopter slowly lifted. He could see Habin in the passenger seat, and he leaned out the window, smiled, and waved.

The helicopter was veering away, climbing to the south.

He waved again, then leisurely reached into his pocket and pressed the button on the remote control.

The helicopter became a fireball and plummeted to the ground.

Collinsville, Illinois
2:30 P.M.

Cody Jeffers stepped on the accelerator and heard the big tires screech as he turned the corner.

A woman in shorts and a T-shirt jumped back on the curb. She screamed an obscenity after him. He grinned as he realized how much he had scared her.

The people in the stands at the stadiums were never afraid of him. They were there for the show, and he had never been the headliner.

Now he was the headliner.

The steering wheel felt smooth and good in his hands. Power. He had never driven a vehicle this heavy even on the circuit.

He passed the bank. Three more blocks to North Avenue. Esteban had specified that it must be at North Avenue.

The neighborhood was getting worse. The buildings were shabby, and prostitutes hung out on the corner.

One more block.

A bunch of teenagers were in the street gathered around a 1987 green Cadillac. Not a good year for Caddys. Flashy, but no guts.

The kids gave him a surly glance as he passed them. He knew how they felt. He represented authority. If he gave them a chance, they'd jump him and cut his nuts off.

Half a block.

There it was. North Avenue.

Now.

Excitement tore through him as he stomped on the accelerator. The next corner. Hit it hard. Do the job.

He was John Wayne.

He was Evel Knievel.

He was the headliner.

The truck crashed over onto its side, knocking the breath out of him.

Cody freed himself from the special protective bars and slowly crawled out of the cab.

It was already happening.

The back doors of the armored truck had flown open and plastic-wrapped money scattered all over the street.

The kids by the Caddy were all over it, grabbing handfuls and running.

Two women came out of the store across the street and ran toward the truck.

"Stop," he yelled. "That's Federal Reserve money."

No one paid any attention to him. Not that he'd expected them to. He would have done the same thing.

People were coming out of the woodwork. It was a mob scene with everyone grabbing the cash and running.

"I'm calling the police," Jeffers yelled. "If you know what's good for you, you'll get away from that money. You're breaking the law."

He waited a moment, then walked away. He'd parked the black Honda sedan two blocks over. He should be out of there in minutes.

As he reached the corner, he glanced back over his shoulder.

They were even crawling into the Federal Reserve truck to get at the money.

Too bad he couldn't wait for the TV and newspaper crews. No one would ever know how well he'd done his job. He had compensation though. More than the headliners on the circuit got.

He touched the money belt under his shirt, where he'd stashed the cash he'd taken from the truck earlier. A little extra to sweeten the pot.

Even Evel Knievel would have envied him this haul.

Des Moines
5:36 P.M.

"Kaldak, where are you?" Yael asked.

"Jeffers's place in Des Moines."

"Are you near a TV set?"

Kaldak stiffened. "Why?"

"Turn on CNN. I was watching TV in the waiting room and there was a news flash. I think it's happened."

He whirled on Harvey Best. "I need a TV set."

Harvey gestured to the living room.

The first thing Kaldak saw when he turned on CNN was the Federal Reserve truck on its side in the street. The crowd surrounding it was pouncing on the clear plastic packages strewn on the ground.

Kaldak had seen those packages before in the poor box at Tenajo. "My God."

A blond newswoman's face replaced the scene. "The driver of the vehicle disappeared shortly after the accident, but this amateur video was taken five minutes after the truck overturned on North Avenue in East Collinsville. A spokesman for the Federal Reserve Bank in St. Louis refuses to comment on the amount of money that was stolen."

Kaldak lifted the phone back to his ear. "Get on another phone, Yael. Call the Federal Reserve in St. Louis. Tell them who you are and let them check with Ramsey for references if necessary. I'll hold on. I'll bet every dime of their money is accounted for."

"You think this is it?"

"I hope not. Maybe I'm wrong. Check and see how the Reserve packages their money." He stared at a replay of the scene in Collinsville while Yael made the phone call. Jesus, they were crawling all over the money, grabbing, running. Kids, adults.

"It's not a Federal Reserve truck," Yael said when he came back on the line. "The last truck checked in fifteen minutes ago. That clear plastic packaging of the money isn't Reserve procedure. They don't know what the hell's going on."

"When did the truck overturn?"

"A little before three."

"Two and a half hours ago." He felt sick as he thought of the damage the anthrax might have wreaked already. "How much of the money was taken?"

"By the time the police got there, the truck had been ransacked." Yael paused. "It's too sweet a setup to be a coincidence."

"If it's Esteban, a demand will be issued almost immediately. I'll call Ramsey and see if they've heard from him. Why the hell would he choose Collinsville?"

"It's not as strange as you'd think. It's across the river from St. Louis, where there's the Federal Reserve Bank. The trucks would be a fairly familiar sight. Esteban targeted one of the lowest-income neighborhoods in the city. When the doors flew open on that truck, those poor devils must have thought they'd won the lottery. How soon before we see signs of the anthrax?"

"Anytime now. There's a hell of a lot of people who are going to need help. I don't know how many will survive. The city should be quarantined and the media has to start broadcasting the—"

"Don't tell me. Tell Ramsey."

"Oh, I'll tell him," Kaldak said grimly. "I told the son of a bitch last night that he should call the president. Old pal or not, the president is going to be looking for scape-

goats and the CIA will be one of them. I hope
Ramsey gets roasted over a slow flame."

"He probably will if he can't pass the
buck. Watch your back, Kaldak."

"Don't worry, I will. Call me if you hear
anything more."

He hung up the phone and dialed Ramsey. It took five minutes to get through.

Ramsey's voice was sharp with strain. "I
can't talk to you now, Kaldak."

"You will talk to me. Esteban?"

"Yes. The demand came ten minutes
ago. Fifty million dollars or he'll target another city. If we pay up, he'll turn over all remaining contaminated currency."

"Were the Palestinian prisoners mentioned?"

"No. Habin's out of it. Esteban assured
us we'll have only him to deal with. And he
told us to check out a helicopter explosion in
Kansas City."

Another barrier eliminated from Esteban's path. "The truck driver was Cody Jeffers?"

"He matched the description."

"But no sign of him?"

"No. I've got to go. I've got the CDC on

the line. Donovan's team is on its way to Collinsville."

"Have they come up with anything?"

"Maybe. They don't know. Nobody knows anything, dammit. Except that I'm to blame. But I'm not going to go down, Kaldak. No way. I'll find a way to save my ass." He hung up the phone.

Kaldak had failed. All these years of tracking Esteban for nothing. Nakoa, Danzar, Tenajo, and now Collinsville. He should have been able to stop him. He should have ignored Ramsey and—

I'll find a way to save my ass.

Ramsey was struggling frantically to survive.

And he was talking to the CDC.

Bess.

Johns Hopkins
7:45 P.M.

In the waiting room Bess shivered as she watched the president's face on TV. He was stern but reassuring. Yes, they had received a message threatening another city, but no one should be alarmed. The contaminated money was being collected and burned. All agencies at his command were at work on capturing the terrorists who had committed this horror.

"He's not telling them how bad it is," Yael murmured. "Bastard. He didn't even tell them there was no cure. He shouldn't be reassuring them. He should be scaring them into going to their homes and staying there. He's only worried about your damn stock market."

The news switched to Collinsville and a long shot of burning buildings. "Riots?" Bess couldn't believe it. "As if the situation there isn't bad enough."

The screen now showed victims being brought into local hospitals, showed quarantine wards, panicky faces.

"Seventy-six reported dead already," Bess whispered. "How many more?"

"Let's hope most of the people stashed the money away for themselves and didn't get generous."

"Oh, God, I hoped I could help. Why couldn't we have had a little more time? Maybe we could have saved some of those people."

"You're doing what you can, Bess."

"Tell that to those people in Collinsville."

"Disasters happen."

"This isn't a disaster, it's murder."

Yael nodded. "So why are you blaming yourself? Esteban is the one who—"

"Get your car and wait outside the emergency entrance, Yael." It was Kaldak, striding into the room. "Bess, I'm getting you out of here."

She stared at him in shock. "I'm not going anywhere with you. Josie is—"

"You'll either go with me or you'll go with Ramsey. Either way you'll have to leave Josie. If you go with me, you'll be free and have leverage to deal for Josie's protection. If you let Ramsey swallow you up, you'll have no power at all. You'll be in some hospital or CDC unit and allowed out of sedation only long enough to give blood samples."

"Ramsey hasn't done that yet."

"He wasn't desperate. He is now. He'll present you as his hidden weapon, and naturally you have to be kept safe. It's a national emergency. Everyone knows individual rights have to be suspended during national emergencies." He turned to Yael. "Hurry, we don't have much time."

Bess shook her head. "I won't leave Josie."

"He's making sense," Yael told her. "Do what he says." He walked out, leaving her alone with Kaldak.

"I'm not going."

"Listen to me." Kaldak's voice was tense, desperate. "For God's sake, listen. I know you hate my guts, and that's okay. But I'm telling the truth. Everything's changed. We've got a panic on our hands, and Ramsey's going to have all the authority he needs. The only way you'll have any power at all is to not let him get hold of you. Ramsey doesn't care about you or Josie, he cares about Ramsey. As long as you're free, you have bargaining power." He gestured to the TV screen on which they were showing the riots. "Can't you see I'm not lying to you? I want you safe. I want Josie safe. Believe me."

She did believe him. She'd had enough experience with Ramsey to know that Kaldak's assessment was frighteningly accurate.

Kaldak picked up her purse and handed it to her. "We'll go down the emergency stairs."

She didn't move.

"Bess, I'm begging you," Kaldak said unsteadily. "Don't let this happen to you and Josie."

Josie. Josie was helpless. Josie couldn't protect herself, and if Ramsey took Bess away, she would have no one.

"I'll go." She strode out of the room.

Kaldak was instantly beside her. "Bess, I promise that—"

"Don't make me any promises. I don't want them from you." She stopped abruptly. "Ramsey's agents. Those two coming toward us."

"Ramsey must have told them to get you." Kaldak's hand was under her elbow, pushing her. "Run!"

She ran. Toward the emergency exit and down the stairs.

Kaldak was right behind her. A door burst open above her. Ramsey's agents. The sound of their footsteps echoed in the stairwell.

Third floor.

Oh, God, the agents were gaining on them. The footsteps were closer.

Second floor.

Kaldak pulled ahead of her and jerked

open the first-floor door. "To the left and through the lobby."

Marble floors, columns, a gift shop.

"Stop them!"

A red emergency room sign over the double doors ahead.

A room full of people. More double doors.

Outside. The screech of tires as Yael pulled up beside them.

Kaldak jerked open the rear door and pushed her inside.

They were on him. Kaldak elbowed one in the stomach and hit another in the chin.

"Take off!" He dove inside the car.

The car jerked forward and Yael raced down the driveway with the rear door still swinging open.

They were on the street, speeding toward the corner. Green light. They could make it.

Bess glanced over her shoulder. The agents were still chasing after them, running down the street. . . .

The light turned red.

Yael ran it.

Brakes screeched.

The agents had stopped and were

standing in the middle of the street, staring after them.

The relief that rushed through Bess dissipated immediately when Kaldak said, "They'll have the license plate number. We need to get out of this car." He reached out and closed the rear door. "Get to the airport quick, Yael."

"And what do we do when we get to the airport?" Yael asked.

"We'll decide that when we're airborne."

"You have a plane?" Bess asked.

"Ramsey arranged one for me earlier. That's how I got to the hospital so quickly after you called, Yael." He smiled grimly. "Don't you think it's fitting that we make our getaway in a plane Ramsey got for me?"

"I doubt if Ramsey will think so," Yael said. "And I'm not at all sure my prime minister will approve either. There's such a thing as abuse of diplomatic immunity. Oh, well, such is life."

"I want Josie protected every minute. I want those guards back on her floor," Bess said. "What if Esteban finds out she's there?"

"I don't think it's an immediate problem. He's a little busy now." Kaldak held up his hand. "I know. It's top priority. We'll take care of it."

"How?"

"I don't know. Let me work on it. I'll see that she's safe. I promise."

She'd told him she didn't want his promises. But he'd lived up to his promises before. Against all odds, he had found medical help for Josie and Josie had lived.

Kaldak was gazing at her, searching her expression. "Okay?"

She looked away from him. "Okay. I'll take help anywhere I can get it. Even from you."

8:16 P.M.

The son of a bitch.

Cody Jeffers stared incredulously up at his face on the TV above the counter, his hands clenching into fists. The picture of him was the one from the group shot at the derby. It had been blown up and wasn't clear, but he was recognizable.

"Anything else?" the convenience store clerk asked.

"No." Cody picked up the cigarettes he'd

just bought, stuffed them in his shirt pocket, and hurried out of the store. He glanced back furtively over his shoulder to see if the clerk was looking at him. No, he saw with relief that the man was waiting on the next customer.

He jumped into his car and peeled off, out of the gas station. The fucking terrorist bastard had set him up. The police would never stop looking for him. Everyone in the country was going to be on the lookout. And he wouldn't have known about it if he hadn't run out of cigarettes.

Don't make any stops, Esteban had said.

Oh, no, don't stop anywhere. If he stopped, he'd hear how Esteban had set him up. Even the getaway car had no radio. He was like a lamb being led to the slaughter.

Slaughter.

His stomach twisted with panic. What was he going to do?

Mama. Mama was smart. She would find a place to hide him. She would think of a way to help him.

He had to get to Mama.

EIGHTEEN

A group of mechanics and pilots were glued to a television set in the office adjoining the hangar.

NBC this time, Bess noticed, but the pictures were almost identical to the ones aired by CNN.

"Walter, we have to get out of here," Kaldak said to a medium-sized man in a red windbreaker. "Are we fueled?"

"Yeah." The pilot didn't look away from the screen. "Fucking bastards. Did you hear? Six more cases and the CDC just announced that there wasn't enough antidote to go around. It's some sort of lab-made germ."

"We have to leave, Walter," Kaldak repeated.

He nodded jerkily. "They ought to bomb the bastards."

"Have they announced who did it?"

"No, but it has to be Saddam Hussein or one of those other weirdos. They ought to bomb them. We should have gotten rid of all of them during the Gulf War."

One sentence the pilot had uttered suddenly hit home to Bess. "You said there wasn't enough antidote to go around. Is there an antidote?"

"Some kind of an experimental one. The CDC pumped blood into a little girl they brought in a couple of hours ago."

"And she's alive?"

"So far." He turned away from the set. "You get on board, Mr. Kaldak. I'll go through the checklist. We'll be out of here in no time." He walked out of the office into the hangar.

"An antidote," Bess murmured.

"Not an antidote," Kaldak said. "It sounds to me like they used the last blood sample you sent them and injected it into the girl."

"How could they do that?"

"They culture-expand and activate the cells from a blood sample and then alter the cells with the immune genes. They've been experimenting with the same procedure with HIV patients. Donovan's team must have accelerated the procedure."

"And it worked. The little girl is alive. It's a start."

Kaldak shook his head. "It's a propaganda move. The government didn't want to admit that there wasn't any antidote so they concocted a miracle cure."

"It is a miracle. She's alive."

His gaze narrowed on her face. "What are you thinking?"

She could feel Kaldak's gaze on her as they boarded the plane and settled into the passenger seats. But he said nothing to her until after they'd taken off. "Well?"

"Tell the pilot to turn west."

"I was afraid of this," Kaldak said. "Collinsville?"

"Collinsville!" Yael repeated.

Bess nodded. "That's where the CDC team is. That's where I have to be."

"You do know there's a quarantine."

"Oh, I think they'll let me in."

"That's what I'm afraid of. You'll be walking right into Ramsey's hands."

"My blood saved that little girl. There may be other people I can help."

"Most of the damage has been done. The anthrax has been so widely publicized that no one in their right mind would open those sealed packets of money."

"That little girl opened one."

"Look, your blood type would have to be compatible. That narrows the chances right there. And how much blood do you think you can give?"

She shook her head.

"He's right, Bess," Yael said.

"He's wrong," Bess said. "Do you think I can hide out somewhere and watch what's happening there?" She turned to Kaldak. "I'm going. Now, you figure out how I can do it and still keep Josie safe and myself out of some isolation ward."

"You don't ask much."

"You owe me," she said fiercely. "You owe me for Tenajo. Now, pay up, Kaldak."

He stared at her for a long while and then stood up and headed for the cockpit. "I'll tell Walter we're going to Collinsville."

. . .

Kaldak didn't return from the cockpit until it was almost time to land at the Collinsville airport. Bess had heard him talking nonstop on the radio, but she hadn't been able to understand what he was saying.

"What have you been doing?" she asked.

"Buckle up. We'll be on the ground in five minutes." He sat down and buckled his own seat belt. "And be prepared for a welcoming committee."

"Who?" Bess asked.

"I radioed the CDC, CBS, CNN, and the *St. Louis Post-Dispatch.*" He smiled grimly. "They should all be eagerly waiting when Mother Teresa reincarnated gets off the plane."

Bess frowned. "Mother Teresa?"

"You," Kaldak said. "You're about to become a national heroine. The courageous, caring woman willing to brave the dangers of the quarantine zone to give her life's blood and minister to the sick."

"Very good," Yael murmured.

"And your sacrifice is all that much greater because you left a sick child to come here, a child you saved from death."

"My God, it sounds like a soap opera," Bess said.

"But it's not a soap opera. It's the truth and can be verified by any enterprising reporter."

"You told them about Esteban?"

He nodded. "I told them about Tenajo. I've shone as bright a spotlight as I could. The media particularly liked the idea of one of their own being the heroine of the piece."

"I'm no heroine," she said with distaste.

"You are now," Kaldak said. "You'll visit that little girl who was given your blood. They'll film you giving the blood sample every day. They'll take shots of you and any new victims brought in. You'll go into the riot areas and show that it's possible to survive this mutated anthrax strain." He paused. "And you'll give interviews about Josie and Emily and Tenajo."

"No!"

"Yes. It's necessary. I want Dr. Kenwood to become the most famous surgeon in America because he operated on Josie. I want the head nurse interviewed. I want the hospital to have to put an army of guards around Josie just to keep away the media."

Her eyes widened as she understood. "And keep away Esteban too."

"I think we can rely on Ramsey for that. He won't dare have anything happen to America's little sweetheart."

"And with every movement scrutinized, he won't be able to stuff Bess out of sight into a facility," Yael said.

Kaldak nodded. "That's the plan."

And it was a sound one, Bess thought. It could work.

"One more thing," Kaldak said. "You're to tell the media the CDC is closer to a permanent cure than their official statement would lead anyone to believe."

"Why?"

"I want Esteban to feel insecure. If he thinks a cure is imminent, he'll try to settle quickly and cut his losses."

"Or distribute another truckload of money."

"No, he won't try that again. Everyone's on guard. He's made his point and scared everyone to death."

"You can't be sure of that."

"I can't be sure of anything. I just have to cross my fingers and hope I guess right." He added grimly, "One good thing. I doubt if Esteban is going to risk coming to Collinsville and try to cut your throat." The plane bounced as the tires hit the runway. "That might be too bold a move even for him."

"I wouldn't bet on that either," Yael said. "He may be clever, but some of his tactics are bizarre."

"Then we'll just have to keep her safe, won't we?" Kaldak unbuckled his seat belt and stood up. He glanced out the window. "There they are. Enough cameras to look like Hollywood on Oscar night."

"I'm going to *hate* this," Bess said.

"Now you'll see what it's like on the other side of the camera," Kaldak said. "Come on. Let's get this show on the road."

Collinsville
11:07 P.M.

The reporters flew toward Bess as she came down the airplane stairs.

Kaldak hung back, watching.

Bess might detest being in the spotlight, but she was smiling and answering questions with quiet confidence. He hadn't expected anything else. When it came to a pinch, Bess had shown she could handle almost anything.

"You son of a bitch."

Kaldak turned at the low hiss behind him and saw Ramsey. "I didn't expect to see you here this soon, Ramsey."

"I was already on my way when I got the call from the CDC that you'd pulled this stunt," Ramsey muttered through gritted teeth. "I'm going to get you for this, Kaldak."

"I told you I wouldn't let you do it to her."

"I should have ignored you from the beginning. Before you let this mess happen."

"Oh, Collinsville is all my fault? You weren't involved at all?" Finger-pointing was exactly the reaction he had expected from Ramsey. "It won't wash. I'm just a peon. You're the man in the driver's seat." He looked at Bess. "And you'll feel like you've been run over by a truck if you let anything happen to her."

"Are you threatening me?"

"Yes." His gaze shifted back to Ramsey. "You think you're desperate? You don't know what the word means. I won't lose her and I won't lose Esteban."

"You've already lost Esteban. We're not even close to catching him. He's cutting every tie that would lead anyone to him. Two hours after Habin's helicopter blew up, there was an explosion in a barn outside Waterloo, Iowa."

Kaldak stiffened. "The counterfeit installation?"

"That's what we're betting. We have specialists out there combing through the ashes."

"Isn't that dangerous for them?" Yael asked. "There's bound to be active anthrax spores in the ink they were using."

"Not if the fire was intense enough," Kaldak said. "Fire's the great leveler. The CDC uses fire to destroy even Ebola."

"Oh, it was intense enough," Ramsey said. "It melted practically everything in sight, including some men who were in the building. We're not going to find anything of value."

"What about Cody Jeffers?"

"He called his mother about three hours ago and she hung up on him."

Kaldak went still. "He called her?"

"He was begging and pleading with her. She hung up before we could get a trace. Since then there's been no sign of him. Esteban probably took care of that loose end too."

"When's the deadline for the money?"

"Day after tomorrow." He glanced sourly at Yael. "The president is taking heat from your government. They keep yammering at him not to give in to terrorists."

"My government is right," Yael said. "There's nothing worse than meeting terrorist demands."

"Having Esteban release contaminated money in New York City is worse."

"Is that what he's threatening?" Kaldak asked.

Ramsey nodded curtly. "Do you know what another incident would do to the stock exchange?"

"I know I wouldn't want to give Esteban the money and have him walk away with any anthrax still in his possession. What's to stop him from using the threat again?"

"Her." Ramsey nodded at Bess. "And you took her away from me, you bastard."

"Too bad. I guess you'll just have to concentrate on finding Esteban instead of harassing an innocent woman."

"Is that the pot calling the kettle black?"

Kaldak flinched. "Yes, I guess it is." He stepped forward and elbowed his way through the mob of reporters. "That's enough for right now. Ms. Grady's very tired, but she'll be glad to talk to you-all tomorrow morning. She still has to go to CDC headquarters in town and give blood."

One of the cameras was immediately trained on him. "And who are you?"

"I'm Ms. Grady's personal escort. The government recognizes the extreme importance of her contribution." He turned to Ramsey. "So Deputy Director Ramsey assigned me the job of making sure that her path is as smooth as possible. Isn't that right?"

Ramsey gave him a lethal glance before he forced a smile. "Of course. It's only sensible that we take excellent care of Ms. Grady."

"He was just telling me he's already sent a force to Johns Hopkins to secure the hospital," Kaldak said blandly. "I'll let him fill you in on the reasons that's necessary while I take Ms. Grady to the CDC headquarters."

The majority of the media people immediately surrounded Ramsey, and Kaldak had to extricate Bess from only two of the more persistent reporters.

"This way." Yael was at their side. "This is Mel Donovan with the CDC."

"We've met." Kaldak shook his hand.

"This is Bess Grady. Mel Donovan. He took over Ed's position at the CDC."

"I'm glad to meet you, Ms. Grady." Donovan shook her hand. "Though I wish it weren't in these circumstances. Our team's staying at the Ramada Inn in the quarantine zone. It's right next door to the hospital. I made reservations for your party."

"Have any more cases been brought in?" Bess asked.

"One. He died an hour ago." Donovan ushered them toward a car parked beside the terminal building. A Collinsville police car with blinking red lights was parked just in front of it. "You heard we used the last sample for a transfer?"

"That's why I'm here." She got into the backseat. "But evidently not soon enough. I hoped—" She shook her head. "It doesn't matter what I hoped. I'm here now. I'll do whatever I can. How close are you to an antidote?"

Donovan shrugged. "We're trying to recreate Ed's records that were destroyed in the explosion, but it takes time." He got into the driver's seat. "Believe me, we've been working around the clock ever since the mutated anthrax came to our attention. This disaster just put more pressure on us. Everyone wants an answer, and we can't give them one."

"Let's get going." Yael climbed into the passenger seat beside Donovan. "Those reporters will be on her again any second." Kaldak climbed into the rear seat and slammed the door. "Yael and I will need cars with CDC stickers so we can move around the quarantine area."

"The mayor's given us the use of his staff cars," Donovan said. "We'll get you the stickers when we get to the hotel."

He waved at the police car and the policeman started his engine. "But don't go anywhere without a police escort. The town is too volatile."

The bitch was smiling and telling them lies.

Esteban sat in his motel room, watching the news reports of Collinsville. He'd been drinking in the devastation that was going to prove so profitable, when they'd cut to the airport and Bess Grady.

She was *lying* to them. The CDC wasn't

close to a cure. He had made sure of that with Katz's death.

But what if people believed her? What if pressure was put on the president to refuse to pay? Those damn Jews were always getting in the way.

She was saying it again.

Fury tore through him. "You lie. Shut up, bitch. Stop *saying* that."

He had turned loose the Dark Beast and shown them there was no way to save themselves. Yet they still thought she could do something to save them. If he was going to win the game, they had to remain frightened and subdued.

He must remove all hope.

Donovan's car encountered a National Guard roadblock two miles from the Collinsville airport but was allowed to pass when the soldier saw the CDC sticker on the windshield.

Bess had grown accustomed to soldiers and guns in third world countries, but they seemed an obscene anomaly in this small American town. Esteban had brought this obscenity down on everyone.

"Lock the car doors," Donovan said over his shoulder. "The hospital is in the riot area."

"Can't the National Guard do anything about it?" Bess asked.

"Right now they're busy just keeping the town quarantined, and the governor doesn't want to use force. These people are victims already. He's asked everyone to stay off the streets until morning, when more troops will arrive."

A few blocks later, they entered the riot zone. Stores with broken windows. People carrying television sets and stereo equipment. Small fires everywhere.

"This is where you want me to show my support, Kaldak?" Bess murmured.

"I may rethink that part of the plan," Kaldak said.

She shook her head. "No, you're right. It's effective showmanship." She was silent, staring out the window. Suddenly she called to Donovan, "Stop the car."

"What?"

"Stop the damn car." She unlocked the door and hopped out. The police car screeched to a halt ahead of them.

The old woman reaching into the broken jewelry-store window.

Focus.

Shoot.

The scruffy little boy carrying a spaniel puppy from a pet store whose burglar alarm was shrilling.

Focus.

Shoot.

"Get back in the car." Kaldak was beside her. "You're giving Donovan a heart attack."

"In a minute." Her gaze had been caught by something in the alley across the street. Two slender figures silhouetted against leaping yellow orange flames. She couldn't tell their age or sex, but they were standing before a rusty oil drum like priests before an altar. "What are they doing?" she murmured. She moved closer.

Focus.

Sh—

My God, they were burning money.

But when we see them tearing up or burning money, we'll know we're really in trouble.

It seemed a long time since Kaldak had said those words. It had been impossible to imagine then.

But it was happening. It was all happening.

So take the pictures. Tell the story.
Focus.
Shoot.
She lowered the camera. "That's enough." She started back toward the car. "Do you suppose it was the counterfeit currency?"

"They evidently think it is, but I hope not. They had it in their bare hands." He held the car door open for her. "And you're not going back to try to rescue them. They're likely to toss you in that oil drum too."

"Someone should warn them."

"There have been police cars cruising the streets with loudspeakers," Donovan said. "We should get out of here. We're attracting too much attention."

He was nervous, she realized. She supposed she would be too if she hadn't been absorbed by the sheer impact of what she was seeing. She nodded, and Donovan gave a sigh of relief and started the car.

Kaldak locked the doors and leaned back.

"You warned me," she whispered as she stared out the window. "I don't think I really believed you."

"I can't blame you. I wasn't a well of ve-

racity at the time." He paused. "But I told you
the truth when I could."

"When you thought it was convenient to
tell me the truth."

"Nothing's been done for convenience
since the moment I met you. I know it
doesn't make any difference to you, but I
promise I'll never tell you anything but the
truth from now on."

"It's too late."

"It's *not* too late. Not if—" He drew a deep
breath and shook his head. "I know. It's not
the time. Forget I said anything."

She would try to forget. She had been
trying to forget Kaldak. Yet here he was beside her, manipulating, guarding, supplying
her needs.

Kaldak made it very difficult to forget
him.

At the hotel, they stopped by Donovan's
room first so he could take blood samples
from Bess. Yael decided to check out the
building security, and Kaldak led Bess to her
room.

He unlocked the door and handed her
the key. "Yael's room is next door and Ram-

sey has agents swarming all over. The floor is wall-to-wall CIA. Don't open your door unless you know who's on the other side."

"I know that. I've gone through all this before. I'm practically an expert by now."

"This stay shouldn't be quite as dangerous. No one's even allowed in the city without the proper credentials, and you don't have De Salmo to deal with any longer." He smiled crookedly. "And who in Collinsville would want to kill the new Mother Teresa?"

"That joke's gone stale. I'll see you in the morning, Kaldak."

"Actually, you won't."

She looked at him.

"I won't be back here until tomorrow evening sometime." He paused. "Maybe not then."

She frowned. "What?"

"I'm going to Kansas. Cody Jeffers called his mother earlier this evening. She hung up on him, but I think he'll call back."

"Why?"

"He's scared and in over his head and she's all he has."

"Then Ramsey can trace the call and get him."

"I don't want Ramsey to get Jeffers. I

Ramsey picks him up, it will be all over the newspapers. I want Esteban to think Jeffers is still free."

"And what will you do if you get him?"

"I'll play it by ear. I have a few ideas, but it depends on how much he knows and how cooperative I can get him to be." His lips curved sardonically. "I'm very good at using people, remember?"

"I remember." She opened the door. "Call me. I want to know what's happening. If there's a chance of trapping Esteban, I don't want to be closed out."

"I'm not closing you out. I'll take you with me if you like."

"You know I can't leave. Donovan's team might need me."

He nodded. "Remember when I asked you what you'd do if you had to make a choice between Josie and getting Esteban?"

"This is a different situation," she said without hesitation. "If it was Esteban instead of Jeffers you were going after, then I'd come with you." She turned and went into her room. "Good night, Kaldak."

She leaned back wearily against the door. Kaldak, as usual, was relentlessly fo-cused on his objective, but life had gone off-

kilter for her. She couldn't walk away from
Collinsville, not if staying there might keep
someone alive. The helplessness she had
felt at Tenajo was still too fresh in her memory. She'd do what she could here. Take one
step at a time.

NINETEEN

The small yard at the Jeffers house was overflowing with reporters and TV cameras. A satellite truck was parked across the street. Kaldak parked two blocks down and walked quickly to the front door.

He elbowed through the crowd of reporters and rang the doorbell.

"Better watch it," one of the photographers warned. "She called the cops when I rang the bell this afternoon and they almost ran me off."

He couldn't blame her. This media circus was overpowering. He rang the bell again.

No answer.

What the hell. He put his shoulder to the door and rammed it with all his strength.

"Shit. Are you crazy?" The startled photographer shot a picture of him as he broke through the door. "You're going to get us all thrown off the property. She'll scream bloody—"

Kaldak missed the last words as he entered and slammed the door shut behind him. The hall was dark but he could see a light streaming from one of the rooms at the top of the stairs.

He didn't have long to wait. A door was flung open and Donna Jeffers marched to the head of the stairs. She was dressed in a nightgown and robe and she was pointing a pistol at him.

"I'm sorry. I'll pay to repair the door," Kaldak said.

"Get out of my house."

"I need to see you."

"You're trespassing. I'd be within my rights to blow a hole in you."

"That's true. But do you think you need

the hassle? You're probably having enough trouble."

"Who are you? A reporter? Police?"

"CIA. Could I come up and talk to you?"

"I've had someone from your department talk to me. I've had someone from every damn department in the government talk to me." She turned on the hall light and her gaze narrowed on him. "You were here before. Breen."

"Kaldak. A small untruth."

"You were looking for Cody." She was coming down the stairs. "It hadn't even happened yet and you were looking for Cody."

"I suspected he was involved."

"Then why the hell didn't you find him? Why did you let him do it? My friends are going to think I've raised some kind of monster. Why didn't you stop him?"

"I tried." He looked at the gun. "Will you put that down? I'm trying to make things easier for you."

"You're trying to catch Cody, like everyone else."

"I want the man who hired him, and I want you to persuade him to help me. But there are people out there who only want a scapegoat. They'll take your son." He paused. "And they'll take you with him."

She was silent a moment. "What do you want from me?"

"When he calls, talk to him but make it very short. We don't want the call traced. If he tries to set up a meeting, do it. And make sure he knows the line is bugged so he won't give himself away."

"He may not call again."

He sat down by the small telephone table in the hall. "We both have to hope he does."

The phone rang a few hours later. Kaldak picked up the hall extension at the same time Donna Jeffers answered the kitchen phone.

"Mama, don't hang up."

"I can't talk to you," Donna Jeffers said. "Are you crazy? I told you the last time not to call me. After what you've done, do you think they haven't tapped my phone? I'll be lucky if they don't arrest me. You've ruined my life, you idiot."

"I didn't mean to do it, Mama. It was counterfeit, but I thought that was all. I need your help. You're all I've got. Can you meet me at the place where I had my ninth birth-day party?"

"No, I can't be involved in this."

"Please, Mama."

She was silent.

"I'll be waiting for you. I know you'll come." He hung up.

Kaldak was surprised to see tears in Donna Jeffers's eyes as she came out into the hall. "Damn him. He's so stupid. They'll put him away in prison and then they'll kill him."

Kaldak wanted to lie to her, but he didn't. "Feelings are running pretty high right now."

"I love him, you know." She wiped her eyes and straightened her shoulders. "But I'm not going to let him take me with him." She gazed at Kaldak defiantly. "You think I'm terrible, don't you?"

"I'm not judging you."

"It doesn't matter what you think. I always did my best for him." She went toward her bedroom. "I've got to do my face and put on some clothes," she said. "Then we'll get out of here. How do you intend to get me through that mob?"

"Same way I came in."

"They'll follow us. So will the police."

"I'll lose them. It may take a couple of hours, but I'll lose them."

"Pizza Hut?" Kaldak asked.

Donna Jeffers shrugged. "All kids like pizza."

Kaldak pulled into the parking lot and shut off the engine. It was just before eleven in the morning and the restaurant was closed. Three other cars were in the parking lot.

"He's probably watching us from a distance," Kaldak said. "Let's get out of the car. I want both of us to be fully visible. He'd get spooked if he drove up and saw me in the car. He might take off again."

Ten minutes passed.

"He's not coming," she said.

"Give him a chance. He'll—"

A black car barreled down the street, pulled into the parking lot, and screeched to a stop. The window rolled down.

"Who is he?" Cody asked. "Why didn't you come alone, Mama?"

"Because I can't help you by myself. You've gone too far this time."

"Who is he?"

"Kaldak." She paused. "He's government."

Cody started to roll up the window.

"Don't you do that, Cody Jeffers." She glared at him. "Do you hear me? You don't run away from this. I'm not going to have them chase you down and shoot you."

"He set me up, Mama. I didn't know anyone was going to die. They'll think I'm just like him."

"Then turn the bastard in, make a deal."

"I'm scared, Mama," he whispered, his eyes glittering with tears. "I've never been this scared. I don't know what to do."

"I told you what to do." She stepped aside and gestured at Kaldak. "You do what he tells you to do and you may come out of this alive."

"I don't want—" He met her gaze and then slumped in the seat. "Okay. What do you want me to do?"

Yes. Kaldak tried to mask his eagerness as he stepped forward. "First, information. I want to know everything you did from the moment Esteban picked you up in Cheyenne."

"Are you still here?" Yael hurried into the hospital room. "For God's sake, haven't they fed you any lunch yet, Bess?"

Bess rolled down her sleeve. "I'm sure ready to eat now. All they've been giving me is orange juice. I bet all the soldiers who've been guarding me have had breakfast and lunch already."

"I'll see if I can get you something. I promised Kaldak I'd take care of you."

"You've all done that. I've been completely surrounded." She smiled. "You two seem to think you're the only ones who can ward off the demons."

"Well, we're damn good at it." He helped her to her feet. "How's the old man who came in this morning?"

"He's got a good chance. Donovan gave him a culture from one of the samples from last night. But it takes a while to prepare the culture, and Donovan needs some in reserve."

"Maybe I'd better keep an eye on him. These eager-beaver doctors may prove a bigger threat than Esteban. You've only got so much blood."

"If you really want to protect my well-being, you can take me down to the cafeteria. I'm starved to death."

"No problem." He hesitated. "Well, maybe two little ones. One, I'll have to bring your lunch to you up here. It's not safe for you to go down to a public cafeteria. Two, there's a roomful of reporters outside with Donovan. They heard about the old man and they're going to pounce."

"I'm surprised you're letting them near me. Everything else is a security problem."

"They've all been searched." He raised a brow. "Want me to try to get rid of them?"

She shook her head. This was just another part of the package she'd bought into to protect Josie. "I'll talk to them. But rescue me after fifteen minutes, okay?"

"Like Lancelot swooping to save Guinevere."

She flinched. "Don't say that. Guinevere ended up in a nunnery."

Yael chuckled.

"Did you see the newspapers this morning? They practically had me wearing a halo. I almost threw up."

"You'll survive. If you don't take any chances."

"I don't have a death wish. If I died, Esteban would win everything he's murdered to get. That's not going to happen. Have you heard from Kaldak?"

"Not yet. But he promised to keep me posted. He's not going to leave us in the dark, Bess."

"Do you always believe what he says?"

Yael nodded. "And you should too."

She shook her head. "You believe in Kaldak. I believe in Josie and you and, most particularly, good old burger and fries." She started for the door. "So let's get those interviews over so you can bring me my lunch."

She had finished the interviews and just returned to the hospital room when Yael's portable phone rang.

"Kaldak," he informed Bess, then mouthed, "I told you so." His smile slowly disappeared as he listened. "I don't think that's a good idea. Goddammit, you told me to protect her and now you want to do this? There's no way I'm going to bring—" He punched the disconnect button "The bastard hung up."

"What's happening?"

"He's found out where Esteban's coun

terfeit is stashed. It's on some farm near the Iowa border. He's heading there now."

Excitement soared through her. "Esteban . . ."

"Don't even think about it. I'm not taking you there."

Emily.

"Let Kaldak take care of him. Stay here, where you can do some good."

Show them the monsters.

Donovan already had extra samples to use in case anyone was brought into the hospital. This was her chance to do what she'd always intended to do.

She could kill the monster.

"I'm going."

Yael shook his head.

"Don't tell me no. I'm going. Take me there, Yael."

"Hell, no." He held out his phone. "Call Kaldak back and tell him to take you."

She shook her head. "He's there, you're here. Take me."

"And how am I going to do that? You're the most visible woman in America right now."

"You managed to get me out of my apartment."

"That was different. It wasn't a quarantine zone. And there's no way I can get you a plane."

"Then find a car for me. Please, Yael."

"It's a mistake."

"No, it's not. I have to do this."

He was silent a moment before he sighed resignedly. "Dammit, I guess you do."

Springfield, Missouri
2:37 P.M.

Something had gone wrong. Jeffers should have been here an hour and a half ago.

Esteban's hands tightened on the steering wheel. With the nationwide media coverage, he would have known if Jeffers had been picked up by the police. And that hadn't happened.

If Jeffers had opened one of the packets, he might be lying dead at the side of some road.

Or he might have found out what was in those packets and panicked. He might be on the run, which was not good. He wasn't bright enough to avoid the search for long.

Whatever the reason for the delay, the

situation was not irreparable. There was a possibility he might not be able to neatly eliminate Jeffers as he'd planned, but the man knew very little.

That Jeffers had been the one who'd hidden the cache of doctored currency at the mill was also a simple matter to solve. Remove the currency, and Jeffers was no longer any threat.

Yes, everything would still fall into place just as he'd planned. All he had to do was maintain control of himself and he could control everything else.

Near the Iowa border
3:48 P.M.

A breeze was blowing and the windmill's blades whirled lazily. "There it is," Cody Jeffers said. "That's where I unloaded the money. I'm not going any closer. You can't make me, Kaldak."

"You don't have to go." Kaldak got out of the car. "Drive to the bridge that's two miles down the road, park out of sight, and wait for me."

"What if you don't come back? What if

someone sees me? You promised Mama I'd be safe."

"Just wait for me." The muscles of his stomach were tense as he stared at the windmill. All those years of searching and it all led here.

No cars in sight. That could be bad or good. Either Esteban had already picked up the currency, or he had not gotten here yet, giving Kaldak the opportunity to set a trap.

Dammit, he wished he'd had time to make the one o'clock meeting Esteban had set up with Jeffers. But it might still be all right. If Esteban had gone to the meeting place hundreds of miles away in Springfield, he shouldn't have had time to get here yet.

If. Maybe. When had Esteban ever done the expected?

He could have skipped the meeting, parked in that patch of woods to the south, and walked to the mill. He could be waiting there for word about the payment.

Or the damn place could be booby-trapped like that installation in Waterloo.

It didn't matter. He couldn't stop now. Esteban was too close.

He started toward the windmill.

A windmill, Bess thought. A pretty stone windmill gleaming in the moonlight. Death was in that windmill, neatly packaged death. She had always liked windmills. She must have taken thousands of pictures of the ones in Holland.

"There aren't any cars around. I don't think Kaldak's here yet, so let me go in first." Yael hesitated. "You won't change your mind?"

She shook her head. It wasn't Kaldak's presence he wanted to check out, but Esteban's. "Be careful."

He smiled. "Always." She watched him disappear into the shadows. A moment later he came out and gestured to her.

She ran toward him. "Kaldak?"

"Not yet." He held the door open for her and she went into the darkness. "But the currency is here. That means we'll have a way to draw Esteban. I'll light the lantern."

It was pitch dark. She couldn't see anything. How had he been able to see the currency?

"I'll do it," Esteban said.

She went rigid.

Esteban lit the lantern across the room. He held a gun in his hand. "Right on time, Nablett. I just arrived myself."

"It wasn't a simple matter getting her out of Collinsville," Yael said. "I was lucky I could do it at all. I think you owe me a bonus."

She stared at him in shock.

"I'm sorry, Bess," Yael said gently. "The deal was just too generous to pass up."

"You're part of this?" she whispered. "You've been working with him all the time?"

"No, I just seized the opportunity when it presented itself."

"He came to me and offered me a way to leave Mexico quickly and unobtrusively," Esteban said. "And any service that I needed in exchange for a small percentage of the ransom."

"Two million dollars may seem small to you but it's not small to me. I grew up on a kibbutz."

Bess felt sick. Anyone but Yael. Yael wasn't one of the monsters. "What . . . services?"

"Why, you, of course," Esteban said.

Murder. He was talking about murder. "Yael saved my life."

"Oh, he insisted he couldn't compromise

his association with the Israeli government. He wants to walk away from this clean. So it couldn't happen when he was supposed to be guarding you."

Yael waved his hand dismissively. "None of that matters. I've burned my bridges by bringing her to you. As I said, I think it deserves a bonus."

Bess still couldn't believe it. Yael's betrayal stunned her. "Kaldak never called you and told you to come here, did he?"

Yael shook his head.

Sweet Jesus, he'd played her so cleverly. He'd known all he had to do was dangle Esteban in front of her and she would do everything under the sun to get to him. "You even told me to call Kaldak back. What would you have done if I'd done it?"

"I'd have offered to call him for you and he would have been conveniently out of range." He met her gaze. "I regret having to do this, Bess. But you were making Esteban very nervous."

"I wasn't nervous. She's only a woman. I always knew that I'd find a way to rid myself of her." Esteban's grasp tightened on the gun in his hand. "And now that you've brought her here, I'm going to have the joy of disposing of her. And, believe me, it will give me the greatest pleasure."

"Don't you want me to do it?" Yael asked.

"You're worried about your bonus? No, she's mine. Don't interfere." He pointed the gun at Bess. "I've dreamed about this moment. Do you know how much trouble you've caused me?"

He was going to kill her.

Terror tore through her. She didn't want to die. There were so many things she still wanted to do.

Dammit, she would *not* die. There had to be a way. Think. Find a way to stall him.

"I'm glad I caused you trouble," she said. "It's going to go on. Even if you kill me, it will go on. They'll never pay you. I've given them enough blood to find an antidote. They'll find it. Tomorrow. Maybe today."

He glared at her. "It's not true."

"It's true." She walked toward him. "They'll never pay you. Why should they? You release this stuff in New York and it's only going to be an inconvenience. No one's going to die." She was a few feet from him. "Except you. They'll kill you. They'll tear you apart for what you did at Collinsville." She thought of something else. "And then the rats will eat you. They'll tear at your flesh and go for your eyes. They'll devour you like a—"

"No." His voice rose shrilly. "Liar. Bitch. It won't—"

She lunged for the gun.

"Puta." He swung the barrel at her head.

Pain.

Falling . . .

Through a dark haze she could see Esteban level the gun at her.

"Esteban."

Kaldak!

Darting out of the shadows behind Esteban, diving between them, bringing him down.

The gun blast was muffled by Kaldak's body. He went limp even as the gun skidded across the floor.

Agony ripped inside her. *"No."*

Bess frantically pulled him off Esteban.

Blood. Blood everywhere. His chest . . . Kaldak didn't move.

Esteban was scrambling across the floor, trying to reach the gun.

She got there before him. Her hand closed on the butt of the gun and she rolled over and pointed it at him.

"Stop her." Esteban was looking beyond her at Yael. "Kill her."

She stiffened.

"But you wanted to do it yourself," Yael said. "I really don't think I should interfere."

"*Kill* her."

"Do you really want to do this, Bess?" Yael asked.

Kaldak. Emily. Danzar. Nakoa. Tenajo. Collinsville.

"I can see you do," Yael said. "Then I suggest you shoot the son of a bitch."

She pulled the trigger.

The bullet tore through Esteban's forehead.

She shot him again.

"That's enough," Yael said. "Once would have been enough."

She whirled and pointed the gun at him.

He held up his hands. "I'm no threat to you, Bess."

"The hell you're not."

"You can waste your time trying to decide whether to kill me or to see if we can save Kaldak. I think he's still alive."

Her gaze flew to Kaldak. *Alive?* There had been so much blood. . . .

Yael knelt down beside Kaldak, his fingers on Kaldak's throat. He nodded. "Alive."

"Stay away from him."

"I do have a gun, Bess. You might consider the possibility that I could have killed you anytime."

"Esteban told you not to interfere."

"Have you ever found me that meek?" He tore a strip from Kaldak's shirt and made a pad. "Now, come and help me. I don't like this bleeding."

She hurried across the room, kneeling, gathering Kaldak close.

"You apply pressure while I call 911," Yael said.

Her hands were already on his chest above the wound. "Call them. Quick."

Esteban was dead and Kaldak was alive. She had been given a miracle and she wouldn't let it be stolen from her. She would not let Kaldak die.

The paramedics carefully placed Kaldak in the ambulance and Bess jumped in and sat down beside him.

She glanced at Yael, who stood outside. "Are you coming?"

He shook his head. "The medics have called the police. I have something to do before they get here. I'll see you at the hospital."

Would he? Or was he taking this opportunity to escape? Yael's actions had completely bewildered her. There was no doubt he'd been in collusion with Esteban. Yet he had held his hand when he could have killed her, and he'd worked beside her to save Kaldak.

The medics slammed the door and a moment later the ambulance was speeding down the road toward the highway.

Kaldak was still unconscious and he was too pale. She wiped her eyes and grabbed his hand.

"Don't you die on me," she whispered. "You hold on. Don't you dare die, Kaldak."

She felt the ambulance vibrate before she heard the explosion.

Her gaze flew to the back window.

The windmill was splintering like a toy as flames engulfed it and clawed at the sky.

TWENTY

Kaldak woke as they were wheeling him into the emergency room. "Esteban?" he whispered.

"Dead." Her hand tightened on his. "Don't talk."

"Are—you—all right?"

She nodded jerkily. "Fine assassin you are. Why couldn't you shoot him or something? Did you have to jump between us?"

"He had his finger on the trigger. I was afraid—reflex action."

"So you let the son of a bitch shoot you."

"Not—my plan. Everything went wrong. I was waiting for Esteban. No time. He got there just before—you."

"I told you not to talk. Do you want to die, you stupid man?"

"No." His eyes closed. "No, I want to live."

"How is he?"

Bess looked up to see Yael standing in the entrance to the waiting room. "Another hospital," she said wearily. "We've got to stop meeting like this."

"How is he?"

"He's in X ray right now. They think the bullet missed vital organs, but he's lost some blood."

"He'll survive. Kaldak's tough."

"Yes. But he's a thickheaded idiot. He had a gun and he didn't use it. He let himself get shot. Did he expect me to be grateful?"

"He probably didn't think at all. Are you grateful?"

"I don't know. I don't know anything."

"Except that you're glad Kaldak isn't dead."

She was glad about that. Everything else was a blur. She leaned her head against the wall behind her. "You blew up the windmill."

"And the money and Esteban with it."

"Why?"

"It was the only way I could be sure that the currency was destroyed. I didn't want it confiscated and put in some security warehouse someplace. Your government is very fond of storing things for a rainy day."

She glared at him. "You worked with Esteban, you bastard."

He nodded. "My prime objective was always to get Habin. He was the one who was going to demand the release of Palestinian prisoners. I had to work with Esteban to make sure Habin was erased from the picture." He smiled slightly. "It was my extreme pleasure to supply him with the bomb he used on Habin's helicopter and the one he gave Jeffers to blow up the counterfeit installation."

"You could have stopped Jeffers from picking up the money."

He shook his head. "I didn't know the details. Esteban just used me as he used everyone else."

"But if it had come down to a choice between ridding yourself of Habin or stopping Collinsville from happening, what would you have picked?"

Yael was silent.

"You would still have chosen Habin," she whispered.

"My country can't afford to have people like Habin alive. We live with the threat of terrorists every moment of every day. My first wife died because of men like Habin." His gaze was cold as he met her eyes. "Yes, I would have sacrificed a hundred Collinsvilles if it meant keeping those prisoners from being turned loose."

Kaldak had once said Yael was more accepting than he was. It wasn't true. The man before her was totally relentless.

He smiled. "You're shocked. Remember I told you that we all have our priorities? Esteban just wasn't as high on my list as he was on yours. You might ask yourself what you would have sacrificed to get Esteban."

"I don't think I would have sacrificed you, Yael."

His smile faded. "I hoped I wouldn't get you killed, but I had to destroy the currency. The only way I could find it was to tell Esteban to use it as a ploy to draw you into the trap." He grimaced. "If Kaldak had called and let me know what he'd learned from Jeffers, that wouldn't have been necessary. By the way, the local police picked up Jeffers near the windmill an hour ago. He was screaming to high heaven about a deal he made with Kaldak."

She didn't care about Jeffers. "You just stood there. You were going to let Esteban shoot me."

"Was I?" He shook his head. "I was only waiting for my chance to be a hero. You and Kaldak didn't give it to me."

"You're not a hero."

"No, I'm only a man with priorities." He turned to go. "I'm leaving for Tel Aviv tomorrow night. I'll stop by in the morning to see Kaldak."

"Do you think he'll want to see you?"

He nodded. "He might be angry that I used you, but Kaldak understands priorities."

"Bullshit."

"Oh, he does. No one wanted Esteban more than Kaldak did, but he didn't take the sure kill last night. I think he understands priorities very well."

Kaldak was sitting up in bed when she came in the next afternoon. "Are you supposed to be up?"

"I'm fine." He scowled. "But they won't let me out of here."

"It serves you right for getting shot." He didn't look well, but he looked much better. His chest and shoulder were bandaged, and his color was almost normal. She set the vase of spring flowers she'd brought on the nightstand. "Was Yael here?"

He nodded.

"He said you'd understand."

"I do."

"Well, I don't. I feel . . . betrayed. I thought he was my friend."

"He *was* your friend."

"Friends don't make you the bait in their little traps."

He was silent.

"I don't care about priorities. It's not right. He shouldn't have done it." Her hands clenched into fists. "And I still like the bastard. That's not right either."

"What do you want me to do? Explain him? Make excuses for him?" He shook his head. "I can't do that. I won't do that. Any more than I would for myself. We both used you and betrayed you. No amount of regret will change that fact. You have to either forgive us or try to boot us out of your life."

"Try?"

"You might succeed with Yael. You won't with me." He said harshly, "I need you. Do you know how hard that is for me to say? I need you and I won't let you go. I don't care if you think I'm a bastard. If you try to get away from me, I'll follow you. God knows, I'm good at the hunt. I won't bother you but you'll know I'm there. And someday I'll be there and you'll need me too."

She shook her head.

"Don't shake your head. It's going to happen."

"Maybe it will. But not because you bully me."

"I'm not bullying you. I'm just telling you how it is." He paused. "Is it Emily? Do you still blame me for Emily?"

"No, not any longer. You didn't know she was going to Tenajo. I don't even blame you for sending me there. It was wrong, but I can understand. Those damn priorities again. You and Yael are obsessed with them."

"No more than I'm obsessed with you."

"I don't want to be anyone's obsession. I have enough obsessions of my own." And Kaldak could very well become one of them.

He had dominated her life from the moment he had entered it.

"Do you think I'm talking about some sick fixation? We're good together."

"You mean sexually."

"Hell, yes, but more than that. And you know it." He hesitated. "I . . . care about you. I don't want you to walk out of my life. I want to stay with you, live with you."

And she wanted to stay with him. The knowledge came suddenly and surely. She wanted Kaldak more than anything else she had ever wanted in her life. But she couldn't have him. Not yet. Maybe never. "And do you want to talk to me about Nakoa?"

He stiffened. "What do you mean? I've told you about Nakoa."

"You haven't told me about your wife and your son. You haven't told me about David Gardiner. And don't tell me you're not that man anymore. Everyone's born with a soul, but it's experiences that make us what we are. I know Kaldak. I don't know David Gardiner. I deserve to know both. I won't settle for anything less."

He was silent a moment. "I'll tell you."

"But you don't want to talk. For God's sake, do you think I want to force confidences out of you? I just want you to be able to let the past go. If you can come to me and say that you've done that, then maybe we'd have some hope of—" She stood up. "This isn't getting us anywhere. It's all too soon."

"I know you care something for me. Stay and let's work it out."

"Right now, I don't know how I feel. I'm sad and angry and grateful, but I—"

"I don't want your gratitude. I want you to— But I'll take the gratitude if you go along with it."

"It's too soon." She moved toward the door. "I can't deal with it. I can't deal with you, Kaldak."

"You're not going to learn by running away."

"I'm not running away. I have things to do. I'm going back to Collinsville and work with the CDC and make sure they have a cure in case this damn mutant anthrax surfaces somewhere else. I have to go to the hospital and check on Josie. Then I'm going to Canada to the ranger station where Tom and Julie left their car and wait for them to come out of the woods. It should be any day now." She had to steady her voice. "I have to be there to tell them about Emily. I'm not running. I have a life, Kaldak."

"I don't. Not yet. But I'm trying. Just give me a little time and I'll get there." He said roughly, "Go on, get out of here. But you can be sure I'll see you later."

She walked out.

She loved him and she was walking out on him. At the moment when he was so alone. What would a man do when the obsession that had driven him for years vanished? She wanted to go back and tell him—

No, it was too soon for both of them. There was too much pain and regret to overcome in one day. Maybe later.

If there was a later.

EPILOGUE

Focus.

Shoot.

"No more, Aunt Bess," Julie said plaintively. "I have to go with Daddy to the grocery store. I promised."

Julie hated shopping, Bess thought. The only thing she hated more was having her picture taken. Bess wouldn't have made her do it, but she wanted a picture to give to Tom for his birthday. "One more."

Julie's curly red hair was shining in the sunlight as she swayed back and forth in the rope swing. The composition was almost perfect.

"And Josie's getting really tired." Julie turned to the tiny girl in the sandbox. "Aren't you, Josie?"

Josie nodded. "Tired. Real tired."

"See?" Julie said with satisfaction.

Josie adored Julie and would have said the moon was orange if Julie had so prompted her. Bess repeated, "One more."

"Hello," Julie said to someone behind Bess. "Are you looking for Daddy? He's at the house."

"No, I'm not looking for your daddy."

Bess froze. Then she turned around.

He was dressed in a dark blue suit and looked elegant and civilized. Hell, he looked wonderful. "Hello, Kaldak."

"Can I go now?" Julie asked.

Bess nodded. "But first you have to be introduced to Mr. Kaldak. This is my niece, Julie."

"How do you do?" Kaldak said. "I've heard a great deal about you."

"Have you?" Julie smiled. "Are you a friend of Aunt Bess's?"

Kaldak looked at Bess. "Am I?"

Bess smiled. "Yes."

"Nice to meet you," Julie said.

Kaldak's gaze went to the sandbox. "Josie? Lord, she's looking wonderful." He crossed to the sandbox and knelt beside the little girl. "Hi, Josie. I don't suppose you remember me?"

Josie smiled and handed him a red plastic bucket.

"Thank you." He reached out and touched the tiny gold earring in her left ear. "I remember these earrings. Pretty."

Josie nodded and then reached out and touched his cheek. "Pretty."

He blinked, astonished.

She giggled in delight at the response and touched his other cheek. "Pretty."

Kaldak chuckled. "I hate to insult you, Josie, but there's something seriously wrong with your judgment."

"Maybe not. She's usually pretty perceptive," Bess said. "You may go now, Julie. Be sure to get the sand off Josie before she gets in the car."

"I know that." Julie was already in the sandbox, pulling Josie to her feet. "Come on, Josie. We'll go turn on the sprinklers and get clean, okay?"

"Sprinklers," Josie repeated, her face lighting up. "Hose. Umbrella."

"No, not this time," Julie said as she started across the lawn, slowing her steps to accommodate Josie's tottering gait. "Not the umbrella but maybe the hose."

"Nice kids," Kaldak said.

"You bet they are."

"It's been over a year. I didn't expect to see you still here. Children's photos are hardly your cup of tea."

"It didn't hurt me to put my career on hold for a while. Julie and Tom needed me. I guess I needed them too."

"How's Josie really doing?"

"Terrific. She's still in rehab, but you saw how normal she's looking. The Mexican authorities found out her grandparents are dead, and there aren't any relatives willing to be responsible for her." She smiled as her gaze followed Josie and Julie. "So she's mine, Kaldak. I'm adopting her."

"That's great, Bess."

"It's more than great, it's a new world for me. What are you doing now?"

"I've been very boring lately. I haven't killed anyone in nearly two days."

"Kaldak."

"Sorry. Actually, I'm heading a research project on a new virus discovered in the Amazon rain forest."

"More germs."

He shrugged. "What can I say? It's my specialty." His gaze fixed intently or her face. "I thought we might go out to dinner."

"Why don't you stay and eat with us? You can meet Tom."

He shook his head. "I want to be alone with you. I want to talk."

"You do? What about?"

"Shoes and ships and sealing wax." He paused. "Dammit, what do you think I want to talk about? Why do you think I'm here?"

"Tell me."

"Do you know how much I've missed you? God, you look great."

"I feel well." What an understatement. At that moment she felt as if she could soar like a balloon. "How are you?"

"Good." Then he said harshly, "No, I'm not. I'm surly and mean and impatient as hell."

"So what's new? You always were."

"You told Julie a lie. I'm not your friend."

"Oh, you will be." She smiled luminously. "There's no way I'll have a lover who's not my friend, Kaldak."

He stiffened.

She said unsteadily, "I've been impatient as hell too."

"Bess." He was coming toward her and the expression on his face . . .

Oh, God, she needed to remember it forever.

Focus.

Shoot.